WONDERLAND

WONDERLAND

WONDERLAND

RACHEL EMBER

HeartEyes Press

Copyright © 2022 by Rachel Ember

All rights reserved.

This book was inspired by the True North Series written by Sarina Bowen. It is an original work that is published by Heart Eyes Press LLC.

No part of this book may be reproduced in any form or by any electronic or mechanical means, including information storage and retrieval systems, without written permission from the author, except for the use of brief quotations in a book review.

RILEY

I stood at the hospital's front doors, hesitating for the first time since I got the call that my grandfather was there and I was the only member of the family who was welcome.

That Grandpa Gene chose me came as a surprise, considering I hadn't seen him in going-on-eight years. But in a family like ours, being the one who's disliked the least isn't exactly an accomplishment. There's not much to like about any of us.

I'd stood outside this hospital eight years ago, on my last day in Vermont. I remembered the tower of concrete and windows like it had been stamped in my mind. Now, here I stood again.

This time, though, I would actually go inside.

Blowing out a breath, I rolled my shoulders, cracked my neck, and stepped into a sour-smelling vestibule. Beyond that, hallways branched in three directions. I squinted at the signs, which were full of medical words I couldn't have pronounced aloud and didn't know the meanings of.

A woman in scrubs came up to me with a polite smile. "Need a little help?"

"Um," was all I managed for a second. Talking to people is either really easy for me, or really hard. When I'm somewhere I don't know how to be, it's *fucking hard*. I swallowed. "I'm here to see my grandpa."

"Okay. Is he a patient here?"

"Well, he's definitely not the chief of surgery," I muttered before I could think better of it. Her smile turned tense, and I winced. "Sorry. Um, yeah, he's a patient. His name's Gene Meadows."

"Super. I can walk you to the nurses' station and—"

Before she could say more, a familiar voice resonated from down one of the hallways. *"Don't you talk to me like that, young lady! I've been wiping my own ass for seventy years!"*

"Never mind," I told the woman helping me. "I know where I'm going."

I followed the sound of Grandpa's outrage all the way to an open door. He was sitting upright in a metal-framed bed, one skinny leg protruding from the hem of his hospital gown. A woman in scrubs stood next to him, and another faced him from a few steps away with her hands on her hips and a disapproving frown. She wasn't dressed like a hospital worker, and she had a notebook under her arm.

"Gene," said the lady with the notebook, "the better you get along with the nurses, the quicker they'll have you ready to get out of here. Do you know when your sister will arrive?"

"Not my sister." As Grandpa Gene's gaze swept across the doorway, he noticed me. He went still, then finished in a completely different, blank tone, "My grandson."

The woman turned to me, some of the tension leaving her expression to be replaced with a cautious smile. "Oh, thank goodness. You're Riley?"

I wasn't sure where to look. It wasn't easy to look at Grandpa, thin and frail and wearing a fucking hospital gown instead of a flannel shirt and overalls. But now that our eyes had met, it was hard to look away.

Still, the lady was talking to me, so I made myself turn to her and cleared my throat. "Yeah, I'm Riley."

She had a kind smile, and she looked exhausted, which I could understand if Grandpa had been yelling at her for a while. "I'm Dolores Manuel. I'm a social worker for the county." She pulled a piece of paper from between the yellow pages of her notebook. "I understand you're able and available to give Gene a hand at home?"

I glanced at Grandpa, but I couldn't glean from his expression how I was supposed to answer. I looked back at Dolores and nodded cautiously.

"Great," she said. "I need you to sign this, and then we'll be all set."

I probably didn't have enough information to take the pen she offered and sign where she pointed, but I couldn't bring myself to try and read the paper. The print was small and close together. It would have been hard to read even if I wasn't distracted by Grandpa's eyes boring holes in me.

"Did you drive here?" she asked when I handed back the paper and her pen.

"No." I'd taken two buses, then walked about a mile instead of waiting for the third one.

"Then I'm happy to give you two a ride home. Is that okay with you, Gene?"

We both looked at Grandpa.

"Sure, fine," he said after a second, like it had taken him a beat to realize she'd asked him a question.

"I'll make a quick call, and we'll get going," Dolores said, and she stepped out. The nurse followed her.

Which left me and Grandpa alone.

Our eyes met, and slowly, Grandpa's blank expression turned into a faint smile. "Aw, kid." He dropped his head back against the squashed little pillow tucked behind him. "Where've you been?"

"You know." I shrugged. "Back in the city." We both knew he wasn't asking where I'd literally been. He was asking why I'd run off to New York and why I'd stayed away. But he didn't call me on my bullshit, and now that I'd said a few words, it was easier to say a few more instead of falling into awful silence. "And now I guess I'm gonna be here awhile."

He grunted. "I just need someone to sign the papers and get me out of this place. You don't have to stick around. I'm fine. This was all an overreaction."

I wasn't sure about that. He looked like shit. But I didn't want to argue with him. Not that we hadn't had plenty of knock-down, drag-out fights without doing each other's feelings any lasting damage, but that had been then. This was now, after years without contact.

"I don't have anywhere else to be," I told Grandpa honestly, making myself meet his eyes and hold them. "If you don't mind me sticking around, that is."

After a second that felt like an hour, he sighed. "Fine. If you're offering, I could use a hand."

My worry spiked. If he was admitting to needing help, he had to feel even worse than he looked.

"Your room's still there," he added.

Those simple words filled my head with memories of Grandpa's place. I thought of the creaky stairs leading up to the bedroom tucked under the dormer window, facing east. The wide swing on the front porch overlooking the woods.

And Peter. A dozen versions of him all packed into a moment's thought: from the bold slip of a little kid I'd first met, to the sweet, nervous preteen of a few years later, to the eighteen-year-old of that last summer, who'd turned hauntingly beautiful during our months apart. That August was the last time I'd seen him, when everything ended with my own declaration that still rang in my ears: *"Have your fancy fucking life, then! I don't need you either."*

Then...Peter's arms windmilling as he slipped and fell. The sickening *crunch* when he'd caught his fall on an outstretched hand, the dull *thud* a half-second later when his head struck the ground—

"Kid? If you stay with me, you gotta help out," Grandpa grumbled. "Deal?"

I swam up from the past and blinked at him, keeping my tone light as I said, "Great. It's a deal."

I waited in the beige hallway while Grandpa got dressed. Staring at my shoes, I tried to push back the tide of thoughts about Peter fucking Landry, knowing it would carry me somewhere I didn't want to go.

I breathed in the antiseptic hospital air, not the woodsy scent of green leaves and rotting logs. I studied the glossy tile floor between the toes of my shoes, not the way Peter wrinkled his nose when he smiled.

When Dolores returned with another hospital worker, pushing a wheelchair, I had gotten myself under control.

I knocked on the door to Grandpa's room. "Are you decent?"

"As I'll get," he called back.

I opened the door, relieved to find he looked healthier already just for having traded the hospital gown for a faded-green flannel shirt. Instead of the overalls I expected, though, he wore jeans and suspenders. The generous belly he'd always had was gone, and maybe with it, he'd lost his aversion to waistbands.

Grandpa noticed the wheelchair, and his eyes narrowed.

Before he could get his hackles up, I put a hand on his shoulder. "Let's just get along so we can get to the lady's car, and you'll be home that much faster."

I thought he might argue, but though he muttered a few inaudible words I was sure were curses, he nodded stiffly. The nurse hovered over him while he lowered himself into the chair, but he didn't need any help.

Dolores drove a dark-green sedan with a trace of rust on the inside edge of its rear wheel well. I wondered what she did for the county. She must have been the one who'd called my mom about coming to help Grandpa. Then, Mom had called me. I hadn't asked for many details as I threw a few things in the bag now slung over my shoulder and bought a bus ticket.

Now I wished I *had* asked questions. I couldn't tell what was wrong with him, or what kind of help he was going to need.

"Okay, Gene, let's get you in the front, here," Dolores said with the take-charge manner of someone who dealt with grumpy people all day. She reminded me of Vicki, a social worker my brother had after juvie and before he turned eighteen. Vicki had been middle-aged, unflappable, tired around the eyes, and wore cable-knit sweaters. Dolores's sweater was a cardigan with big plastic buttons, but everything else matched up.

When Grandpa was settled and Dolores had closed the car door, I took a step toward her.

"So, what's going on with him?"

"Just old age and stubbornness, honey," she said, giving my shoulder a squeeze. "The rest of it is for him to tell you, not me."

She had a point, and maybe if she'd spilled all of Grandpa's personal details to someone she'd just met, I would have judged her for it, at least a little. But I knew that if I asked Grandpa, he'd be pissed.

I got into the car, watching the back of Grandpa's head and his stiff shoulders as Dolores drove us out of town and to the two-lane blacktop that led to Grandpa's place.

As a kid, I'd been amazed by how Vermont towns just ended, suddenly becoming the country. Growing up where green space was the exception, not the rule, had made the quick transition out the car window seem like a magic trick. It still took me by surprise. As the years had passed since my last visit, I'd continued to think about this part of the world all the time. But I'd begun to wonder if it was as green, open, and fresh as I'd remembered, or if my memory had been playing tricks on me. It hadn't been, though not everything was the same.

There were now a few big houses where I remembered small ones or empty pastures. Some were pretty fancy, including the massive, three-story colonial no more than an eighth of a mile from Grandpa's, with marble greyhounds posted on either side of its driveway entrance.

The contrast between that gaudy place and Grandpa's was almost funny.

When I was thirteen, I'd arrived here for the summer, and was greeted by a pile of rusty junk lying just past the mailbox, in plain view of the road. That kind of thing was par for the course at Grandpa's place. He'd drag home some treasure with grand plans of fixing it up or using it for something, and instead it sat where he'd dumped it and he never touched it again.

From what I could tell, that same pile was still stationed by the mailbox, a mailbox that leaned at the same angle I remembered from years before.

When I realized the barbed-wire gate wasn't stretched across the end of the driveway anymore, I leaned between the front seats. "What happened to the zebras?"

"Zebras?" Dolores gave us a disbelieving look as she slowly guided her car over the potholes in the gravel driveway. "You've got to be kidding me."

"I had a few," Grandpa told her, then said to me, "They died. They were as old as you, and that's old for zebras."

The zebras had been mean as hell if Peter and I bothered them, but they'd mostly kept their distance, roaming the property at will within the bounds of the sagging barbed-wire perimeter fence. The sight of their stark stripes through the trees or in the meadows had reinforced the park's magic for me.

"What about..." I started to ask, then hesitated, unsure I wanted to know.

Grandpa looked at me out of the corner of his eye and answered anyway. "He's just fine. He's still young for a tortoise."

Relieved, I leaned back in the seat, watching the house come into view. It was kind of absurd-looking—the original, square, story-and-a-half had a metal shed tacked on one side, and a more typical, but still awkwardly boxy addition stuck to the other.

Rusted cars were rowed up on the other side of the clothesline in the backyard, and the tall grass in the front yard made it clear Grandpa still hadn't taken up mowing.

Through anyone else's eyes, the place probably seemed like a dump. But my chest filled with warmth at the sight. For years I'd assumed I'd never set foot here again, but no other place had ever felt like home.

Dolores was glaring at Grandpa. "A *tortoise*?" she demanded. "Are you two messing with me?"

Grandpa's eyes met mine in the rearview mirror, and we both chuckled.

Dolores sighed, long-suffering, and put the car in park. "I'm going to come check on you in a week," she informed Grandpa. Then she twisted around to look at me. "You too, honey. It's really generous what you're doing, by the way. Maybe he won't say it, but I know your grandfather is very grateful."

"He's getting free room and board." Grandpa jerked on the car-door latch, but it must have still been locked.

Dolores ignored him, looking steadily at me. "And as you're his caretaker, I'm trusting that he will share what you need to know about his health and treatment."

"I have been taking care of myself since that kid was in diapers," Grandpa muttered, pinching the manual lock with his thumb and forefinger but failing to get a good enough grasp to pull it up and escape.

"Part of my job as Gene's caseworker is to ensure that he not only has a support system, but that he's willing to use it," Dolores continued, raising her voice pointedly. With that, she faced forward and popped the locks.

Grandpa threw open the door and practically jumped out, like a horse leaving a starting gate.

But I hesitated there with Dolores, remembering Vicki, and how she'd seemed genuinely sorry during her last visit, when she told Quint she wouldn't be back now that he was no longer a minor. Dolores seemed to mean well, which was more than could be said for most fucking people.

"Thanks, ma'am." I scooted across the seat to get out.

"You're welcome, honey. And good luck. You're going to need it."

By the time Dolores pulled away, Grandpa was almost to the porch steps. I watched him walk. He shuffled his steps like his right leg wasn't bending the way it should, and when he reached the first stair, he leaned heavily on the wooden railing.

"Well?" he barked at me without turning. "You coming?"

I jogged the few strides it took to catch up to him, staying close as he went up, just in case he should fall. He didn't, but he took each step slowly and deliberately.

Under our combined weight, the stairs sagged noticeably. "These steps could use some work," I told him.

"Well, you can make that your first order of business. I told you there was work to do around here."

If the front door locked, I'd never seen the key. Unlocked front doors—another enigma to a city boy like me. Grandpa went inside, leaving the door open for me to follow. I stepped through —and froze.

So much had been the same outside that I wasn't prepared for the change *inside*.

Grandpa had never been much of a housekeeper. I didn't think he'd ever run the old vacuum in the hall closet, and he'd probably never touched a dust rag. But he'd picked up after himself and didn't leave dirty dishes in the sink overnight or laundry on the floor.

Now, though, stuff was everywhere. Boxed, stacked, piled… as though eight years ago Grandpa had packed up half the stuff to move, then changed his mind and stayed put. And then the filled boxes, piles of mail, and heaps of odds and ends had somehow grown and multiplied of their own volition. The result was strange teetering towers on every tabletop, and heaps of clothing and random junk in every corner. The house had always had too many hallways and corners, but now it felt more like an animal's den than a house.

Grandpa must have known that seeing the house would surprise me because he looked anywhere but at me as he tossed his jacket onto a pile of clothes on the bench inside the door. Shoes were stacked under the bench, three-deep. I recognized one pair of rubber boots as something he'd bought for me when I was sixteen. Had they been sitting here since?

"Grandpa," I said slowly, knowing I shouldn't say anything but unable to stop myself. "What the fuck is going on?"

"Huh?" He glanced at me. "What are you talking about?"

"I'm talking about the house!" That wasn't exactly true. I added a few things up in my head. Grandpa had needed to find someone to look after him once he was released from the hospital. But even though he looked a little stiff on his feet, he seemed to be getting around fine. Now that I'd seen the house, I had to wonder if maybe the thing that was wrong with him had less to do with his body and more to do with his head.

But fuck if I knew how to ask about any of that. So, yeah, we could start with the house.

He gazed around as though trying to see the place through my eyes. "I got a bit... behind on things, I suppose."

"There's got to be more to it than that."

He looked at me sharply and huffed a breath—almost a laugh but humorless. "Ain't that the truth."

And while I stared, wondering what the fuck he was talking about, he trudged down the hall to the downstairs bedroom and closed the door firmly behind him.

PETER

Three weeks later

Initially, I was surprised to see an older, balding guy in a Carhartt jacket at Vino and Veritas, the trendy, inclusive bookstore and wine bar on Church Street. But then I reminded myself that you couldn't judge a book by its cover, and then I snorted at myself for coming up with a book pun while sitting in a bookstore, and then I wondered if maybe I'd had a little too much caffeine if I was carrying on a conversation with myself.

I wasn't sure how it happened, but at twenty-six, my lifestyle was basically that of a retired senior citizen. On weekday mornings, I enjoyed a cup of coffee at my favorite bookstore while reading the copy of the local paper they kept around for customers.

Today, though, Carhartt Guy had beaten me to the paper, and I'd been sipping my coffee and resentfully watching him thumb through the pages for forty-five minutes.

We got the paper at home too, but I was too busy avoiding my mother to share it with her.

"Maybe you should go over there and arm-wrestle him for it," Briar whispered, stopping next to my table with a hand on his hip. "You know, you *could* get it online and read it on your phone."

He was right. I *could* get a digital copy on my phone. That's what I'd done while I was at Harvard for seven years and still reading my hometown paper a few days a week.

Maybe my need to stay up-to-date on what was going on back home had been my first clue that I wasn't one-hundred-percent happy to escape Vermont for Harvard, after all.

"It's not the same," I hissed back. Briar, of all people, should understand that. I'd never seen anyone treat books as lovingly as he did, and I doubted he had the same reverence for their electronic versions.

"You're like an old man trapped in a twenty-six-year-old body," Briar observed in a normal voice, shaking his head.

I bristled, even though I'd been thinking the exact same thing. "Because you're *so* immature, Mr. Has-A-Five-Year-Plan-To-Buy-A-House," I shot back with a smile. I liked Briar—I was surprised how much. I didn't make friends easily, and Briar and I hadn't known one another long. Briar's boyfriend, Jamie, was the younger brother of my friend from law school, Aaron.

I practically shot out of my chair when I saw Carhartt Guy head for the door, leaving the newspaper unclaimed.

"I'll leave you to it," Briar said, shaking his head as he walked back to the display table, where he'd been swapping out books of photography for cookbooks.

"Bye," I called absently as I snatched the paper off the table and shook the glossy advertisement pages out of it.

Like every old gossip in town, I went to the legal notices first. I liked to think I had an excuse—I was always amused when I saw my aunt's law firm, Sprysky and Gentry, printed as a contact at the bottom of a notice. Today, the firm had three.

Most of the page, though, was taken up by a list of names printed by the tax assessor—all the people who were in arrears on their property tax and scheduled for foreclosure. This column was probably being avidly read all over town.

I glanced over the notice the way I'd skimmed everything else, ready to flip back to the front page to read today's headlines—and stopped dead when I recognized a name.

"Oh, shit." Generally, I didn't blurt out profanity in public, but the words escaped me before I could stop them. I looked up guiltily to find Briar frowning at me from the display table.

He wandered back over with three books in the crook of his arm. "What's up?"

"Nothing. Sorry." I bit my lip. I hadn't heard the name Gene Meadows in years, but when I was a kid, he'd been as close as family. And his property, which everyone just called the park, had been my escape from reality every summer.

Now it was up for tax sale.

Briar was still looking at me like he worried I'd stumbled over a traumatizing obituary, so I swallowed and tried to explain. "The tax foreclosure list went out today, and an old family friend's name is on it. Gene Meadows."

"Tax foreclosure?" Briar echoed.

"Yeah. If you don't pay them, eventually they sell your property for you and take the tax bill off the top."

"Damn," Briar murmured. Then he tilted his head. "Gene Meadows. That name sounds familiar."

I wasn't surprised. Briar was a transplant, so he wouldn't necessarily know about the park. Though it was something of a legend among the older generations, it had closed in the eighties, and people my age without family in the area tended not to realize it was even there. But people still gossiped about the local, semi-reclusive man who'd won the state lottery. "He won two million dollars about five years ago."

"That's right!" Our eyes met. I assumed his mystified expression matched mine. Neither of us bothered to ask the obvious question: why the hell would a millionaire be in default on a five-figure property tax bill?

"Maybe he just forgot to pay," Briar suggested with a shrug. "I heard he's pretty eccentric. And when people around here call someone eccentric, it has to be serious."

I huffed out a breath, not quite able to laugh.

"Hey, are you okay?" Briar perched on the edge of the chair across from mine. "How well do you know him?"

"Well, when I was six, he told me to call him Uncle Gene. But I haven't seen him in years." I felt like the world's biggest asshole. Gene had been my uncle Frank's friend. I hadn't been back to the park since I was eighteen, for about a thousand reasons, but Uncle Frank had kept me updated on Gene even after I went away to school. Nothing much, just a quick anecdote about his quirky friend during our monthly phone calls.

But right when I started law school, Uncle Frank had gotten sick, and now he was gone.

I could have checked in with Gene myself, of course. But I hadn't. For someone who rose to every academic challenge, I was terrible at doing the hard things that really mattered.

That thought made me flinch.

When I was away and busy with school, I'd had an excuse not to stop by and say hi to Gene.

But I was back in town, without even a real job to keep me busy, and I knew he might be in trouble, so what was my excuse now?

I blinked at Briar's confused face, and asked, "Could I get a to-go cup to pour this into?"

I didn't often drive east into the outskirts of town toward the park. The road Gene lived on was a remnant of another time, when Burlington's neighboring towns were still truly small and the only people competing for rural land were farmers. Now, half the acreage this close to town had a big, new house on it and a lawn service.

Not the park, though. At least, not yet. It made me a little sick to wonder how many enterprising real estate developers were salivating over the possibility of snatching up the valuable land at tax sale.

I needed to figure out what the hell I was going to say to Gene when I showed up on his doorstep, but the closer I got to the park, the less I was thinking about Gene.

Inevitably, following this stretch of blacktop made me think about a different Meadows: Riley.

Not that thinking about him was anything new. I'd been doing a lot of that lately. I didn't know whether it was being back in Vermont, where we'd spent all those summer days together, or just having extra room in my mind now that I wasn't immersed in the grind of law school.

Over the years, I'd lost my resolve and looked him up online several times, every time wishing I hadn't because it left me miserable for days. Not that there was much to find. He had a few accounts where he never posted anything publicly, but occasionally someone would post photos of him. So I'd seen him transform from a lanky teen into a taller, broader, bearded, and even more beautiful version of the beautiful kid I'd known.

But it made me strangely sad too, to know that the Riley in my memories was lost in more ways than one. The Riley with smooth cheeks and a scrawny chest, who had given me so many firsts—my first kiss, the first hand on my dick that wasn't mine. That last summer, when we'd taken the plunge into blowjobs, we'd basically worn out our knees clumsily and worshipfully sucking each other off. Somehow those fumbling firsts with Riley were more powerful than any encounters I'd had since, and I'd had my share of objectively good sex.

I knew other stuff from the occasional social media stalking, too. I'd figured out he worked in a restaurant somewhere, and that he could make even a kitchen apron look sexy. There was a photo of him with a pretty girl wound around him, her dark hair in a braid, one of his hands hooked casually around her neck, him grinning at the camera, her eyes riveted on him. I wondered if he was bi. I wondered if he was out as queer at all. I wondered, often, if that pretty girl was his girlfriend.

I turned into Gene's driveway, and my stomach twisted. I wasn't ready to be here yet. I pushed down on the brakes, hard and abrupt. Before I actually saw Gene, I needed to climb out of the ocean of old feelings I'd let myself tumble into.

Slamming on the brakes turned out to be a good thing in more ways than one, because someone familiar was sunning himself smack dab in the center of the pitted gravel driveway.

Grinning, I put the car in park and got out, walking up to crouch a few feet away from Gene's pet tortoise, one of the reasons why visiting Gene when I was a child had always felt like slipping into Neverland.

"Hey, Lemon," I crooned. I wasn't sure, but he seemed bigger than the last time I'd seen him, a sandy-colored boulder on leathery feet. He slowly turned his head toward me, and I knew he recognized me too when he took a slow step in my direction and his beak opened expectantly.

"I don't have anything on me, Lemon, sorry," I said with sincere regret. There was nothing I would have enjoyed more than popping a strawberry or a chunk of melon into his mouth like old times.

Today was one of those rare, warm late-February days, close to fifty degrees, but it wasn't going to stay that way for long, and worry spiked in my chest. "Kind of cold for you, isn't it, buddy?" I knew Lemon had a mind of his own, but he was pretty far from his heated habitat up at the park, where he hung out through all but the warmest months.

All tortoise-related concerns fled, though, when I heard the unmistakable sound of a shotgun cocking. I'd never fired a gun in my life, but I was born and raised in a constitutional carry state, and more specifically, I'd spent a lot of time in my formative years around Uncle Frank and Gene, who seemed to be armed at all times.

My head jerked up, and sure enough, at the bottom of the

wooden steps to Gene's rambling house stood the man himself. It took me a half-second to recognize him. He was thinner than he'd been the last time I'd seen him, with whiter, flyaway hair, but I'd know the stance of Gene Meadows with a gun in hand anywhere.

"Can I help you?" he called in a chilly voice.

I rose from my crouch with my hands raised. He wasn't aiming the gun at me, but I remembered how Gene felt about uninvited guests. *And* he'd found me harassing Lemon.

"Hey, Gene. It's me, Peter. Peter Landry. I just came by to say hello."

Gene instantly slung the gun over his shoulder and pushed back his hair with his free hand. "Peter! Damn, kiddo, is that really you?"

I laughed, leaving the car where it was and walking toward the house. "Yeah, it's me. I know it's been a while."

He propped the gun against the porch, his movements slow and stiff, but when he faced me again, his grin was wide. "Damn right it has. The last time I saw you, you were a skinny little beanpole, and now look at you." He held out his arms, and after a moment's hesitation, I stepped close and hugged him. I'd been taller than him since I was fourteen, but I remembered him as someone larger than life, and curling my arms around his now bony shoulders hurt my heart a little.

"I guess the roosters have really come home to roost," Gene said as we pulled apart. He squeezed my arms, and I realized that while his tight grip might have something to do with him being happy to see me, he was also using me for balance. I grasped his arm to steady him in return.

"Roosters, huh?" I wrinkled my nose. I couldn't remember what the saying stood for, and regardless, I was just one rooster, wasn't I?

Before he could clarify, the front door creaked. It hadn't occurred to me that Gene might not be alone, but it didn't exactly surprise me either. Gene had never been one for girlfriends or roommates, but he'd always had friends coming and going.

So when I glanced up without bracing myself, I was gut-punched.

Riley.

And not some daydream-slash-hallucination of the boy I'd known—which wouldn't have come as a complete surprise, considering how I could tumble into my memories if I let myself.

No, this was the *real*, present-day Riley, the one with the height and the breadth and the beard, staring at me like he was seeing a ghost.

My heart thundered, and my whole body turned hot. The last time I'd felt like this had been the summer after my first year of law school, when a distracted driver had veered into the bike lane and their side mirror had grazed my thigh.

Apparently, my head and heart thought this was another near-death experience, because once again, my life was flashing before my eyes. Except, it wasn't my whole life. It was the nine summers between my ninth birthday and my eighteenth.

Running through the woods so light-footed, I was half convinced my body weighed nothing in the shade of those old trees, knowing Riley was right behind me.

Watching the sunset from the top of the old Ferris Wheel in Meadows Park, but having a hard time looking at the horizon when the light was falling on Riley, making him even more beautiful than usual.

The first time Riley kissed me, so gently, when we were fourteen.

The last day of that last summer, when we fought like never before—an argument we never finished because in the middle of it, I fell fifteen feet and snapped my arm like a dry branch.

Waking in the hospital to find Riley gone, and sending a couple hundred unreturned text messages in the weeks after that.

All those images, sensations, and feelings were like a pool, and I dipped underwater and resurfaced a second later in my real, present life, with Riley still staring at me and Gene gripping my arms.

I had the absurd thought that maybe Riley had thought I'd died that day I broke my arm. I'd bled a lot, and it had been that, as much as the pain, that had caused me to lose consciousness at some point while Riley had bolted toward the house with me in his arms. If he'd thought I was dead, that explained the radio silence ever since. If he'd thought the long, embarrassing texts I'd sent for weeks before finally giving up were actually from a ghost, no wonder he hadn't answered any of them.

Gene clapped me on the shoulder a few times, hard enough to shake me out of my reverie.

"Look, Riley!" He was beaming, either oblivious to, or more likely enjoying, the fact that Riley and I were both shocked as hell. "It's Little Pete, all grown up."

Pete. That's what my uncle Frank used to call me too.

I dared a glance at Riley, almost expecting him to have vanished. The moment felt surreal. But he was still there, still staring. Finally, though, he cleared his throat, and I heard him speak in the low, husky voice I'd never forgotten, one that had been slightly incongruous with the teenaged version of him but fit the grown-up version perfectly.

"Hey, Peter."

Hey. *Hey?* I kept staring at him, tightening my grip on Gene while his fingers kept digging into my arms, no longer sure who was clinging to whom.

"So," Riley went on, his eyes sliding away from mine, then glancing back again. "What's up?"

When I'd imagined running into Riley again, we hadn't *exchanged pleasantries*. He hadn't looked at me warily, like I might pick up Gene's gun and point it at him at any moment.

No, when I'd imagined seeing him again—because of course I had, especially lately, when he'd taken over my thoughts more and more often—he'd told me he was sorry. He'd begged me to forgive him for leaving without a word, for making me wake up in the hospital only to find out that a severe concussion and a broken arm were the least of my wounds. My heart was broken, too.

Gene's voice lowered. "You okay, Pete?"

I blinked into Gene's worried face, shocked again by how frail he seemed. I relaxed my grip on him, forced a smile, and nodded. I was here for Gene, not Riley, after all. I needed to get my head straight.

"Yeah, of course." I hesitated, then asked, "Are *you* okay, Uncle Gene?" The honorific I'd always used for him rolled off my tongue, feeling wrong and right at the same time.

He squeezed my arm, his smile fading as he apparently filled in the blanks on the timing of my visit. "Oh." He let go of me and immediately transferred his grip to the porch railing, leaning against the post. "You saw the paper."

"Yeah... I know it's none of my business, but I wanted to see if I could help."

He shook his head and said in a stiffer tone, "I appreciate that, but I have it all handled."

"Grandpa," Riley said. I winced at the sound of his bewildered voice. "What's he talking about? What was in the paper?"

My thoughts spun. Riley didn't know about the foreclosure?

Gene grimaced, then looked over his shoulder, and instead of answering the question he'd been asked, said, "What the hell is Lemon doing out, Riley?"

Riley shrugged. "I don't know what he's doing all the way down here, but I've been leaving the door open for him."

"Kid, do I have to explain how tortoises are cold-blooded? He doesn't go out this time of year!"

I'd heard the two of them get into short shouting matches a hundred times, which had made me nervous even though their altercations always ended with laughter or grumbles and a quick hug. It was the Meadows' communication style.

But this time, Riley didn't shout back. He looked like he wanted to—I didn't have to know him anymore to interpret the way his nostrils flared as he took a deep breath and let it out—but he didn't. "I'll put him back in."

"Good." Gene turned to me with a bright smile. "Pete can help. Can't you, Pete?"

"Um… yeah," I choked out. Because what else was I supposed to say?

"Great. His chariot's in the shed. No, the garage, I think. When you get back, we'll have a chat." He bent slowly to retrieve the shotgun.

I met Riley's eyes—we likely wore the same stricken expression—but just as when we were kids, Gene gave us our marching orders and we fell in line. Riley came down the steps to hover behind Gene as he made his way up, and I took a few steps back to give them space.

Now that Riley was turned away from me, I was free to stare at him, drinking in the way he'd changed—that beard, fuck—but equally, the ways he was the same. His dark hair still fell past his collar like spilled ink, and there was an ease and strength in the way his body moved. He was *unfairly* good-looking. The kind of guy who'd turn heads on the street. I certainly couldn't look away, even as Gene reached the door, batting at Riley when Riley tried to hold on to his elbow to balance him.

When I knew he would turn back any second and see me watching, I turned around completely, my back to the house, closed my eyes, and took a few deep breaths.

I could do this.

We'd just been kids. I didn't know Riley anymore, and he didn't know me.

The past was the past.

But if that was true, why did all my *feelings* about Riley seem as strong as ever? Why did I want to simultaneously yell at him and hug him, and why was there a faint sting of tears in my eyes?

I needed to get my shit together. I'd help haul Lemon up to the park, all while saying as little as possible. Then I could address the one and only reason I was here: helping Gene.

Because there was no one else for me to care about in the Meadows family. Definitely not.

RILEY

Peter Landry.

Grandpa had been right. Peter wasn't the same kid who'd run all over the park with me for nine summers. He looked different. His uncle had always called him Little Pete, but the nickname didn't fit now. He was still as slim as he'd ever been, but he had to be almost as tall as my own six feet. Also, he wasn't wearing the baggy clothes he'd been partial to as a kid, trying to look bigger than he was and creating the opposite of his intended effect. Now his clothes fit him like a glove, from his gingham button-down shirt to his navy corduroys.

But his face was the same. Bright blue eyes, neat golden hair, and skin that looked lightly tanned even in the dead of Vermont winter. He looked like a California boy, which I used to tease him about. The joke didn't seem funny now—last I heard, California was exactly where he'd like to be. It shouldn't have mattered whether he was on the other side of a state line from me or all the way across the country. I hadn't expected to see him again either way. Still, I'd hated that he'd apparently wanted to be as far from every memory of us as he could get without crossing an ocean.

I tried to help Grandpa inside, but as usual, he made it clear my help wasn't welcome. When the door had closed behind him, I turned around to find Peter facing the opposite direction, his shoulders slightly hunched, and before I could remember it was wrong, my eyes ran a greedy route over his body. There was a telltale, faint roundness to his shoulders that hadn't been there before, suggesting a layer of muscle where before he'd been just bone and sinew. His ass was small and tight and slightly rounded too, and his legs looked a mile long in the slim-fitting pants.

Cursing myself, I closed my eyes and counted down from five. I could do this.

I opened my eyes, cleared my throat so he'd know I was coming, and started down the steps.

Peter took a few steps forward, as if to keep his distance, before turning with a guarded expression. "I guess I should have called."

"Yeah," I said, jogging down the stairs and not realizing what I was saying until I'd said it. I winced. I hadn't meant to agree that he should have called first. It was just nervous mumbling into the silence after he'd spoken. I stopped at the bottom of the steps and shoved my hands in my pockets.

Peter's eyes narrowed. "I had no way of knowing you'd be here."

"I know," I rushed to say, but then couldn't think of anything else, so I just looked at Peter while he glared at me.

After an awkward beat, Peter nodded toward the garage. "Chariot's in there, apparently." He strode toward the manual garage doors before I could warn him that he'd be lucky if any of them were still on their tracks. I'd cautiously checked out the garage while I was doing an inventory of the entire house, feeling like I should know the extent of what Grandpa and I were dealing with.

But to my surprise, when Peter grabbed the handle on the near side of the two-car garage and pulled, the door rolled open with a squeal of metal-on-metal. The low-riding, reinforced wheelbarrow that Grandpa had been using to haul Lemon around for decades was immediately inside, as though it was the last thing to have been wheeled in.

And it probably was, because just like the rest of the house, the garage was piled with an accumulation of old junk; most likely, there wasn't anything usable aside from the cart.

I braced myself for Peter's reaction, but he didn't seem bothered by the mess. Maybe the state it was in looked normal for a garage.

"If you can just help me get him in, I can take it from there," I said, falling into step a safe distance behind Peter as he wheeled the cart toward where his car was idling in the driveway.

"I told Gene I'd help you," Peter said stiffly. "I don't mind."

"Okay." I badly wanted to know what it was he'd read in the paper about Grandpa. I had the wild thought that Grandpa's hospital visit had been mentioned, but that was ridiculous. The doctors and Dolores wouldn't even tell *me* what had gone on with his stay there. There was no way anyone had written an article about it.

Curious as I was, I wasn't going to ask. I could see that I was one wrong word away from making Peter lose the tight hold he had on his temper.

He'd been like that as a kid, too. Bottled up. A stark contrast to me at the same age. I'd had no sense of how to keep my grip on the Meadows temper, which had made Peter's self-control seem like an asset. But now I knew how bad it felt to let things build up with no outlet.

Peter set the wheelbarrow on its legs and leaned into his car to turn off the engine. When he reemerged, I'd decided it was better that the tension between us snapped now than while we were trying to wheel a hundred-pound tortoise through the woods.

"This is weird."

He stopped short, and the blank expression from before shifted to one of reluctant amusement as he rubbed the back of his neck. "Yeah."

He'd reached up with his right arm, and it looked strong and perfectly functional.

He must have seen where my gaze had strayed because he held his arm out, twisting his wrist one way, then the other, his expression cool again. "It healed fine, if you were wondering."

I *had* wondered. Obsessed, really. Grandpa had called after I'd fled back to New York to assure me that Peter was going to be fine. He'd called again when Peter got his cast off. But I'd only heard messages. I'd been so stubbornly determined not to see or speak of Peter ever again. Now it seemed ridiculous, but I'd been eighteen. I'd *been* ridiculous.

I felt ridiculous now too, staring at Peter like I'd forgotten how to string more than two words together. Which was exactly how I felt.

He turned away from me abruptly, back on task.

Lemon had maneuvered himself off the driveway and was busy digging in the yard a few feet from Peter's car. He was worse than a gopher. Good thing Grandpa was pretty much the opposite of a landscaper, because Lemon could have trashed a flower bed or a vegetable garden in five minutes flat.

Peter positioned the wheelbarrow, and then we stood to either side of Lemon and lifted from beneath his carapace. Working wordlessly together, we hoisted him in a smooth arc into the wheelbarrow. When he was in place, Peter put a staying hand on his shell.

Lemon, familiar with his chariot, withdrew his head partially into his shell and settled in for the ride.

"You want to push or walk?" he asked, still without looking at me.

Peter had asked me that question so many times, and I'd always given the same answer. Pushing was the hard job. "Push," I said.

So that was how Peter and I arranged ourselves. I got the wheelbarrow handles, and he walked alongside with one hand on Lemon's carapace, absently scratching with his fingertips as we walked toward the trees. I caught the affectionate smile he aimed at the tortoise and found myself feeling jealous of a reptile.

We'd managed to load the tortoise and get underway without making eye contact. Though I glanced at Peter several times, his gaze was always firmly forward.

My heart was beating harder and harder from the strain of being close to him.

Didn't he want to tell me I was an asshole for leaving without saying goodbye? For leaving him while he'd been in the hospital, sedated?

Maybe he was over it. It had been eight years, and Peter had met so many people and done so many things.

"I didn't know you were in Burlington," I said when the silence became too much for me to take.

For a moment I thought he wasn't going to answer, but then he shrugged. Keeping the wheelbarrow steady for Lemon meant slow strides, and we'd only just left the yard where the house and old outbuildings were clustered and stepped into the shelter of the trees.

"I moved back last summer, after graduation."

He *lived* here? I was too surprised to do anything but blurt out my reaction. "Really?"

He stared ahead and nodded.

"Grandpa told me you were working in LA."

He glanced at me, and the moment of eye contact made my breath catch.

"I was." He dragged his teeth over his lower lip as he faced forward again. "I didn't realize he was keeping tabs on me. Uncle Frank…"

"I know he's been gone for a few years. I'm sorry."

"Thanks."

Peter rubbed small circles on Lemon's carapace with the heel of his hand. Lemon didn't like being touched on his head or his legs, but he enjoyed neck scratches and being petted or scratched on his shell. Of course Peter remembered that.

I shouldn't have bothered him with questions, but my curiosity won. "You said you've been living here since last summer?"

I saw a touch of color in his cheeks that I didn't think could be attributed to the slow-motion exercise of following Lemon the hundred yards from the driveway.

"I live with my parents. It's temporary." He cleared his throat. "Or at least, living with them is temporary. Living in Burlington… I don't know."

I had no idea what to do with this revelation. The last couple of summers we'd spent together, all I'd wanted was for Peter to admit to the possibility that he might want to live in my favorite place on earth, a place I saw him as wildly lucky to have lived in all his life. But his ambitions had always been for bigger and farther away. I'd always known on some level that the summers before we finished school were all I'd get of Peter's life, and I'd greedily eaten them up. It was only after we graduated that I'd begun to feel despair at losing him instead of gratitude at having him in the first place. I'd planned my grand gesture on the Ferris wheel as my last stand, but I started a fight instead. And then Peter fell.

I could still see him falling. His face frozen in a silent scream, his arms windmilling. I could still remember the sound of him hitting the ground, and then the piercing wail when he'd caught his breath several seconds later and used it to scream.

"A little more this way," Peter murmured.

I automatically adjusted the wheelbarrow's path. "You still remember your way around."

"And you still have no clue." I could see the corner of his lopsided smile.

I snorted. "Nope."

I'd figured the creek that threaded through the trees between the house and the park had to be dry in order for Lemon to have passed. But it was more of a mud hole at the low point in its banks where the trail crossed it. I frowned down at my clothes, which consisted of one of my three pairs of jeans, a flannel shirt I'd borrowed from Grandpa's closet, and my crappy but only pair of shoes. I wasn't too worried about myself, but Peter's pristine outfit was more of a concern.

"Why don't we go up to the road?" There was an old access road that used to be the public entrance to the park; a quarter-mile of crumbling asphalt. But it also featured a low-water bridge.

"I'm not going to backtrack half a mile just to avoid getting dirty," Peter said tartly. "I'll be fine."

"I'll have to go fast so the wheel doesn't get stuck," I warned.

"I'm ready," Peter assured me. "Just do it."

I pushed the wheelbarrow forward. Peter and the front tire of the wheelbarrow hit the mud at the same moment. Of course, as soon as his leather shoe was sucked ankle-deep into the muck, Peter stopped short.

Unwisely, I hesitated, and with the loss of momentum, the wheel lodged almost instantly. I barely managed to stop the wheelbarrow from tipping and spilling Lemon as my own feet sank.

I swallowed my first laugh, but when Peter jerked his foot free of the mud only to leave his shoe behind in the process, I couldn't stop the laugh that followed.

He lifted his head to glare at me. We were basically shoulder to shoulder, and he'd stretched out his arms for balance as he stood with one socked foot raised. His fingers grazed my shoulder, and then he rested his palm flat against me.

I'd been wrong; we weren't the same height. He was probably two inches shorter, which put us about on par with how we'd been as kids. Back then I'd loved the way that, when we faced each other and kissed, he'd had to stand slightly on his toes to reach me. Having his body strain and lean against mine that slightest amount had been almost as good as having his mouth on mine.

I knew he was only touching me to stop himself from toppling over, and I had both hands occupied with the handles of a wheelbarrow full of a hundred pounds of sulcata tortoise and my feet stuck in the mud, but his touch still carried a burst of electric heat that made my eyes flutter and my stomach swoop.

Then I looked down at his mud-flecked, exposed sock and lost the leash on my laughter.

"Goddammit," Peter muttered, but I could hear the smile in his voice too, and when I glanced up, I saw a flash of his familiar grin that always started on the right side of his mouth and took a second to turn up the left side too. "Don't laugh at me. Help me."

Turned out, we had to help each other. We were both stuck, and so was Lemon's chariot. By the time we'd hoisted the tortoise out of the wheelbarrow and set him on the opposite bank of the creek, then fished through the squelching mud to find Peter's shoe, then dragged the wheelbarrow free and up onto dry land, we were thoroughly mud-covered and wheezing with laughter.

Also, we were wet enough to be shivering, which made me worry for Lemon.

I caught Peter's eye, hating to interrupt the moment, my arm still burning where he'd touched me. "We'd better get him inside. It's getting colder."

Peter's smile vanished, too. "Yeah."

We got Lemon loaded up and headed out of the trees. Stepping into the clearing had always seemed like a grand reveal of the park, since the very first time Peter had shown it to me when we were nine.

A gated, wrought-iron fence encircled the half-acre. Looping welded letters arced above the entrance gate, spelling out *Meadows Park*. Young trees and brush were clustered at the entrance. The path was pitted and obscured by encroaching grass, and the scaffolding of the small roller coaster and the steel pinwheel of the Ferris Wheel bled with rust.

I'd hesitated at the edge of the clearing without realizing my muddy feet had stilled. Peter, back in position to my right and a step ahead of me, his hand splayed on Lemon's shell, stopped too. The sun struck his face, and he squinted against its glare. There was a pattern of mud droplets on his cheek like a tattoo, and total understanding in his blue, blue eyes.

Peter and I had been so close, for so many years, that we could say a lot to each other without saying anything. I'd assumed I'd lost that, and that I'd never find anyone I could build it with again. But apparently it wasn't lost, after all, because as our eyes locked, I knew exactly what he was thinking.

When we were nine and I was visiting Grandpa for the first time, Peter was already an expert on the park. He'd been my guide to every inch of its wonders. At the end of the tour, he'd asked me what I thought.

"It's magic. The best place on earth."

His eyes shined now just like they had back then when he'd nodded and solemnly agreed, *"Exactly."*

PETER

The problem with Riley Meadows was that I reacted differently to the idea of him than I did to the reality.

In theory, I was still mad at him, and would be forever. But in reality, I couldn't go twenty minutes without grinning at him like an idiot.

Maybe that was because the park *wasn't* reality. It was a magical dimension shoved into the mundane. Nothing else explained how I'd turned into Gene's driveway as a rational adult thinking about tax foreclosure, and now I was covered in mud, helping wheel a hundred-pound reptile toward ten-foot iron gates laced with ivy.

Being in the park had always felt like stepping into a fairy tale, and I guessed that was a magic I'd never outgrow.

Being in the park *with Riley* might have had something to do with it, too. Riley, who was smiling at me while I smiled back, his golden eyes warm and a lock of hair in his face.

I tore my eyes away and patted Lemon's shell. "Almost there."

As kids, we'd occasionally collected Lemon from some distant corner of Gene's property if there was rain in the forecast. We'd needed all our combined strength to roll him in his chariot up that last hill, our feet slipping in the grass and the backs of my thighs burning just from my half of the load. But grown-up Riley managed the task all on his own. He grunted softly with the effort but barely broke his stride up the slight grade toward the gates.

I followed, tipping my head back to take in the full view of the Ferris wheel that loomed front-and-center inside the gates. It was locked into the exact position it had been when I saw it last, with the gap for the missing passenger basket at two o'clock.

We'd climbed the Ferris wheel for years without getting hurt, which in hindsight was probably a miracle. I could remember almost losing my grip more than once. But I'd never fallen, not until the very last day I'd come here.

The memory made me swallow. I didn't remember anything after the moment of the fall. What had stayed fixed in my mind was Riley's horror-struck expression and his outstretched hand reaching for me in vain as gravity had overcome me.

I didn't remember the impact or the immediate pain. Riley must have gotten me to the house somehow, but I didn't remember that either. Only waking up in the hospital, and hurting, and then hurting more because Riley wasn't there and wouldn't return my texts and…

I stumbled over a patch of weeds. Wandering alongside Lemon and lost in my thoughts, I hadn't been looking where I was stepping. "Fuck." I leaned heavily on Lemon to catch myself, and he must have noticed the harder pressure because he extended his head a little from his shell and turned it my way, jaw dropping open hopefully. I snorted. "Sorry, buddy. My pockets are still empty."

"You okay?" The low rumble of Riley's voice was going to kill me if I didn't wrap up this surreal visit soon and get out of here.

"Fine," I said, without turning my head his way. I could keep a better handle on myself when I wasn't looking at him.

We had to take turns passing through the gates. They used to open and close smoothly, but now their rusty hinges had them wedged open, the gap between them just large enough for Riley to slide the wheelbarrow through.

Then we walked on under the shadow of the Ferris wheel, but I didn't look up at it again. Instead, I focused on where I was stepping.

The main park wasn't large, just a couple of acres. In addition to the Ferris wheel, there was a small roller coaster, so old that some of its support structure was made of wood instead of metal, and the wood had failed in spots, causing pieces of the structure to buckle.

There was also the Octopus—our name for the ride with long metal arms capped with airplane-shaped baskets. When the Octopus had been operational, the metal arms had undulated up and down while the entire ride turned in a circle.

Two round roofs on supports stood over the open space where the carousel and the bumper cars had been. The carousel horses had been sold—a sore subject with Gene that I'd learned as a child not to mention—and the bumper cars had never been operational in my lifetime, though that never stopped Riley and me from burning away many summer afternoons in the two cars that had remained nose-to-nose since the day the ride had been turned off for good.

The office stood to one side, a cylindrical two-story building embellished to look like a tower castle.

Then there was the greenhouse. Because it was a round building with a green roof, whichever Meadows ancestor had designed it apparently hadn't been able to resist the opportunity to add a stucco turtle head jutting from beneath the roof overhang at the entrance, and two clawed, scaled legs to either side. Paint had worn off the turtle's face in the past eight years, including most of the black from its eyes, leaving it looking like it was sleeping.

At the sight of his home, Lemon extended his head farther and pushed a little at the lip of the wheelbarrow with one foot.

"Let's stop here," I told Riley, before Lemon tumbled out on his own. We lifted him out.

"How has Gene been handling this big guy?" I wondered,

grimacing with relief as we deposited Lemon's substantial weight on the ground. He ambled toward the open doors to the greenhouse like going home had been his idea all along.

"He has help. He pays a teenager from town to come out."

"So, how's he doing? Health-wise."

Riley shot me a sharp glance, but then he shrugged. "He's okay, I guess. You coming in?" He walked into the greenhouse after Lemon, and I followed, giving Riley a wide berth where he waited to close the doors behind me.

The light was dimmer inside. Though the walls were transparent, there was no direct sunlight this time of day.

I took a deep breath of warm air that smelled strongly of Lemon—which was to say, not great. I had loved the big dude since I first saw him when I was about five years old, but he stank.

Lemon himself made his way eagerly toward a scattered pile of dry hay while I looked around.

All in all, the greenhouse seemed in pretty good shape. It was warm from a combination of refracted sunlight through the glass and supplementary heat from a few discreetly positioned vents. I knew where they were because I'd come out with Uncle Frank the weekend he'd helped Gene hook up a brand-new heating unit during my freshman year of high school.

Gene had always gone above and beyond to keep the greenhouse up. The same couldn't be said for the rest of the park. Not that Gene didn't love every inch of the place. Over the years, he had gotten ambitious about one project or another, but most things never got past the planning stage. He and Uncle Frank would sit on the porch while Gene waxed on and on about his grand plans for the park if only he could get it fixed up and reopened.

He'd declared he was repainting the office building one summer, using the cherry picker while standing on an old truck he'd bought. He'd conscripted twelve-year-old Riley to drive the truck in slow circles around the tower for hours. But the truck gave out before he'd run out of paint, and had to be towed out of the park to the eastern edge of his land, where it was now rowed up with a couple dozen other junk vehicles.

Then, one weekend during the school year, Gene had decided to get one of the old popcorn machines running again. I'd ridden along to Montpelier, wedged between Uncle Frank and Gene on the single bench seat of Gene's old pickup truck. But by the time the machine was ready to be picked up, Gene had lost steam again. As far as I knew, the popper was still parked somewhere in the garage, now probably under a pile of the junk I'd seen while we were getting the wheelbarrow. I doubted it had been so much as turned on since it was fixed up.

Maybe Gene's energy for everything else came and went, but Lemon needed the greenhouse to survive. No matter what, Gene had kept the creaky ventilation system working, regularly maintained the heater, and ensured that Lemon's hay supply never ran out.

Riley was cutting the twine on a hay bale now, his jeans pulling tight over his ass as he bent over. Damn it, looking at him at all was completely unsafe. His ass, his thick thighs, the bow of his back... everything about his body made me stare.

I turned away and leaned against the concrete divider between the designated tortoise area and the flamingo pool. The flamingos had been before my time, but getting another flock was always on the reopening to-do list Gene had laid out to Uncle Frank again and again.

I'd never seen the pool with water in it, but around the big concrete bowl in the floor, there used to be mature tropical plants. They seemed to have been pulled out, leaving mounds of arid dirt. Nothing could survive in Lemon's pen without him mauling it to death. But with Lemon as the only living thing inside, the greenhouse felt desolate. I couldn't blame Riley for wanting to let Lemon roam outside despite the questionable weather.

Riley looked at me as he dusted hay off his sleeves. "Thanks for helping."

"No big deal. You gave me the easy job." Except for the part where I'd gotten stuck in the mud, but then, it had felt so good to laugh with Riley that I couldn't even regret the sacrifice of my favorite pair of suede ankle boots.

"You probably want to get back to the house to see Grandpa."

Right. Between finding Riley here in the flesh, the tortoise wrangling, the mud bath, and seeing the park again, I kept forgetting the troubling reason I was visiting in the first place. The foreclosure. Which I was pretty sure Riley knew nothing about, based on his confusion earlier.

I nodded. "Yeah. But if there's anything else you need help with—"

"Nah," he interjected before I could even finish, which made me frown. Maybe the sense of lingering closeness when our eyes had met had been all in my head. One-sided.

We trudged back the way we'd come, the wheelbarrow rattling along easily now that it was empty, and a heavy silence fell between us.

Half my mind was spinning with frustration. I had this opportunity to see Riley again, to talk to him about something that mattered, and I wasn't seizing my chance. The other half of my mind just wanted to get out of this encounter unhurt.

Torn, I didn't know what to do except let my feet carry me to Gene's house by muscle memory, my head down and my mouth shut.

Gene was waiting on the porch. He waved and leaned over the railing when he saw us come out of the trees. Riley took the wheelbarrow back to the garage, and Gene gestured for me to sit beside him in the Adirondack chair with the chipped green paint.

"What'd you boys do, go for a swim?" Gene crowed, taking in my mud-caked calves and trashed boots.

"We probably should have taken the road," I admitted, sinking into the chair.

Gene shook his head, chuckling. "Nothing wrong with a little dirt. It's good for you. You used to know that, Pete."

I breathed out a laugh. The funny thing was, he was right. I'd been so carefree when I ran wild at Gene's place. My classmates and professors at Harvard had probably always thought of me as a country boy—they couldn't conceive of any other kind of lifestyle in Vermont. But I was also known for being immaculately dressed, painstakingly analytical, and risk-averse. They wouldn't recognize the version of me that seemed to exist only in the park.

While I was lost for a moment in my inner musings, Gene had turned solemn. "So, you wanted to talk?"

I nodded and sneaked a glance at Riley, who was headed our way and definitely within earshot.

Gene waved in dismissal before I could ask whether he wanted me to say anything more in front of his grandson. "He was going to figure it out sooner or later, Pete. Don't tie yourself in knots."

Riley paused on the stairs. "Find out about what?"

"The park," Gene said simply with another wave of his hand. "The taxes."

Riley looked from me to Gene and back again, obviously bewildered. "What about the taxes?"

Gene leaned back in the chair and stretched out one leg, tapping the heel of his boot against the porch. Then he glanced at me like he wanted me to answer instead.

So I spoke for him, hesitantly. "The property taxes haven't been paid in... a while. Which means the assessor can auction off the park on Gene's behalf and take the taxes out of the proceeds."

Riley's stare was blank. For a moment I thought maybe I'd used too much legalese and he hadn't tracked what I'd told him, but then he rounded on Gene.

"How is that possible?" Riley's voice was rough, like he was trying to rein himself in, but even so, his voice rose as he went on. "You have millions of dollars, and from what I can see, you haven't spent a cent of it! Why wouldn't you pay your taxes?"

Gene jerked up his chin. His obstinate look was one I recognized well, from his face and his grandson's. "That's my business."

"Did you hear what Peter said? You could lose the park if you don't pay!"

"And that's what's wrong with this government," Gene snapped, crossing his arms. "What right do they have to charge me taxes on land that's been in my family for six generations? That's what I'd like to know!"

"So, what, you're refusing to pay taxes because you don't *believe* in taxes? They don't care, Grandpa! The only one who's going to learn a lesson when you lose the place is *you*!"

I watched them with growing alarm. Gene had always been eccentric, and some of his political arguments over the years had made me shake my head. Uncle Frank had had an anarchistic streak, too. But I couldn't believe Gene would risk the park in a philosophical protest about the concept of property tax. Especially considering he'd already been paying the same tax for decades.

I twisted in my chair to face him. "Gene, there's no way around it."

He glanced at me, blotchy red stains on his cheeks, easy to see through the white wisps of his beard. His eyes were unmistakably sad, but his mouth curled into a stiff smile as he leaned over to pat my knee. "You're right, Pete. I know it. I just wanted to make the tax collectors sweat a bit. Make them think about things. There's not going to be any sale. I'll pay those bastards well before that."

Everything he was saying made sense. I knew he had the money, and it would be in character for Gene to make a big deal out of a random whim. And yet, as he spoke, dread formed a gnawing pit in my stomach.

I smiled back, probably no more convincingly than Gene, and covered the cool fingers gripping my knee with my own. "Okay. I think that's a good idea. I could even take the payment in for you, if you want. I'd let them know you're paying under protest."

He squeezed my knee again, then slipped his hand from beneath mine and got to his feet. I rose along with him. "Not necessary, not necessary. I want to do it myself. But thank you, kid. You know, it's about time for my nap. Don't be a stranger, you hear?"

He hugged me to him with one arm, and I submitted, trying to think of something else to say that would ensure the taxes got taken care of, but coming up short. I squeezed him back, patting his back. "Okay, Uncle Gene. I won't."

RILEY

When I was a kid, Grandpa's grouchiness was my favorite thing about him. He was never grouchy with *me*. Everyone else got his prickly side, but I got his sly grins. He'd made me feel like we'd been keeping a secret from the wider world, even if I hadn't known exactly what it was.

Since I'd been reunited with Grandpa, it was hard to imagine feeling immune to his temper.

"Stop hovering," he snapped, eyeing me from his chair while I bent over him to make sure he'd counted out the right amount of Tylenol into his palm.

"What do you need it for, anyway?" My gaze skimmed over him nervously. "Is there something wrong with your leg?" He favored the right one when he walked, but I was pretty certain at this point that an injury hadn't put him in the hospital. He was sick, and it wasn't just manifesting in the mounds of junk.

"You get to be my age, and you'll have a stash of this stuff in your house too. And one in the truck, and one in the shed." He dry-swallowed the pills and set the uncapped jar back on the table next to his armchair. "Now let me breathe, kid!"

I took a step back, frustration welling, but I didn't know what to do with it. Grandpa wasn't the only reason I was on edge, but I refused to think about the other reason.

Of course, the thoughts slipped through anyway, like they always did. A rush of memories of Peter over the years, like a slideshow in ultra-fast-forward. Except that what used to be the last slide—Peter, cheeks mottled red and flinching while I yelled at him, then *falling*—was replaced with a new one, of a grown-up Peter with incredible legs and really good hair.

It had been three days since Peter was at the park, and still, every time I heard a car on the driveway, I practically ran to the window, thinking it might be him. But inevitably, it was only the mailman or one of Grandpa's friends stopping for a glass of tea on the porch. Peter had no reason to come back. Even if he wanted to help Grandpa, now that he knew I was here, he wouldn't just drop by.

I didn't have the bandwidth to let Peter crowd my thoughts while I was trying to deal with Grandpa, so I pushed him aside as best I could and crossed my arms. "If you won't let me help you, maybe we should call someone else."

Grandpa jerked up his head and scowled at me. "Like who?"

"Aunt Tabby's a nurse."

"Please. Tabitha works in a hospital, but that doesn't make her a nurse!"

I frowned. "She wears scrubs."

Grandpa looked at me like he thought I was trying to make a joke. I hadn't thought about it, but he was probably right that Aunt Tabby didn't have any special skills. If I remembered right, she'd gone into her hospital job directly from waiting tables.

"Not to mention, she didn't even have the decency to apologize for her boys after they came sniffing around," Grandpa went on, mumbling.

"Wait. Mick and Stevie were down here?"

I could tell Grandpa hadn't meant to tell me that. He folded his arms and shrugged. "Yeah, a few months back. They didn't stay too long after I told them I wasn't interested in funding their startup."

"Startup?" I echoed. "You mean that video streaming thing where they charge people to watch them play old video games?" Not that there was anything wrong with making money from silly videos. I didn't live under a rock; I knew people made money doing it. But my cousins were low on work ethic, and the streaming was just the most recent in a long list of things they'd been sure would make them rich with minimal effort.

Grandpa shrugged again and scratched his arms. "Maybe. It was some damn thing. I told them I couldn't help, and all of a sudden, they had somewhere else to be." He looked out the window, his jaw tight.

Those two could be charming when they wanted to be, and then bite you in the ass, like every snake in every fable.

"They shouldn't have done that. It's your money, and you shouldn't be giving it away."

He made a noncommittal sound but didn't immediately change the subject. My heart picked up speed. For weeks I'd tried to figure out a way to approach this topic, and suddenly—accidentally—here I was, with the perfect opportunity to ask him what I really wanted to know.

"So... do you have any ideas about that?"

He didn't look at me. "What?"

I held in the urge to sigh. Maybe there was something going on with him mentally, but for the most part he'd proved himself as astute as ever. He knew what I meant. "Do you have any ideas of what to do with the money? Come on. I remember how you used to talk about what would happen if you won." Anyone who bought tickets once a week, the way Grandpa used to do, thought about how they'd spend their winnings. Why else would they buy the tickets?

Grandpa only grunted. Since he hadn't shot me down yet, I pressed on, well aware I was shuffling out onto thin ice.

"You used to say you'd invest most of it in the park, right? Fix it up. Are you still thinking of doing that?"

He pushed himself up from his chair abruptly, startling me. "I'm going to rest in my room."

So much for not getting shot down. At least I'd been able to touch on the subject, though, which was further than I'd gotten before.

When I heard Grandpa's bedroom door close and the faint, twisting, metallic sound of its lock, a fresh wave of worry churned through me.

I'd had this same feeling yesterday, when Grandpa got back from a trip to town with a friend. I'd asked if everything was settled with his past-due taxes, and he'd waved me off, saying something vaguely reassuring, but he hadn't answered my question directly. Maybe I should have insisted on seeing the receipt.

I wandered into the kitchen, now a cocoon of piles of mail and magazines and empty containers on every surface.

Thinking about the tax problem made me think of its unlikely messenger. Of course.

Even in the face of Grandpa's enormous problems, which I had no idea how to help him solve, I couldn't help it when my thoughts strayed to Peter.

Living with regret about Peter Landry was part of my daily life, a familiar twist in my chest. But seeing him again had twisted me up in a whole new way.

I'd known there was something special about Peter since the day we met, when he'd raced through the woods like a deer and I'd been running as fast as I could to keep up. On the receiving end of Peter's easy smile and sparkling eyes, there had been no way I could do anything but smile back and go wherever he led me.

Three days ago, when Peter showed up, I learned I still had the magnet in my chest that reeled me toward him and gave me the sense that all was right in the world when he laughed. No one else had ever made me feel that way.

But daydreaming about Peter wasn't going to help Grandpa.

I shook open a trash bag and picked up some of the stuff on the kitchen floor. When I tried to throw stuff away with Grandpa close by, he got pissed. But he was shut in his room, and I doubted he'd come back out anytime soon.

I was sure there was something he wasn't confessing about the taxes. He'd acted like he had everything under control. And he should have, considering it was a question of paying some money and he had money in ample supply.

Still, doubts nagged at me.

After I'd been staying with him a few days, I'd given up on asking Grandpa questions, and poked around the house instead, looking for the answers he wouldn't give me. Every time I thought I might have found a box of documents or something else relevant to Grandpa's health, they turned out to be full of truck stop receipts or random junk bought at yard sales and never so much as unpacked.

The cumulative frustration thrummed through me. I'd been deliberately picking up actual trash from the floor that I was sure Grandpa wouldn't notice was gone, but now I paused and scanned the countertop instead. To the right of the sink were rows and rows of pickle jars, lids screwed on tightly and filled with varying levels of green vinegar. I itched to drop them all into the bag.

If I did, I'd be inviting a raging fight with Grandpa. But maybe a fight was what we needed. For better or for worse, sometimes that was how two Meadows got their points across.

I winced at the *clink* of each jar and the *whoosh* as I swept a pile of old mail off the table and into the bag, but the sounds didn't bring Grandpa running. I tied off the first bag when it got heavy, set it on the floor, and had shaken out another bag when something caught my eye.

I'd cleared enough of the counter by getting rid of the jars that I could see the old breadbox wedged behind a stack of unopened cereal boxes. It was blue tin, a little dinged up, with hand-painted trout lilies in little clusters.

I pulled it onto the cleared section of the counter and pushed up the lid. I'd half expected a withered loaf of bread that predated the pickle-jar collection, but the only thing inside was a mason jar stuffed with a few five-dollar bills.

I huffed out a breath of amusement. The past had crept up on me again. Inevitably, while I'd stayed with Grandpa, there had been days when the weather had been too wet to play outside. Trapped inside and forced to entertain myself, I'd gone on secret treasure hunts, looking for the jars stashed throughout the house.

Grandpa hated banks. He'd always said so. When we went into town for ice cream or gas, he'd often refill his wallet from whatever jar was closest at hand. I'd seen him empty one from the top shelf of the coat closet, and another from inside the heavy glass umbrella vase by the door.

I hadn't thought much of it when I was a kid. Grandpa squirreling away his money was just another way that Gene Meadows was unlike anyone else.

Caught up in the memory, I left the unfilled trash sack beside the full one and wandered into the dining room. I had to move some boxes to make space to duck under the table. Sure enough, dead center in the middle of it was a jar, glued by its lid. It was empty, though. I never remembered this one being empty. Usually it was full, and if the coil of money was arranged right inside, I could read the numbers printed on the outermost bill. Often it was a hundred.

Then I checked all the usual places—the hall closet, the umbrella vase, the box next to the back door where he kept firewood. In each one, the jars were there but empty.

Noise in the kitchen drew me back there to find Grandpa elbows-deep in the bag I'd filled, pulling stuff back out, his expression furious. He saw me and pointed a quivering finger. "Who the hell do you think you are? These are my things. I told you!" He put handful after handful of crumpled mail on the table, pickle jars rattling each time he shoved his hand inside the bag.

As I looked at him, a few things slid into place. The money jars. Banks. The lottery money. Sadness and panic squeezed my throat like twin fists.

"You never listen," Grandpa spat at me. "None of you kids ever listen!"

"Grandpa," I finally managed.

"Don't talk, listen! I told you that you could stay here and help out, but I meant with the things that I need help with. I don't need any help in my own damn house!"

"Grandpa!" I raised my voice just enough so he'd know I was serious, and he paused for the moment I needed to get my question out. "When you won the money, what did you do with it? Did you put it in the bank?"

His scowl twisted into something I couldn't read, but I caught what looked like a mirror of my own wide-eyed panic, and for a second I couldn't breathe.

I answered my own question. "You didn't. You put it in the house somewhere." I gazed around, overwhelmed all over again by the sheer volume of *stuff* wherever my eyes landed. "And maybe you forgot where."

He scoffed. "You think I'd put two million dollars in this house?" Relief rushed through me, but it didn't last long, as he went on, "I got an aluminum case and buried it in the park." His derisive tone faltered as he added, "And *then* I forgot where."

Fuck.

Inside would be bad enough. Combing through the stuff in here could take weeks.

But the park? Finding a fucking needle in a haystack would be easier.

"In the park," I echoed, my voice rough. "When?"

"A couple of months after it came, when it was warm enough to dig. I had it in the house at first. Thought I might put it in the walls. Stuff the mattress with it." He looked around as though dazed. "I had this nightmare, over and over, that it would catch fire and that would be that."

I didn't point out that he was naming one of the reasons people put their money *in the bank*, but it was a close call. I swallowed. "Okay. So you buried it. And you don't remember where?" I tried to keep my voice level.

He shook his head. "Don't remember the night much at all. I woke up from another one of those damn dreams, got a shovel, and dug until my hands bled. I rolled the safe into the hole off the back of the old ATV. Finished filling it in just in time to watch the sun come up."

I rubbed my forehead. "But you don't remember where?"

He looked at me, his eyes so haunted, I couldn't bring myself to feel angry, only sorry for him. But I knew he wouldn't want to be pitied, so I didn't offer any comfort.

"I kept a little of it here in the house. But that's spent now. And the rest…"

I leaned heavily against the old kitchen table. "Maybe you could hire someone to look for it, or—"

"No goddamn way!"

I grimaced, but his reaction didn't surprise me. Of course he wouldn't trust a stranger to go looking and not try to keep at least some of what they found. Or claim they found nothing and keep it all. I wasn't nearly as distrustful of people as Grandpa, and even I could see his point.

"It should have been easy to find," he muttered, crossing and recrossing his arms. "Ten paces off the south side of the ride. I said it a hundred times, so I wouldn't forget."

"What about… I don't know, a metal detector?" I tried.

He rubbed his jaw. "Don't work on aluminum."

Which was probably why he'd chosen aluminum. My flare of hope receded. Just after Grandpa had buried the money, there might have been evidence of disturbed ground or trampled brush. But now? *Five years.* Five years of the grass growing and the trees spreading. I'd seen how much the place had changed since I'd been gone.

At least he had *some* idea of where he'd buried it. Or did he? Maybe he'd gone only five paces to the south, or three. How the fuck long was a *pace*, anyway? And what had he used to plot direction? An actual compass, or his gut?

"Grandpa," I said on a sigh. "This is a fucking mess."

I expected him to shout at me, but instead a bark of laughter escaped him. He dropped the trash bag, and I heard glass breaking. Grandpa trailed a shaky hand over the top of his head, where his white hair was thinnest.

My heart thudded once more with despair, and then in the next beat, I felt a pulse of something else. Determination, maybe. A little hope. And most of all, growing like a flame in my heart, purpose.

The park was bounded by a fence, and it was big, but the task wasn't impossible. I could dig up every inch of it if I had to.

"I'm going to find it."

He shook his head slowly, still so white-faced that looking at him made my eyes sting. He looked every day of his almost eighty years. "Maybe it's not there. Maybe someone sneaked in and took it."

"Why would anyone go looking? Did you tell somebody?"

"Just you. You really think you can find it?" His voice had become very small, his eyes wide with hope, like if I thought I could do it, he'd believe I could do it too.

"I'll find it," I said firmly, hoping I didn't turn out to be a liar. Then I hesitated and added, "But I'm going to need a little help."

"I don't get around like I used to. Can't stay awake either. I try not to get too far from my chair."

"I don't mean you. Somebody else. Not just anybody," I clarified before he could protest. "Someone you trust."

Grandpa was friendly with a lot of people, but I knew he didn't hand out real trust lightly. With Frank gone, there was only one person—besides me, apparently—that I knew Grandpa would share his secret with.

Understanding dawned in his expression. "Pete."

"Yeah." Despite having just discovered the full extent of Grandpa's bizarre mess, my heart sped up at the knowledge that I had an excuse to see Peter again. He wouldn't be able to say no, not when Grandpa needed him, even if agreeing to help meant being around me. Though it had hurt to see him a few days before, it had also been the best day I'd had since the last one we'd spent together. I would take the bad with the good.

Grandpa smiled as though all his massive problems were already solved. "My two boys. Of course you'll find it if you work together."

The weight of his trust settled heavily on my shoulders, and I really, really hoped I deserved it.

PETER

I could hear Aunt Iris's low, steady voice as I approached her office after waving to Jen, the receptionist. By Aunt Iris's tone, I instantly knew someone had crossed her, and they were about to be very sorry.

I paused in the hall right outside her door, not *intending* to eavesdrop. It wasn't my fault her voice carried.

"If you think you're going to steamroll my clients just because they happen to live in Vermont, then you're twice the ignoramus you assume them to be."

Aunt Iris was my godmother, not my actual aunt. She and my mother had been best friends since they were in elementary school, and Iris and her partner, Tom, had no kids of their own but were happy to spoil me whenever possible. Her general life philosophy was the promotion of inner and outer peace, but when she was defending a client or a principle she believed in, no one was scarier.

"I spent ten years in Washington, and I assure you, I have a few senators on speed dial who would love to know that the EPA wants to run roughshod over a citizen's constitutional right to due process."

She must've scared whoever was on the other end of the call

sufficiently because I heard her gruff farewell and the receiver hitting its cradle. I pushed open the door. Aunt Iris was at her desk, her silver-streaked brown hair in a braid, and she was wearing a violet tunic with orcas embroidered on it. She looked up and beamed at the sight of me.

"Honey! I knew you'd come by today. This morning while I was meditating, I caught a distinct whiff of citrus. You can ask Tom. I came in to breakfast thinking he'd made me orange juice, but there wasn't a piece of fruit in the house!"

According to Aunt Iris, citrus was the scent of my essence. I smiled back and came over to kiss her cheek before sliding into the chair across her desk.

"Do you have court today?" I asked. The crocs by the door were a modest black, which as far as I knew she only deigned to wear as a concession to the rules for attorney attire at the courthouse.

"Yes, but not until after lunch. Which gives us plenty of time to chat." She looked at me over the half-moon lenses of her glasses. "How do you feel about taking a case?"

I groaned.

"Just a little one!" She held up her thumb and forefinger a half-inch apart. "Teeny tiny."

"Aunt Iris, we've talked about this."

"I'm just asking! You can say no."

"I don't even work here!" I pointed out, not really expecting the protest to slow her down.

"It's just a *small* case," she insisted. "And it's brand-new, so you can run solo with it. You won't be giving us the nod to put your name on the sign by agreeing. You'll just be doing a favor for a family friend."

"You're not just a family friend," I muttered, and she beamed at me again.

"I know, honey. I'm family, full stop. It's not a favor for *me*; it's a favor for my friend, Marion."

Aunt Iris said the name like I should know who she was talking about. I squinted, trying to remember.

"The artist," she prompted.

"Oh, the one with the rabbits?" There was a local artist who dealt entirely in rabbits—she painted them and sculpted them from clay or found objects. I remembered attending a show with Aunt Iris when I was maybe eleven or twelve, and feeling like I'd gone down Alice's rabbit hole.

"Exactly!" She flipped a few pages on the legal pad in front of her, then tore out a sheet of notes and handed it to me. "Here. This should be everything you need to know."

"I didn't say yes," I reminded her absently as I read, tilting my head to follow the slant of her tight cursive. "Are you sure this is everything I need to know?" I asked, bemused. "All it says is: 'Marion. Vicious rabbits. Party fence.'" I glanced up with a snort. "Plus my name, with a question mark."

"And the address and phone number," Aunt Iris confirmed with a nod.

I looked down at the page again. If only the attorneys I'd worked with in the Los Angeles law firm could see me now, taking the lead on my very own, vicious-rabbit case. A thought like that might have stung last summer, when I was still grieving the death of my Big Law ambitions, but now I just smiled to myself, picturing their horrified expressions.

"It shouldn't take long. One strongly worded phone call or demand letter should sew it up. And if you record your time, I'll cover it out of that reserve we have for pro bono work."

"Pro bono work done by the lawyers in your firm, which I'm not." I thought about scooting her notes back across the desk, but for some reason, I folded the sheet of paper in half and held on to it instead. "I'll talk to her. We can call it a free consultation."

"Excellent. Marion will be so relieved. She wouldn't want just any unfeeling stranger traipsing around her labyrinth, but you have such a sweet energy about you. I'm sure she'll take to you right away."

I felt instant regret for agreeing to whatever I was now entangled in. "Did you say *labyrinth*?"

Of course, it was too late to escape the tide of Aunt Iris's meddling. "Did you want to use that empty office down the hall? Though there might be a little clutter in there still. Tom put some of the odds and ends in there when we were getting the space next door ready for Aaron. Oh, wouldn't it be nice for the two of you to settle in here together at the beginning of the summer? Then the workplace energy would only have one reorientation instead of two. We'd all lose a lot less sleep." She leaned forward. "Is that why you came by? Have you made a decision?"

I held up a hand as if it would keep her at bay. "I'm not here to get hired. I came to drop off this." I dug in the hip pocket of my navy chinos for the thumb drive and set it in the middle of her desk. "Mom was busy, and I was... free."

"Are those the photos for the historic district application? Already?" Aunt Iris actually looked surprised, and I snorted.

"Have you met my parents? I'm surprised it took them an entire forty-eight hours to get what you asked for." The historic resources board, which my parents had been members of since before I was born, was helping a neighborhood apply for historic district status with the state, and the application required exterior photographs of every building. "I guess the light wasn't right on Friday, so they waited it out." I rolled my eyes. "You have no idea how many times they said the word *stickwork* in the past month while they've been revving up for this. I've started flinching every time I hear it, like a trauma response."

"Now, Peter. Don't be unkind," Aunt Iris said reprovingly. "They're passionate about history and architecture. Passion is commendable."

I sighed. "You're right. Anyway, I'll let you get back to work." I got up and returned to her side to dutifully kiss her cheek. She smelled like dandelions and hairspray, the way she had for as long as I could remember.

"Tell Marion I sent you!" she reminded me as I reached her office door.

"Will do."

I glanced at the folded paper in my hand as I traipsed out of the firm's building and onto the street.

Maybe I'd call Marion—did she have a last name?—from Vino and Veritas. I'd made the bookstore my home away from home while I was studying for the bar, stuffing extra money in the tip jar like I was paying rent. Why not let it be the place where I made calls on bizarre legal errands from my aunt?

The sun was shining today, making the walk down the wide pedestrian mall that encompassed this block of Church Street even more pleasant than usual. It was almost as warm today as it had been when I'd gone out to the park. I wondered if that meant Riley had let Lemon out again, and whether Gene had given him hell for it.

I shied away from letting my thoughts stray too far toward the Meadows, though. I was just getting my head above water again after seeing them the other day. Every morning I thought about driving back out there. I told myself it was because I wanted to ask Gene more about the tax matter, maybe twist his arm into letting me help. But mainly, I wanted an excuse to see Riley again.

The Vino and Veritas building had a bookstore on one side and a wine bar on the other. The spaces were separate except for a shared main entrance. I turned right, entered the bookstore, and looked around hopefully for Briar. I was bad at remembering his schedule, but I thought he was working today. I didn't find Briar, but there was another familiar face behind the coffee counter in the corner.

"Hey, Autumn. Could I get a double soy latte?"

She glanced up and wrinkled her nose. "I guess."

"You guess?"

She shrugged as she stepped in front of the espresso machine and pulled a lever. "I just can't believe you always ask for *soy* milk, Peter Landry." She pulled a clean spoon from a crock. Her delicate features, freckles, and strawberry-blonde hair made her look more like a forest sprite than someone who could do much damage armed with nothing but a teaspoon, but I still leaned away when she pointed the spoon at me.

"I'm sorry?"

"You'd think someone who was born and raised in Vermont would have more respect for the dairy industry." She reached for a carton of soy milk and glared at it before pouring it into the pitcher.

"Some people are allergic to dairy," I pointed out.

"Are *you*, though?"

"No," I admitted, then frowned. "Wait, don't you and your brother have a hemp farm?"

She looked at me like I'd said something completely beside the point, then looked back down as she inserted the steam wand. "Yes. But we don't make fake milk out of it."

She set down my coffee while I chuckled, then took a sip, enjoying the taste of the house blend with the perfect dash of sugary, imitation-dairy goodness.

"Maybe it's fake, but it's delicious," I informed her.

Autumn started talking again, something about hemp, and how she and her brother weren't interested in dairy replacement products, and why, but I was distracted by a flash of motion outside the windows.

There was no reason for this particular passerby to catch my eye. At this time of day, Church Street always had a steady stream of foot traffic. And plenty of people had dark hair, wide shoulders, and flannel shirts. But maybe I had a sixth sense for Riley Meadows. I knew him in just a glimpse of the back of his head and the set of his shoulders.

"Ignore me all you want," Autumn said, sailing around from behind the counter. "I've got a shipment to unpack. If you need a refill, ring the bell." She patted my arm in passing.

Riley walked in. I knew I should look away, but where he was concerned, I'd always had a shitty sense of self-preservation.

I'd spent an hour looking at him out of the corner of my eye while we'd hauled Lemon up to the greenhouse, but I hadn't *stared*.

So it was just now that I was fully taking him in, down to the little details. His beard was short, thick, and neatly groomed. It looked fucking good on him. As a kid, his messy dark waves had hung to his shoulders, and when we were out in the park, he'd often tied his hair back into a half-ponytail just to keep it out of his face. Now his hair was shorter, but just long enough on top to look deliberately tousled.

I managed to stop admiring the breadth of his chest and walk over, almost not feeling my feet, my latte quaking slightly. "Hi."

He cleared his throat, his voice low and full of gravel. "Hi."

"So, what are you doing here?" It was an offhand question, just something meaningless to prevent an awkward silence.

His expression turned wary. "Right. Me, in a bookstore. Pretty ridiculous."

"That's not what I meant," I hurried to say. "Fuck, of course I didn't mean that."

His jaw ticked, but after a second he nodded shortly. "Okay. I'm not here for a book. I was looking for you. Your mom said you were probably here or at Iris's. I stopped here first."

"You talked to my *mom*?"

"Yeah. She was in the yard when I came by your house."

"You went to my *house*?"

He narrowed his eyes, probably because I was acting like a complete fool. "Yeah. I was looking for you, like I said."

"Right." I glanced at my feet. "Well, here I am."

"It's about Grandpa."

My eyes flew to his. "Is he okay?"

"Yes. Well, sort of."

I frowned.

Riley sighed. "I'll explain it, but not"—he glanced around the bookstore—"here."

"Okay, that's fine. Should we go somewhere else?"

Riley shook his head again. "I have to take Grandpa to a doctor's appointment. Can I get your number?"

"You already have it."

He blinked at me.

I bit my lip. "Or maybe you don't. There's no reason you would remember it. I just meant, it's the same one I've always had." Fuck, what were the words coming out of my mouth? I couldn't stop them now that they'd started. "Do you want me to write it down, or...?" *Unflappable,* an esteemed judge had once called me during an intense mock trial debate. If only she could see me now.

"You don't have to," Riley said, his quiet voice interrupting me and silencing me more effectively than a shout. "I remember it."

"Oh." I looked at my shoes again. "I know yours, too."

He made a small noise, then cleared his throat. "I'll text you, and we'll figure out a time for you to come out to the park and talk?"

I had to swallow to stop myself from saying yes before he'd finished asking the question. After a beat of silence, I nodded.

"Good."

We looked at each other. His eyes were still like a hawk's, in their color and their intense focus. I was pinned by them. I didn't know how long I would have stood there, just looking at him, if he hadn't taken a deep breath and turned away first.

As soon as he was gone, I wanted to kick myself.

What got into me when Riley was around? I was supposed to be mad at him. I had *good reason* to be mad at him. When he wasn't right in front of me, all the hurt was so much easier to remember. But when he *was* right in front of me, all I wanted was to be near him, to have him close as a shadow, the way he'd been when we'd raced through the park as kids.

"Who was *that*?"

I spun around to find Briar behind me. Going by the little pebbles of foam packing material clinging to the cuff of one of his sleeves, he'd been in the storeroom.

"Riley," I said without thinking. "Riley Meadows. I guess."

He raised his eyebrows. "You *guess*?"

"I need to go," I said, which was nonsensical because I was holding a mug with the Vino and Veritas logo on it, still full to the brim. But I could tell by the look in his eyes that I wasn't going to be able to shake off his curiosity if I stuck around. "I don't feel so well." I put the latte in the bus bin by the counter with a wistful parting glance. What a waste.

"Okay," Briar called, looking more confused than ever as I waved over my shoulder midway through my beeline for the door. "I hope you feel better!"

I hoped I felt better, too. The question was whether spending more time with Riley was going to remedy what had been ailing me since law school graduation, or only make it worse.

There was only one way to know for sure.

7
RILEY

I didn't know how else to do it, so when Peter showed up the next morning, I sat down on the front porch steps and told him everything. The whole situation was an impossible mess, but it didn't take all that many words to lay it out. Grandpa, banks, the mason jars, and how that attitude when he had thousands of dollars had transferred directly to the millions he'd won. His increasing paranoia, and the night he'd blistered his hands digging in the dark.

At some point in the telling, Peter dropped down onto the step next to me and put his elbows on his knees, then his head in his hands. When I finished, he lifted his head again.

"That's…" Peter began, then stopped again. "It's wild. *Shit.* Poor Gene."

I nodded, unsure what else to say. Then I realized I hadn't even done the hardest part—I hadn't asked for his help. I'd only planned the half of the conversation where I told him what was going on, and now I didn't know how to ask him to wade into it with me.

Peter's matter-of-fact tone interrupted my spiral. "I'll help you look."

Of course Peter was already one step ahead of me, offering

help without waiting for anyone to ask him. Just as he had when Lemon had needed to get back to the greenhouse a few days ago.

Just as he always had, all the years I'd known him.

Because under the taller, leggier, sleeker exterior, Peter was still the same person who'd led me through long, hot days of make-believe in the park, who'd heard all my secrets, who'd been the one, that July day when we were fourteen, to close the last inch between our mouths and seal our first kiss.

Damn it. I'd missed him so much.

"Thanks," I managed, my voice tight. "We might not be able to find it, no matter how hard we try. Not in time to get the taxes settled."

He shook his head, and his hand landed on my knee, almost like he'd touched me without thinking, the way he used to. He'd always been so tactile, and I'd loved that. But right now, we both froze as soon as he made contact, and after a second, he snatched his hand back.

"We'll find it," he said firmly, looking forward. "We'll divide the park into sections, and we'll make a plan. We'll search every inch of it if we have to." He cracked a smile that didn't quite reach his eyes. "It'll be fun."

The back of my neck was hot, and I was trying not to look at him directly for the same reason I didn't stare into the sun. But I couldn't help curling my hand over my knee where Peter had touched me, like I could contain the burst of electricity still dancing on my skin from the brief weight of his hand through a layer of frayed denim.

"If you say it, then I guess it's true." It was my old line from when we were kids, and I'd always meant it—Peter had seemed to know *everything*, constantly telling me the names for types of grass or talking like an adult about what was in the news—but he'd always taken it as a joke.

Apparently he still did, because I glanced at him just in time to catch his smile, so of course I smiled too.

Just as he had when his hand landed on my leg, Peter pulled

back a second later, this time by breaking eye contact and standing up. "Does Gene still have those old maps of the park? We could make a photocopy or maybe trace the one from the seventies with the aerial view."

My gut clenched as he made for the front door. "Wait!" I scrambled to my feet.

"What?" Peter looked bewildered. "Are you okay?"

I forced myself to draw and slowly release a breath. "Just... wait. Grandpa's not—he—hasn't been himself."

He tilted his head. "You sound like you don't want me to go inside. Is there something different about the house?"

I bit my lip and shrugged.

Peter's expression softened, and his hand lifted from his side, almost like he was going to reach for me again, but this time he stopped himself. "Hey. Whatever it is, it's fine. I love Gene. You know that."

Love. The word rolled off his tongue so easily that I felt a flare of strange jealousy for Grandpa. Ridiculous.

I looked away. "I know you do."

"So...?"

"Okay. Go on in."

Even though I'd meant what I said, I still held my breath as Peter slowly opened the door. He stood at the opening for a few seconds, then walked inside step by deliberate step, leaving the door open for me to follow.

He was probably really good in court, I thought, watching him take in what he was seeing. He was doing a much better job controlling his reaction than I had when I'd first seen it. The only way I could tell he was bothered at all was because his throat jumped when he swallowed.

"How long?" he asked softly.

I shrugged, keeping my voice equally low as I answered, "I don't know. I found stuff that looked like it was from at least four years ago." Newspapers with the date on them; the postmarks of the oldest mail. But I figured things started to slip for Grandpa around five years before, when he'd lost the money. Or maybe when he'd won it.

Peter looked away, nodding like he'd formed an answer to a question he'd only asked himself. He'd told me when we were younger that he sometimes carried on whole conversations in his head. He'd been seven or eight when he realized not everyone did the same. He'd told me about it like it was something to be ashamed of, but it had just made me even more fascinated with his mind.

Now, I could see him going back and forth with himself through the subtle shifts in his expression. How his eyes strayed to the left, then to the right, like he was watching a miniature tennis match only he could see.

"Grandpa's probably in the living room." I could hear the murmur of the TV. "We can ask him about the maps."

We found Grandpa where I'd expected him to be. He blinked at Peter for a second before seeming to really register his presence.

"Pete! You're back again." He rocked a few times in the chair before he was able to tilt himself more upright. I fought the urge to help him because I knew he'd snap at me if I tried.

"That's right. I couldn't stay away." Peter walked over and squeezed Grandpa's shoulder, then crouched next to his chair and looked at the TV. "What are we watching? Oh, the PBR. Of course." He grinned.

"Frank got me into it," Grandpa admitted with a wistful smile.

"Me too." Peter pointed at the screen. "Is that TJ Curtis?"

"No, no. TJ doesn't ride in the PBR anymore. He's all-in with the PRCA."

Peter nodded knowingly, and I walked around behind Grandpa's chair, where I could see the screen and try to figure out what the fuck they were talking about. Oh, right. Bull riding.

"You know about this shit?" I asked Peter incredulously.

He tipped his head back to smile up at me, and the line of his throat and the way his hair fell back off his forehead caught me off-guard. Heat raced under my skin, even though we had Grandpa and the canyon I'd dug between us.

Fuck, I had to be careful, or I was going to say or do something I'd regret.

"Sure," Peter said, seemingly oblivious to what he was doing to me. He looked at the screen again, leaning one elbow on the arm of Grandpa's chair. "Bull riding is the only sport you can't fix." He glanced at Grandpa and winked.

Grandpa barked out a laugh. "Damn. I forgot he used to say that."

I smiled because Peter was smiling. "So, Frank was into cowboys?"

Still chuckling, Grandpa shrugged. "Oh, I don't know about that. I think he mostly rooted for the animals." He patted the arm Peter had rested on his chair. "You're here to give us a hand, Pete?" he asked, his tone light, but his fingers curled to grip Peter's sleeve.

Peter twisted around and put his other hand over Grandpa's. "Yep. Don't worry about it, Uncle Gene. Riley and I know the park inside out. We'll probably find it before dinnertime." He caught my eye.

"Knock on wood," I mouthed, earning a wry smile as he straightened back to his full height.

"Have you still got any of those old maps of the park? It would help us look."

Grandpa frowned, and his expression got tighter as he glanced around the living room at the nearest hills of stuff.

"You know what, never mind," Peter said. "I know where to find one."

I followed him toward the front door. "You know where to find a map of the park from the seventies that isn't in this house?" I murmured to Peter when I was sure Grandpa wouldn't overhear.

"Yeah." Peter looked resigned. "I just have to go back into town to get it." He glanced at me. "Want to come along?"

I tried not to seem too eager. "Sure."

"Good. It'll be better with you there. You can be a buffer."

"Buffer?"

"Yeah, like a human shield." He went out the front door and into the sunshine, and I chuckled as I followed him, closing the door behind us.

"Now I'm wondering if I should have agreed to go along. Where exactly are we going?"

"The Historical Society," Peter said grimly.

"Oh, I get it." I reached for the passenger door of Peter's car. "You want me to protect you from your dad."

"He always liked you," Peter said as he got in the car.

"He was just being nice," I corrected, pushing the passenger seat back so my knees weren't crammed into the underside of the dash.

"No, he really liked you."

He seemed to mean it, but I still had my doubts. Peter's parents were picture-perfect—they lived in a big, perfect house, in a perfect town, and had a perfect son. I'd been the kind of kid that other kids' parents tried to avoid.

"He always said you had a creative spirit," Peter went on. "If he hadn't liked you, why do you think he spent all that time with you, wandering around in the archives?"

"To be nice." But it was true that Peter's dad had never seemed impatient when I'd followed him around his workplace. It hadn't happened often, but when Grandpa was busy or couldn't watch me, Peter's uncle or his parents would. And because Peter's parents both worked, we usually wound up at the tiny county museum Peter's dad oversaw, or in the lobby of the office building his mom managed, more often than we were at their house.

By the time we were teenagers, no one worried if we were out at the park alone, so those last few summers, I'd barely seen the Landrys. Except on my last day in Burlington, when they were white-faced and clinging to each other in the hospital parking lot.

I'd wanted to ask them how Peter was, but I was afraid their answer would break me.

When quiet fell between us, I fidgeted in my seat. Maybe I should stop waiting for the right moment and just come out and say it. Apologize. I owed Peter that. I took a deep breath, but before I could speak, a ringtone came over the car's speakers. Peter must have placed a call.

After a second or two, Ken Landry's familiar voice said, "Hello?"

"Hi, Dad. Are you at work?"

"Yes. It *is* eleven a.m. on a weekday."

"Can we come by?"

"We?"

"Yeah. I'm with Riley Meadows. I'm helping him with something for the park."

There was a long pause, and then static as Ken must have released a heavy breath against the speaker. "Riley Meadows! There's a name I haven't heard in a while. Wow. You're helping him, you said?" He lowered his voice. "Are you sure that's a good idea? Damn, buddy, that summer after your arm, it was—"

"Dad," Peter interrupted, his voice tight and a flush climbing past his collar. "I've got Riley here with me. In the car. You're on speaker. Can we head over? We need a copy of the old aerial maps of the park."

"Oh! Yes, sure. Come on over." He cleared his throat. "Hi, Riley!"

"Hi, Mr. Landry," I answered, unable to tear my eyes from the side of Peter's face as he drove on, his eyes firmly forward.

"Okay, Dad, we'll see you soon." Peter hung up before his dad could say anything else. Silence fell in the car again like a stone.

I wasn't good with words. When they were written down, they ran around on the page, and it was worse if they were on a screen. When I tried to pin them down in my head and speak, the results were hit or miss. The only times they came easily were when I was totally relaxed, or when I was mad as hell. And when I was mad, I only managed to say the wrong ones.

Staring out the window, frustrated with myself, I watched the country turn into the city in what seemed like a blink. Vermont magic. I *was* going to apologize to Peter. The words and the moment would come. But I didn't have either of those things right now.

"Here we go," Ken said cheerfully, leaning close to his computer screen. The fan on the dusty old machine was whirring so fast, he had to raise his voice for us to hear him over it. "This is what you wanted, right?" He pivoted the monitor toward us, knocking over a jar full of paper clips in the process. "Oh, dang it."

I knelt on the floor and started gathering up the escaped paper clips.

"Thanks, Riley."

"No problem, Mr. Landry."

"Call me Ken," he reminded me. I nodded awkwardly. Ken kept stealing glances at Peter, like he still couldn't believe Peter was willingly in my company.

That made two of us.

Ken's office was an interior room in the Historical Society's old commercial building, a block off Church Street. He had so much stuff piled in there it reminded me of Grandpa's house. Except, I had a feeling that if Ken wanted to find something in his towers of books and loose-leaf paper and folders, he'd know exactly where it was.

When I got off the floor with the paper-clip jar refilled, Peter had already confirmed that Ken had the right document, and Ken had printed it out on a boxy printer that was serving as a table for a lamp and three stacked banker's boxes.

"So, what is it you two are working on?" Ken took the paper from the tray and handed it to Peter, who glanced at it, nodded, and passed it to me. I stared at the hand-drawn map, remembering the full-color brochure Grandpa used to have and wondering if it was lost forever. The flattened, black-and-white version was nothing compared to the original, but it would work for Peter's plan to create a grid for our search.

"Just investigating some possibilities for the park's future," Peter said casually. I shot him a glance, startled by the effortlessly delivered not-quite-lie.

"Would Gene reconsider applying for the state historic register? If he did that, he'd be eligible for—"

"Grants. I know, Dad. I've been listening to you and Mom talk about this stuff for years."

"I know it's Gene's business, not ours. But if you need any ideas... Has he checked with the local economic development programs?"

"Dad." Peter's tone was short, and I winced on Ken's behalf, but he only shrugged.

"Well, so long as you know we're here to help. Do you boys need anything else?"

"No. Thanks. We'll take it from here." Peter got up and stepped carefully around a wooden butter churn that was inexplicably sitting in the middle of the room.

"Thanks, Ken," I chimed in, his first name feeling awkward in my mouth. He quirked a smile at me as he accompanied us into the open first story of the building, which also served as the museum floor.

We went into the museum's research room to draw a grid over the map, and then Peter threw together a simple spreadsheet we could open on our phones, labeling the columns and rows to correspond to the sections on our map. Then he scanned the map with his phone and saved it to the cloud for good measure.

"Are you sure you're a lawyer, or are you a professional treasure hunter?" I asked Peter on our way out, just as a handful of people were coming in, most of them older, carrying baskets, and several of them with pieces of fabric draped over their arms.

Ken emerged from his office, checked his watch, then gave his wrist a little shake. "Is it noon already? It must be." He huffed. "If I had to decide between telling time by my watch or by the quilters, I'd pick the quilters every time."

One of the group, who had a basket in each hand and her hair in two long white braids, registered our presence, homed in on Peter, and headed our way.

"Ken! That's your boy, Peter, isn't it?" She beamed at Peter.

"That's him," Ken said with a warm smile for Peter that I found hard to look at, like I was seeing more than Ken should go around showing just anyone.

"I thought so! The picture of his mother, isn't he? But so tall!" She reached up as though she wanted to pat the top of Peter's head, but because she couldn't reach, she tapped her forefinger against his nose instead.

I swallowed a laugh.

"I'm Marion," she announced to Peter. "You're my lawyer! Although," she added, planting a hand on her hip, "you haven't called me yet."

"I just got your information yesterday." Peter looked a little dazed—whether from the nose tap, the very large white rabbit on the front of her knitted sweater, or her carrot earrings, I wasn't sure.

"Marion!" called one of the group from where they'd settled at a wide square table in the corner. "We need you!"

Sighing, the woman gave Peter another once-over, then leaned toward him, closed her eyes, and sniffed.

Peter caught my eye, and the slight panic on his face made my ribs creak with the urge to laugh.

Marion opened her eyes. "Iris wasn't wrong. You *do* have a sweet energy," she said decisively, then pointed at him sternly. "You had better call me tomorrow, young man. Avoiding a client is unprofessional in any field." And with that, she went to join the rest of the quilters.

Peter opened his mouth, and I could tell he was straining

against the instinct to argue. Instead, he said, "That's a very good point. I will definitely call tomorrow."

I glanced over my shoulder as we headed for the door and discovered that Marion's sweater had a rabbit knitted on the back, too. This time, facing away, with some kind of large, soft ball stuck to the fabric right at the small of her back as a tail.

I shook my head and grinned to myself. God, I loved Vermont.

PETER

We were both quiet as we drove back to Gene's.

"You should go around to the park entrance," Riley suggested when we reached Gene's driveway, breaking the silence. "We won't be able to get past the gates, but we can walk up there without worrying about the creek."

Getting stuck in the mud together had been a highlight of my year, but I could barely admit that to myself, much less Riley. I nodded and continued to the next intersection and the corner of Gene's property, then another eighth of a mile or so to the drive to the park, which was completely overgrown. The rusty gate bore a pitted sign threatening trespassers. On its other side, two fallen trees blocked the way. But there was enough room for me to nose the car up to the gate and be well clear of the road.

We slipped through the gaps in the gate's bars, walked around the fallen trees, and continued up the driveway. At one time, the surface had been asphalt, but over the decades it had disintegrated into black gravel and patches of grass, becoming more like a path than a road.

"So, what do you do in the city?" I dared to ask eventually. Work seemed like a safe topic. Well, it didn't feel like a safe question when someone asked me, but generally speaking, work and the weather were neutral conversation starters.

"I basically quit my job when I came out here," Riley said simply, not seeming to notice that I was in the midst of a nervous internal debate. "But I was working in a restaurant."

"What kind?" I knew the answer from stalking him on social media. I'd seen the name mentioned in a comment, and I'd looked it up. It was a good one, with a Michelin star.

"Kind of upscale, I guess. I worked in the back of house. Stocking dishes, setting up preparation areas for the chefs. Grunt work."

"Why'd you quit?"

"I told them I needed time off for a family thing and that I didn't know how long I'd be gone. When it turned out to be weeks instead of days, my boss said they couldn't hold my place."

"That sucks."

He shrugged.

The park was ahead of us—the entrance gates, the upper curve of the Ferris wheel, and the parapet of the office tower visible. The drive was lined with old, regal white pines, evenly spaced. I imagined pulling up here when the park was open, how grand it would have felt.

"How's your family? Well, other than Gene." I'd never met anyone in Riley's family, but I'd picked up enough clues back in the day to put together a picture.

"Well, Quint is in jail. No surprise there."

I winced, but it was true that I wasn't entirely surprised. Riley's older brother had been in juvie at least once back when we were kids, and in every story Riley had told about him, he'd been getting into some kind of trouble.

"My mom and dad are the same as always. They work, they party, and then they work some more. Mom had to quit cleaning houses when her back got bad. She's in a call center now. Dad's still in construction."

My heart thrumming like a trapped bird, I decided to ask a

question that barely felt natural. But it was, right? "Are you seeing anyone? A girlfriend?"

I was staring determinedly at the Meadows Park sign at the entrance when I asked, but out of the corner of my eye, I saw Riley's head jerk in my direction.

"Why would you ask me that?" His voice was gruff. "Of course not. You know I don't... that I'm not into women."

"I didn't know that," I said lightly, kicking at the asphalt-turned-gravel with my next step. "You could be bi. You could have just been experimenting." Referring offhand to our relationship as teenagers as "experimenting" made me feel a little sick.

Riley stopped in the middle of the drive and put his hands on the back of his head, exhaling long and hard. I stopped too, turning to him cautiously, and watched him glower at his feet. I could sense that he was riding the knife's edge of his temper. Back when we were kids, he was quick to get angry. Not at me, not usually, but in general. He'd been—mercurial. I could see he still was, but better at regulating his emotions so they didn't explode.

When he gazed at me, his expression was pained, and he looked as miserable as I felt. "Is that what it was for you? Experimenting?"

The sick feeling in my gut doubled. "*No*," I said immediately, dragging a hand over my face. "Of course not."

"Do *you* have a girlfriend?"

"I'm not seeing anyone," I said stiffly. I hadn't answered his entire question, so I went on. "I have dated women, though." Barely. I *slept* with women, but I never called any of them a girlfriend. "I'm not gay. I'm bisexual."

Riley nodded slowly, and his eyes slid down my body in a way that made me shudder. The constant tension between us kept my senses on a hair trigger. A sexual charge could build in an instant.

"I'm gay," he said flatly, staring somewhere between my navel and my knees.

Fuck, if we didn't stop talking and start walking again, he was going to watch me get an erection right in front of him. The snug gray jeans I was wearing would hide nothing.

I pivoted and strode away, willing myself to settle down. "Sorry," I called over my shoulder without looking at him. Safer that way. "It's none of my business."

"It's not?" he asked from behind me. I was a fast walker. He'd have to run to catch up.

I focused on the gates with the random thought that if I reached them, I'd be safe from this conversation. Like touching home base in a game of tag. I walked a little faster. "Of course not. We were... Back then, we were just kids. It's been eight years."

We were just kids. It's been eight years. The words rolled off my tongue, these rote lines I knew so well because I repeated them to myself all the time when I needed to convince myself that my feelings for Riley were something I should shake off. Move on from. Knowing on a deeper level I never would.

I slipped through the narrow space between the wedged-open, stuck-in-place gates. I was leaner than Riley, and it took him a little more time to squeeze past.

I could feel the conversation closing in, cornering me somewhere I didn't want to go. I hesitated, slowing for just a few steps, and that's all it took for Riley to reach me, his hand closing around my elbow.

"I'm so sorry," he said in a rush.

His palm was large and warm and held me firmly, yet also like I was fragile. Not quite the uncertain, sometimes painful grappling we'd done as overzealous teenagers, but still familiar. I was frozen, and made briefly speechless by that touch.

My head caught up to the moment a second later, and I frowned at his words. "Sorry?"

"For your arm. And for leaving. And for never calling you or answering your messages."

Oh. The apology I'd thought I'd wanted. It was happening, and I'd missed it because I was so distracted by being a half-step away from his body, by the promise in the way he held my arm that his touch would be even better than I remembered.

I'd been angry as recently as a few days ago. But it had faded. It was impossible to be angry with Riley when he was close, more than a memory. When he was shyly watching me when he thought I hadn't noticed. When he was touching me.

It was impossible to be angry, but it was *very* possible to be confused. "Why did you leave? Why didn't you ever call?" I asked, my voice a choked murmur.

He bent his head. His thumb rubbed up and down the inside of my forearm just below the elbow he still held in the warm, firm cradle of his hand. "You almost died because of me."

That brought me up short. I snorted. "What?"

He gave a tiny nod, and I saw his eyelashes flutter, like he was on the verge of tears.

I turned into him so we were face-to-face, his head bent between us, and I squeezed his right arm, then ran my hand up his bicep and back down. "Riley, God no. Is that what you thought? It wasn't that bad. It just bled a lot." That was a thing with head wounds, apparently.

His grip tightened infinitesimally on my arm, then eased again. "You were unconscious, and then when you *did* wake up, you weren't making any sense. I thought I should run for help, but I didn't want to leave you alone. So I carried you into the trees." A small, broken laugh escaped him. "And I fucking got lost."

"Riley." I got a little closer to him and put my hand against the side of his face, urging him to look at me. His beard was surprisingly soft against my hand, but I felt the faint bristle against the thumb I slid under his jaw. "That wasn't your fault, either. You were scared."

"It's a few hundred yards of trees," he said on a groan, but he looked up at me. His eyes were wet, turning them to liquid amber. His pulse throbbed against the pad of my thumb. "You were in my arms, bleeding, and it was my fault. And I thought you'd die like that, and the last things we'd said to each other would be that stupid fucking fight. Gene called the ambulance, and then they wouldn't let me go with you. They said the police might come by to talk to me."

Alarm surged through me. I'd never heard anything about that. "What? But it was an accident."

"They only had my word on that."

We'd been *kids*. But thinking of Quint, I could only imagine how terrified an eighteen-year-old Riley had been, covered in dirt and my blood, told to wait for the police.

He leaned into my hand a little. "I sneaked off and tried to go by the hospital," he said, shocking me all over again.

"*What?*" I'd *definitely* never heard anything about that.

"Yeah. But they wouldn't let me around you without asking your parents, and I was sure they hated me more than ever. I assumed they'd call the cops. So… I got on a bus."

I pulled loose of his grip so I could put my arms around him and hold him hard against me. "Riley. God."

A tremor ran through his body, and then he melted against me, his strong arms so tight, they restricted my breath. I rubbed his back, then stroked the back of his hair. We were close in height, like we'd always been. He was still that crucial inch or two taller, but I could easily hook my chin over his shoulder. And his body was big and warm and strong against mine. We'd both changed, and grown, yet somehow in relation to one another, our bodies were the same.

And now that my body was pressed against his, it had the same desperate need for him I'd never felt since, which I'd chalked up to just being a teenager's overactive sex drive.

I was hard, and he was hard against me. I could tell he noticed because his hands clutched my waist and he growled into my ear, "*Peter.*"

I groaned. "Office?"

"Fuck yes."

We staggered apart, and Riley grabbed my hand. The tower-shaped office had been our hideout. The door was held closed by a rock Riley kicked out of the way. Inside, it was dim and musty, but familiar, too. Riley paused in the lower room, cast in the jagged light that fell through a single broken window. He still held my hand, but he felt far away. I held him tighter, gripped by the strange feeling that if he released my hand now, even for a second, the physical reconnection would stop and we might never grab it again.

But Riley's expression was conflicted. "Peter, I don't know if—"

I backed toward the counter that encircled half the room and planted my ass on the edge of it, inside a gap between the old office chairs our younger selves had kicked apart for similar purposes once upon a time.

I wet my lower lip, and Riley's eyes latched on to the glimpse of my tongue and darkened. I shuffled my feet apart to make room for him, my breaths coming in fast pants that matched the rhythm of my pounding heart.

He let go of my hand as he stepped close, his hard thighs between mine, his hands sliding up my sides. It felt so good to have him close, touching me, that my head was light.

He kissed me hard, square on my lower lip. I felt the rough grazing of his teeth as he sucked at my lip and stroked it with his tongue.

I grabbed his shoulders, partly to keep myself from collapsing back against the counter, since his kiss had apparently melted my spine, and partly to pull him down, closer, so I could get more of his mouth.

He murmured a noise against my mouth that sounded appreciative, and then I felt the gust of his chuckle when I hooked a leg around him and made him stumble forward, pinning my hips tightly to the edge of the counter with his own.

As our dicks slotted together through our clothes, we both gasped, still kissing with increasing desperation.

"What do you—" I managed.

"Can I—" he breathed at the same time.

We blinked at each other, laughing roughly, and he fisted my shirt. "Can I take this off?"

"Yeah," I said, blinking, and he leaned away to help me wriggle out of it. The kiss of the cool air on my hot skin made me shiver, and then the slide of his palms and the brush of his thumbs over my nipples made me moan.

"You're even more gorgeous than you used to be," he said, nudging his nose against my cheek, then kissing my neck. "Fuck."

I splayed my hand over his chest, clutched at his flannel shirt. "You too. Off."

He wore an undershirt beneath. I peeled it off his abs while his arms were still tangled in the flannel layer, then raced my knuckles up and down the firm ridges of his stomach.

"You got... bigger," was the most sophisticated statement I could make.

He finally got free of his shirt and smiled at me playfully through tousled hair. "I'll show you something bigger."

I snorted, but then couldn't help letting my fascinated gaze roam past his beautiful, lightly haired chest to the waistband of his jeans. The bulge there *did* look even more impressive than what I remembered.

"Perv," he said, with the same warm affection he'd used when we'd swapped that pejorative as horny teenagers desperately in love with each other.

I blinked hard and shoved off the countertop to launch myself at him, wrapping my arms around his neck and standing on the balls of my feet so that we were the exact same height and I could take his mouth the way he'd taken mine—with my tongue and teeth, like I wanted to get inside him.

Which, incidentally, I did want, but *that* kind of fucking was probably unrealistic up against the counter in the office of an abandoned theme park.

But if I couldn't fuck him the way I'd dreamed of when we

were kids—without ever having the nerve to actually initiate—I could go for the next best thing.

I slid to my knees and pressed my cheek against the tented denim to the left of his zipper.

"Peter," he breathed, his voice wobbling, and I watched his face as I slid my hands up his thighs. The thick muscles there were trembling faintly beneath my palms.

"I've thought about this for years." I rubbed my cheek against the hard shaft straining against his jeans, for me. "It was never as much fun with anyone else."

His eyes widened, like the admission surprised him. It surprised me too. I wasn't always this honest, but I didn't know another way to be, not with Riley. Even after all these years.

"Fuck," he said, seeming to suddenly unfreeze. One of his hands slid into my hair, while the other wrestled with the button at the top of his fly. My mouth watered in anticipation. Then he was pulling out his cock, over the band of his underwear. Hot and throbbing. I stuck out my tongue and licked his knuckles where he grasped himself, and he made a low, growling noise that was very familiar to me *and* my dick, which was painfully hard under two layers of clothing, begging me to reach in and jack it.

But my hands were occupied, yanking his jeans down a few more inches, then his briefs, so I could tilt my head and suck one of his balls into my mouth like a large piece of candy.

His hand tightened in my hair. "Fuck, fuck, *fuck*. I've thought about this too. Nobody does it for me like you do."

Does it for me. Did he mean in general, or this particular act?

My head and my dick warred for dominance a moment, but considering I had one of his hot, hairy balls in my mouth and my nose buried in the short, thick hair at the base of his cock, my head didn't have a fair chance, and I shook off the passing thought.

I let go of my mouthful, and he held me by the head and fed his cock past my lips, staring down at me. With his dark eyes seeming to glow and his bare chest displayed, he was so beautiful that looking at him almost hurt.

I sheathed him all the way down on the first try.

His cock was the same size it had been back then, despite his teasing a few minutes ago. It was big and perfect, stretching my throat exactly the way I'd remembered, the way I'd dreamed, waking in a sweaty twist of sheets, for years after he was gone.

We'd perfected this, he and I. Mouths and cocks and hands and kissing. We'd been so desperate for each other, we'd never made it to anything else, but the way we pleasured each other had never left us wanting. I gloried in him the same way now that I had when I'd first been brave enough to take him all the way.

He remembered what I liked, it seemed, because when my eyes watered and my throat convulsed reflexively around him, he only pulled out a little before easing back in with his hand caught fast in my hair.

God. My hips jerked forward. I was so turned on, I was thrusting unconsciously at nothing. I rolled my palm hard against my erection, the zipper of my chinos and the button biting painfully into my shaft not enough to divert the impending orgasm that had drawn my balls tight. I'd never come in my pants before, not even back then. Riley would have never allowed it. But maybe there was a first time for everything?

My eyelids fluttered, and because he was staring at me like I was something worth memorizing, Riley didn't miss it. And he hadn't forgotten what it meant.

"Don't." My eyes widened as he punctuated the word with a short, firm thrust that hit the back of my throat. Then he pulled me off him by my hair, and stared down at me while I gasped, the head of his cock resting spit-slick against my lower lip and chin. "I want to make you come," he said in a low, commanding voice I definitely *didn't* remember from when we were kids. He hadn't grown up just in body, apparently.

I forced my hand away from my crotch and grasped his thigh instead.

His nails rasped against my scalp as he gave my hair an approving stroke. And then he cupped the back of my head again and slid his cock back inside my hungry mouth.

This time he wasn't slow. He was quick, and he stayed deep in my throat, so that all my attention had to be focused on taking in what little bursts of air I could through my nose, slackening my jaw and turning myself over to him as he fucked himself to orgasm. He started to pull out to come, our old habit, but I clamped my hands around his hips at the last second to hold him close, and swallowed every hot pulse instead.

He shuddered, and swore, and said my name like I was a saint in his church, and then he dragged me up by my underarms, set me on the counter, stripped me to my ankles, and knelt between my splayed knees.

It hardly took any time. The scrape of his beard, the hot oasis of his mouth, and the rough pressure of his hands were so familiar and so different at the same time, I felt like I was having an out-of-body experience.

I tipped my head back when I came, and he kept me in his mouth, sucking me gently, swallowing like I'd swallowed, a new capstone to our old tradition. The thought made me laugh, but I was so on edge, it could have been a sob too. A long, labored breath with a note. He squeezed my knees as though in answer, but kept his mouth on me like he'd never stop the gentle pressure, even as I started to soften, making it feel like I was still coming a solid minute after I was milked dry. The sensation was so incredible, I didn't want it to end, but as the pleasure edged close to pain, I took a sharp breath and gripped his shoulder, and he immediately let me go.

He didn't pull away, though. He turned his cheek against my leg and rested his head on my thigh, his soft hair falling on my wet, softening dick. A memory jolted me. He'd always been like this after we'd come. Like as close as we'd gotten while we fucked, it still wasn't close enough.

I curled my arm around his shoulders as best I could given the position I was in, and tentatively ran my other hand over his head, almost expecting him to pull away.

He didn't.

But he hadn't collapsed against me so that we could stay entangled, hearts fused together, for as long as possible, drunk on mutual exhilaration. I could feel tension in those shoulders I embraced, and it was building in my body too.

As the drive to come and make him come ebbed away, I wondered if I'd just made a big mistake.

Now wasn't then.

We weren't two kids desperately in love, worshiping each other any way we could. We were two grown men who didn't know one another anymore.

RILEY

"You used to do the same thing when you were a kid," Grandpa observed from his recliner.

I turned from the living-room window I'd been peering out of. "What?"

"Sit at the window and watch for Peter." Grandpa's smile was wistful. "I'd get a call from Frank that they were heading over, and if I let you know, you'd immediately go watch for them, like they might beam in a second later."

I remembered that, actually. Except half the time, I was too restless to watch from the window, instead waiting at the end of the driveway where I'd see him coming sooner. Looking back, maybe it had been a little pathetic. But I'd never worried about being vulnerable with Peter. I'd never tried to hide how much I wanted to be around him.

My phone buzzed with a text, and my heart sank even before I pulled it from my pocket. I had a feeling I knew what it would say.

Sure enough, in the message thread with Peter there was a new text, short enough that I could read it without much of a struggle.

Peter: *Can't make it today. Sorry.*

Fuck.

I dragged a hand through my hair. I wasn't exactly surprised that Peter was making himself scarce. Yesterday had been awkward.

Well, first it had been amazing. But *then* it had gotten awkward.

After Peter had blown my mind, he hadn't said anything while we got dressed. And when he'd finally spoken, all he'd put words to was a strategy for digging up the first quadrant of the park, starting with the spots that fell roughly into the ten-paces range.

He'd been all business, looking my way without ever looking me in the eye, and speaking in this level, matter-of-fact tone that drove me out of my mind, like he was just going to pretend nothing happened in the office.

Damn it, getting hold of Peter again had confirmed what I'd already been pretty sure of—that the old magic was still there between us. Holding Peter, kissing him, coming with him, it was a Technicolor experience. Everybody else I'd ever been with had only been in black-and-white.

"What's the matter, kid?" Grandpa murmured. At some point, he'd gotten out of his chair and had come up behind me. I hadn't noticed him until he spoke and his hand curled around my shoulder.

"Oh, nothing. Peter can't make it today." I glanced at Grandpa but didn't quite meet his eyes. I didn't want him to see I'd made myself all misty. What had I thought? That making Peter come would absolve me of abandoning him back then? Or bridge the canyon of shit that ensured we couldn't be anything more than unlikely childhood friends?

That rift between us had already been wide when we were kids. But now? God, Peter was a *lawyer*. And my highest professional achievement had been getting bumped up from dish duty at my old job.

Grandpa patted my shoulder and started for the door. "Well, on the bright side, that means you're available to drive me into town for coffee."

"I'm your chauffeur now?" But I got up and followed him, relieved to have something to do other than sit at the window like a sad dog.

"What goes around comes around, kid. I remember driving you all over the county, looking for that *Alexander* movie at Blockbuster. I never knew you were so into history."

I snorted. I was pretty sure Grandpa was aware that Peter and I had been obsessed with the movie because of the combination of Jared Leto and Colin Farrell, not the subject matter.

I grabbed the keys, leaving my coat on the rack by the door. I knew from going out to check on Lemon earlier that the weather was warm enough I wouldn't need it.

I took it as a good sign that Grandpa had obviously noticed I'd tidied up around the foyer, but hadn't yelled at me about it. There were now just two pairs of his shoes under the bench, and he stepped into his well-worn slip-ons. I tried not to hover in case he stumbled while he was trying to balance on one foot at a time. He glanced at me, at how close I was, but didn't yell at me about that either.

Maybe we were turning a corner.

"Is your coffee place still Baylor's?" I asked him as we got in the truck.

"I'm sure as hell not going to Starbucks," he replied, and I chuckled as I rolled down my window to get some air moving through the cab of the truck. The upholstery smelled a bit like feet when the truck had been sitting in the sun.

Baylor's was an old filling station. So old that the attendant had to come out and read the pump to know how much gas you'd put in, then figure the price for you at the register. I was happy to see there hadn't been a single update since I'd come here with Grandpa last. Even the owners, Mr. and Mrs. Baylor, looked the same and were right in their places—Mrs. Baylor behind the counter, Mr. Baylor pouring coffee for the customers sitting in plastic chairs at small tables clustered by the case of lottery tickets.

The sight of the tickets brought me up short. It wasn't that I'd *forgotten* that there were millions of dollars buried in the park that I'd promised to find. But thankfully, it didn't stay at the forefront of my thoughts at all times, or I'd lose my shit.

"Well, goodness me," crowed one of the old coffee drinkers, a man with a flat-brimmed hat and overalls. I remembered him from back in the day, though I couldn't recall his name. "It's that grandbaby of yours, Gene, isn't it? All grown up and looking city."

"Yeah, that's Riley. Don't you give him a hard time, Curtis." Grandpa squeezed my elbow like he was presenting me to his friends, and gazed at me with the same warmth I remembered from when I was a kid. I hadn't felt like I deserved it then, this casual pride, but I really didn't deserve it now. At least back then I'd had potential. People liked kids; they always assumed they'd grow up to do something that mattered, and they gave them the benefit of the doubt. I wasn't a kid now. It had been a long time since anyone had looked at me like that.

Damn it, I was going to get misty again. I smiled and nodded and murmured hellos to Grandpa's friends, and Mr. Baylor dragged over a stool from behind the counter for me when Grandpa took the last chair.

The coffee was the familiar thin, bargain-brand stuff that sometimes tasted a little burned. I'd drank it back then because Grandpa made it seem special to be invited to have a cup with the adults. Apparently, everyone assumed I'd have one today. Mrs. Baylor doctored it for me just like old times, with so much creamer, it was almost white. The sugar coated my tongue and made the coffee even worse than it would have been otherwise, but I smiled at her gratefully and drank the whole cup.

"You're still a New Yorker, Riley?" asked another face I vaguely remembered. She was some kind of farmer; I remember that much. She was also frowning like residency in New York City was a tragedy. "What is it you do down there?"

"I used to work in a restaurant."

Her face brightened. "You don't say? That is one thing I will say about New York. Great food."

Several of the group pulled faces and groaned. "Don't talk about your trip to New York City again, Kendra. We've all heard about the damn *guh-no-key* a hundred times."

"My daughter invited me for a visit," Kendra said, happily ignoring the protests from her friends. "I figured I had to say yes. I stayed on an awful little folding bed and saw about a dozen rats, but she took me to this Italian place that was *heaven*."

"Oh, yeah?" I tilted my head. "What was it called?" Even in New York, there were only so many unforgettable restaurants, and they each made it their job to know about one another.

Before she could answer, another man in the group interjected, "Speaking of city, look who the cat dragged in."

Along with everyone else, I looked to the door. A tall guy about my age had walked in. He had kind of an old-school haircut, and even though I knew nothing about fashion, I could tell his business-casual dress was impeccable. He was about as stark a contrast to Baylor's ambiance as Peter had been in the park the day he'd shown up in those fancy shoes.

"It's nice to see you too, Mr. Brown," the sharp-dressed guy said cheerfully. He turned a warm smile on Mrs. Baylor and took an envelope out of the interior pocket of his sport coat. "I came by to drop this off. And for a cup of coffee to-go."

"Oh, thank you, sweetie," Mrs. Baylor said with a grin, taking the envelope. "I appreciate you bringing this by. I know I should get better with the email, but it still stresses me out."

"Is that those paint swatches?" Mr. Baylor asked. "You work quick, Chase." He poured coffee into a paper cup.

"No, Virgil," Mrs. Baylor said irritably. "It's a…" She glanced at Chase.

"Branding kit," he supplied with a smile.

"I just can't wait to have a look." She tucked the envelope under her arm.

"Give me a call and let me know what you think," Chase said.

Mr. Baylor slid the lidded cup across the counter. "Put your money away," he said gruffly when Chase began to open his wallet. "You got a busy day ahead of you?"

"Always." Chase glanced my way, catching me eavesdropping. Not that I could help it. The interior of Baylor's was so small, I was only a few feet away from their conversation. Meanwhile, Grandpa's crowd had struck up a rousing discussion on commodities prices that I couldn't have followed if I'd wanted to. "Hi," he said when our eyes met. "I'm Chase Ashton."

"Riley Meadows." I tilted my head toward Grandpa. "His grandson."

"Riley Meadows," Chase repeated. "What a coincidence. I had a call yesterday from Ken Landry at the Historical Society. He said he was going to give you my number to talk a bit more about historic designation and grant opportunities."

My mind spun at the thought that Ken had made a call on my behalf. I wasn't sure whether to feel annoyed or grateful.

Grandpa finally extracted himself from the conversation at the tables and looked around, eyes narrowed. "What's that? He says he talked to Ken?"

"Yes, sir. I'm on the Chamber of Commerce Board, and we help with those applications."

"Don't act like what you do has anything to do with that Chamber," Mr. Baylor said reprovingly. He turned a serious look toward Gene. "Chase goes above and beyond. He's a good kid. If he's offering you some help, then you're very lucky."

"I've told Ken I don't want some crony from Montpelier poking around my property," Grandpa said gruffly. "Writing down every tree and rock for one of their Google maps."

"Grandpa, it's fine," I murmured. "He was just asking."

Grandpa pushed back his chair like he hadn't heard me, fixing a full Meadows glower on Chase, whose eyes widened in surprise at the animosity. Or possibly Grandpa's suggestion that the Vermont government was making maps for Google.

"Hey, now, Gene," Curtis said in a low voice, because of course we'd gotten the attention of everyone in the tiny station. "You know these kids. They get excited about all this 'economic development' nonsense and don't see what's obvious to old folks like us."

Grandpa barely spared Curtis a glance.

Chase picked up his coffee cup, his smile careful. "I didn't mean any offense. But if you're interested in speaking more, give me a call. You folks have a good day." He left the building at a measured pace I had to admire, considering that the emotional charge in the air made *me* feel like bolting.

Grandpa sat back down, and a long second of silence ticked by.

"You all are the reason young people think we're hopeless," Mr. Baylor informed his customers. "Chase is a good kid," he reiterated.

"So you said," Grandpa muttered.

"He does marketing, is that right?" Curtis asked.

"Public relations," Kendra corrected. "Doesn't he work with the outfit that got hired by that developer who's looking to rezone something south of town? The ones who've been sniffing around after your ground?"

When Curtis frowned, another man clapped a hand on his shoulder. "Don't look like that, Curt. We know you aren't gonna sell out."

Awkward silence descended again.

To my relief, Grandpa pushed his chair back. "You all stay out of trouble," he said, the familiar words of farewell from all our visits here. Mrs. Baylor slid a Snickers bar across the counter and winked at me on our way out. I almost protested—I was a grown man now, not a kid—but I just smiled at her and took the candy instead.

"Why would anyone care if Curtis met with a developer?" I asked Grandpa when we were back in the truck. I started the engine, then paused to open my candy bar.

Grandpa noticed my prize and huffed a laugh. "Yvonne's still giving you treats, huh?" His smile faded as he considered my question. "Curtis owns a lot of land the developers want. It's close to town. And he has to be tempted because it's rocky acreage. Never was much good for farming or anything, really, except a little grazing."

"So why doesn't he sell it?" I thought of the big houses along Grandpa's road. I bet if a developer was interested, Curtis probably stood to make a lot of money.

"Most people who've been here a few generations would rather the development didn't come. I happen to be one of them. I'm a Meadows, after all. We don't like change." He winked at me. "But I wouldn't give Curtis a hard time if he decided to cash out. If they don't build on his land, they'll build on somebody's."

I thought that over as we drove back to the park, noting the changes along the way with a fresh perspective—not just homes, but a glossy new car dealership and a suite of offices, too.

I was a Meadows, and I had the brown eyes and short temper to prove it. But maybe I was different from the rest of the family when it came to change. A part of me found it… exciting. I liked the idea that a place I already loved was thriving, growing. Sure, sometimes change was for the worse, but that felt easily overshadowed by the possibility of change for the even-better. Kind of like the young trees I'd watch grow over time, where the woods faded away and the clearing opened at the park. They were already strong and sturdy when Peter and I first climbed them over a decade ago, but now they strained several feet higher and cast wider pools of shade.

Turning into Grandpa's driveway, I thought of Peter. Kind of an odd segue in my thoughts, maybe, but I was used to it. And maybe it made me a fool, but I thought that between him and me, maybe change could be a good thing too. Maybe we were like those trees. Harder to climb than before, but once you got up into the branches, you were even closer to the sun.

PETER

Maybe flaking out on Riley and spending all day hiding at Vino and Veritas wasn't my proudest moment, but I didn't let myself think about it too closely. At sunset, I wandered from the bookstore to the wine bar to meet Aaron, who was in town for the weekend, and his boyfriend, Jeremy.

Sometimes it was hard to believe I hadn't known Aaron longer. Granted, he grew up outside a small town forty-five minutes from Burlington, but that wasn't *that* far, and we were only a year apart in age. We'd had so much in common—and not just the area where we were from—that we'd hit it off quickly when we'd met at Harvard during my second year of law school and his first.

Now he was planning to join Aunt Iris's firm after he graduated in a couple of months. Aaron and I had had the same Big Law aspirations when we were at Harvard, and yet we'd both wound up back home.

"Hey, Peter!" Aaron got up from the table they'd grabbed and hugged me. "I'm glad you could make it."

"You should have come with us to the maple festival today," Jeremy added, squeezing my shoulder in greeting and dropping back into his chair. "I ate. So. Much."

"I told you," Aaron said with a grin, returning to his own chair, "Peter abhors all things maple."

Jeremy frowned. "I thought you were trying to be funny when you said that. I assumed it *had* to be made up." He blinked at me. "Peter, are you..." He leaned over the table and finished in a stage whisper, "A Vermont native *who doesn't like* maple syrup?"

I pulled out the third chair at the little table where they, naturally, had squeezed two chairs so close that their shoulders pressed together. They were like this. It was both adorable and annoying how happy they were together. In our friend group there were somehow *three* nauseatingly happy pairs of boyfriends who seemed to be vying for some kind of cutest-couple prize.

Jeremy looked at me insistently. "But seriously. Let's talk about this. Did you have a traumatizing experience involving waffles? Go to one too many maple festivals? Walk in on your parents doing a scene involving—"

"Hi, can I take your orders?" Thank God a server interrupted Jeremy before I had that visual burned into my brain for life.

We ordered our drinks, and when the server left, Aaron picked up the conversation. "Some people just don't like certain foods," he said reasonably.

I refrained from asking where that reasonableness had been when he'd found out I liked soy milk in my lattes. He'd been just as outraged as Autumn. His family operated a small dairy farm, and even though Aaron and his siblings weren't taking up the family business, they loved it.

"Actually, my particular maple-sugar problem has an origin story," I confessed. "When you were a kid, was there a food you really, really loved?"

"Spaghetti and meatballs," Jeremy said immediately. "But the kind that comes in a can."

I laughed, and Aaron shook his head incredulously. "I can't imagine spaghetti and meatballs from a can being served at your house."

"As if Delia Everett would ever allow canned spaghetti inside her home! The scandal!" Jeremy clutched at his heart dramatically. "But one of my friends' parents were really into convenience food. And whenever I stayed at his house, I ate a whole can all by myself," he said smugly, like eating mushy meat was a huge accomplishment.

"Okay, so maple sugar was my mushy spaghetti and meatballs."

"You say mushy like it's a bad thing," Jeremy said. "The lack of texture on those things is an honest-to-goodness scientific miracle."

Aaron elbowed Jeremy and shook his head, smiling. "You're such a disaster. Peter's trying to tell us his origin story."

He looked at me pointedly, and I rolled my eyes, chuckling, and went on. "My parents rationed it to me because, you know, child, sugar." They both nodded. "But one weekend, I stayed with Aunt Iris, and she made maple cookies especially for me. The problem was, Aunt Iris was never very good at telling me no. So she let me eat however many cookies I wanted. Which turned out to be all of them."

Aaron grinned. "And now the thought of maple flavor makes you..."

"Want to barf," Jeremy finished helpfully.

"Yep. Kind of inconvenient, living around here." I squeezed my lemon slice into the glass of water that had been on the table when I sat down. "Now, Aaron," I went on seriously, "how bad is your senioritis? Have you even taken notes in any of your electives this semester?"

Aaron smiled ruefully because of course he was still being a diligent student. He updated me on some of the faculty drama, and then we moved into quick updates on classmates of mine and where they were working.

When our food came, Aaron said, "What about you? Did Iris talk you into working at the firm yet?"

Jeremy grinned. "Of course she did. Peter has taken the lead on a very important case," he informed Aaron. Jeremy was part-timing at Sprysky and Gentry while finishing his senior year at Moo U, where he was starting law school in the fall.

"It's not even a real case," I protested, while registering with alarm that I still hadn't called Marion. I was a little afraid of the piece of her mind I was going to get for taking so long. First thing in the morning, I'd call her. For sure.

"Peter, every client's issue, no matter how small, is very important to them," Jeremy said solemnly.

I narrowed my eyes at him. "You're quoting Aunt Iris."

He shrugged and smiled. "The lady is wise. And I think it would be pretty awesome if we could work together. Are you at least thinking about it?"

I wasn't sure what to say to that. I was carefully not thinking about the future because when I did, a giant chasm of indecision opened before me, threatening to swallow me forever if I took another step. It was paralyzing.

"I guess," I said. "But for now, I'm busy helping out a family friend." Oh, shit. Why had I brought that up?

"Oh? Anyone we know?" Jeremy asked, not looking at me. Aaron had gotten fries, and Jeremy hadn't, and now Jeremy was casting longing glances at Aaron's plate.

"Probably not. Gene Meadows. He was close with my uncle."

"Why is that name familiar?" Aaron asked, cocking his head. Then his eyes widened. "Wait, isn't that the guy who won the lottery a few years ago? He owns an old amusement park. My parents talked about it when the story broke. They remembered coming into Burlington as kids just to go there."

"Yeah. That's Gene's place. It's been closed since the early eighties, though."

"What are you helping him with? Something money can't buy, I suppose," Jeremy said with a careless smile.

My face probably did something funny before I controlled my response, but neither of them seemed to notice because Jeremy finally broke and reached for a couple of Aaron's fries. Aaron responded with a resigned sigh and passed him the ketchup.

"Gene's a little forgetful. He misplaced some stuff around the place, and I remember my way around from when we were kids. I'm helping Riley look for the... missing stuff." God, when had I become such a bad liar? I felt a little guilty for not telling them the whole story, and I knew Aaron and Jeremy wouldn't tell a soul if I asked them to keep it to themselves, but I wasn't going to break Gene's confidence.

"Wait, who's Riley?" Aaron asked.

"Gene's grandson."

"Is he the guy who came in here looking for you the other day?" Jeremy asked. "Whoever it was, Briar said he was super hot."

Aaron's head swiveled in my direction. I could only shrug. After all, Riley *was* hot. Objectively speaking. And subjectively speaking. Aaron looked surprised but not shocked or anything. He knew I was bi, but I'd only dated women at Harvard. If you could call my occasional, strictly business hookup arrangements dating. "Oh yeah? Is he from Vermont?" Aaron asked.

I shook my head, then hesitated. Technically, Riley was from New York City, but on a deeper level, I was pretty sure Vermont was as much a part of him as any other place. "He, um, used to spend summers here. But he's always lived in New York."

"Oh, cool," said Jeremy, leaning around Aaron to steal another fry. "Is he our age?"

"He's three months and one day younger than me," I said absently, then froze and looked up into their surprised faces.

"So you *know* him," Jeremy said, narrowing his eyes and leaning forward slightly. He was going to make a really good litigator one day.

"No," I said immediately, then bit my lip. "I mean, we spent a lot of time together when we were kids. But I don't know him now. Until a few days ago, I hadn't seen him for eight years."

"Okay, we're gonna need more than that." Jeremy rotated his wrist in a go-on gesture.

There was no way I was going to tell them about the park, and the summers, and Riley.

Was I?

The funny thing was, I *wanted* to. The whole story was bubbling up inside me. I'd never told it before. I'd never had to. Everyone who knew me back then already knew how I spent my summers, and by middle school, about the faraway best friend I was texting constantly. And by the time I was around people who didn't know all those things, it hurt too much to think about Riley, much less talk about him.

But after everything he'd told me—why he'd left, why he hadn't answered my texts and calls for the five or six weeks before I'd finally given up—the memories didn't hurt as much anymore.

I took a deep breath. "When I was little, I used to go everywhere with my uncle Frank. And his best friend was Gene Meadows. And when I was nine, Gene's grandson Riley started spending the summers here, too."

When I concluded the story with how I woke up in the hospital, followed by weeks of unreturned texts and calls, we were on our second round, Jeremy had all but licked the crumbs from Aaron's plate, and my friends' eyes were wider than ever.

"So, I guess you can see why I don't talk about him," I finished at last. "When I say it out loud, though, it sounds…"

"Really, really romantic?" Aaron murmured.

"No," I hissed. "Just dramatic. Not… not like real life." I rubbed the bridge of my nose. "I don't know what it is, but my head is all mixed up when it comes to him. I'm not myself." I caught Jeremy and Aaron exchanging a glance and narrowed my eyes at them. "What?"

"I mean, are you sure about that?" Aaron asked gently.

"Sure about what? That I'm not myself when it comes to Riley?"

"It sounds like you and Riley are different in a lot of ways, but there must be something about him that resonates with you."

Jeremy nodded, sliding his hand over Aaron's where it rested on the table. Aaron turned to him as they linked their fingers. "Sometimes the people who seem the most different are alike in the important ways."

Did they *have* to make heart eyes at each other with me sitting *right there*?

I groaned and buried my head in my hands. "You two are as bad as Briar and Jamie, I swear."

"Aw, thanks," Jeremy said sweetly.

I couldn't look at them without smiling, even though they were ridiculously sappy and I didn't believe in romance. Not at all. Okay, *sometimes*, but only when I was under the influence of the park and Riley Meadows and a few thousand hours of childhood memories.

Aaron took pity on me and stuck their joined hands beneath the table, like I wouldn't notice them if they were out of sight. "I always wondered why you didn't really date at Harvard. I remember that one girl in the master's program who told everyone she was using you for your body and that you'd scheduled your breakup in advance at the four-month mark. I thought she was being funny, but then *bam*. Around came August 1, and you were single again."

"Jill." I smiled faintly. "Yeah, she and I did it right."

"No wonder you were emotionally unavailable. You were already in love with Riley."

My eyes snapped to Aaron's. "Excuse me?"

He shrugged apologetically but didn't walk back the comment. "It's true, isn't it?"

"You're *worse* than Briar and Jamie," I amended flatly. Aaron's brother and his boyfriend subsisted on a diet of doughnuts, crullers, and romance novels, from what I could tell. Briar even ran an all-romance book club out of Vino and Veritas. "Obviously *they* would turn it into this whole"—I waved a hand—"*romantic* thing. You two are supposed to be more reasonable."

"You mean about the fact that you fell in love with your childhood best friend after spending several summers in an abandoned amusement park and sharing your first kiss on the Ferris Wheel?" Jeremy deadpanned. "Yeah, nothing *romantic* about that. Not at all."

I pressed my lips together. I wasn't sure how to say what I meant—that to me, the stories in those books Briar and Jamie were so obsessed with were a fantasy, and I didn't understand the point of spending time reading them, much less expecting that kind of stuff to happen in real life.

Of course, several of my friends, present company included, seemed to be doing a pretty good impression of that very phenomenon, but that was beside the point.

"We were just kids. Kids experience things in a hyperemotional way."

Aaron ducked his head like I might not notice his smile. "Whereas adults are too wise for silly things like feelings."

I sighed, utterly failing to translate my thoughts into words, even though supposedly, that's what I'd spent three years of law school learning how to do. "That's not what I mean. But those summers... they weren't real life. It was like being in a dream, running around in that park. Like, I don't know, we never outgrew the ability to make-believe. Somehow, going into the woods toward the park felt just as much like an adventure whether we were eight or eighteen." Or twenty-six, but fuck if I was going to admit that out loud.

Aaron's eyes got a little misty, which was the opposite effect I'd intended to have.

"My life is *not* a romance novel," I told them firmly. "Nothing is going to happen with me and Riley." Aside from what had already happened. Which I was pretending *hadn't* happened, and that meant I wasn't going to tell Jeremy and Aaron about it. "Nothing except some long, very awkward hours of digging holes, finding nothing, and getting increasingly frustrated."

"All those hours, forced to be together," Jeremy murmured with an exaggeratedly dreamy expression, then laughed and dodged when I swung gently at his arm with the back of my hand.

"Wait, digging?" Aaron asked. "What exactly did Gene lose out there?"

I shook my head and let out a shaky breath. "You wouldn't believe me if I told you."

"Well, if you need help, let us know," Aaron said immediately—and meaning it because that was the kind of guy he was. Digging holes looking for undisclosed lost property of someone he didn't even know? He'd be there. And Jeremy was nodding along unreservedly because like he'd said, he and Aaron were alike in the ways that really mattered.

I smiled gratefully at them. "Thanks. I'd probably take you up on it, but Gene's a pretty private guy."

"Well, if you change your mind, let us know."

From the stage behind me, I heard someone tuning a guitar, and I twisted around to see who was playing.

As it turned out, the band was really great, but even excellent live music couldn't pull me into the present. A part of me was still lost in yesterday. The park. Riley. The weight of his head on my leg when we'd finished each other off, sweaty and gasping and lost. Avoiding him wasn't going to save me from falling for him all over again. Or was that the right phrase? If I imagined love as a tumble, I'd already hit the ground where Riley was concerned, long ago. And I'd never gotten back up.

PETER

I drove up to Gene's house the next day with my heart in my throat. Riley didn't make me suffer through knocking on the door. He jogged down the porch steps as I walked up, then seemed to consciously slow his strides with his hands shoved in the pockets of his jeans as he closed the distance to the car.

It was another warm day, but there was a hint of briskness in the air that made me wonder if we were going to get one of those cold snaps my dad cheerfully called Second Winter.

Riley's flannel sleeves were rolled up, and he looked so good that all I wanted was to press my face into his shoulder and breathe deep. But instead of touching each other, we stopped abruptly at a short distance, like magnets turned the wrong way.

"Hey." He raked a hand through his hair, which messed it up more instead of smoothing it out. No matter how many times he pushed it back, his hair wanted to fall forward. He hadn't had that problem when it had been long enough to tie back.

"Hey. Sorry about yesterday."

He shrugged. "It's okay. You don't have to come here every day."

"I said I would," I reminded him gruffly. "I want to help."

We both looked at the ground, like our shoes were the most

interesting thing about one another. Riley was wearing old hiking boots, unlaced, the cuffs of his jeans tucked carelessly inside. The way someone wore shoes shouldn't be hot, but it made me imagine how easily he could kick them off and step right out of those jeans...

"I know you have your own stuff going on too," Riley went on. I glanced up at him, but he was still looking down, his eyelashes ridiculously long and dark against his cheeks.

"Not really," I said honestly.

"Job stuff, I mean," he protested.

I shook my head.

He looked at me at last, frowning. "Aren't you a lawyer now?"

"Sort of." I wasn't sure I wanted to be one at all, but I left that unsaid.

His frown deepened. "What about that lady with the rabbit sweater who said you're her lawyer?"

"I wouldn't call that legal work. Mostly, I followed her around her yard for a couple of hours and learned more than I ever wanted to know about Flemish Giants."

His eyes widened, and a snort escaped him that I could tell he hadn't meant to let out. "Flemish *what*?"

I breathed out a laugh. "They're a kind of rabbit."

First thing that morning, I'd finally called Marion. She'd instructed me to come to her place for an in-person meeting. The whole trip had been surreal, starting with the video she showed me on her phone, which she'd recorded while a tired-looking sheriff's deputy explained that her neighbor had accused her of letting "attack rabbits" run free. I'd seen the fearsome creatures myself, lounging in the garden like something out of *Alice in Wonderland*.

"They're accurately named," I assured Riley. "I didn't know rabbits could be that big. They're the size of basset hounds, I swear." I laughed again and found Riley looking at me with one side of his mouth curled up, a flash of familiarity in his changed face. Because back when we were inseparable, Riley had always laughed when I laughed. It was automatic. Before he even knew what I was laughing at—and even if we'd heard the same joke and he didn't think it was particularly funny—*my* laugh made him laugh, every time.

As soon as our eyes met, his smile vanished. Still, the moment had lit up that old connection, the one we'd proven two days ago could still fully ignite if we let it.

I cleared my throat. "Anyway, yeah. I did help Marion, but it wasn't really legal advice. It was more like mediating a dispute between neighbors."

"But you're a lawyer," he insisted. "You went to school and took the test."

"Yeah, I did." I didn't add that if I wanted to do anything other than rabbit-related negotiations between bickering neighbors, I would need help from someone with actual experience.

"I guess what I'm saying is, you have other stuff you could be doing. So, thanks."

"You're welcome." I rubbed my hands against the tops of my thighs. "Should we…?"

"Yeah, we should get to work."

Riley pivoted and headed for the trees. I scrambled to get my messenger bag from the back seat of the car and jogged after him.

We hopped over the creek where the banks were high and narrow. If for some reason we missed the short jump, it would be a messy fall, but taking the short leap across was an old habit I apparently hadn't forgotten. I remembered the first time we'd dared each other to do it, and how my heart had hammered. I'd landed on the far side and felt like I'd crossed the Grand Canyon.

I hadn't meant to match pace with Riley, but the same muscle memory that carried me over the creek put me shoulder-to-shoulder with him as we walked on, though far enough apart that we couldn't accidentally touch.

"So you went to school, took the test, but you're not working for your aunt yet?" Riley asked. "Why not?"

"I'm not sure," I confessed. "Aunt Iris would love nothing more."

"I remember when we were kids and people would ask the usual question: what do you want to be when you grow up? Fuck, I hated it when people asked me that. But you always had your answer ready."

Riley's comment took me by surprise, but only because he remembered a small detail like that. He was right. I'd been telling people I was going to be a lawyer, just like Aunt Iris, since I was six.

"Well, I was a kid. And I was pretty sure that being a lawyer meant being a professional fairy godparent, which is really only accurate in Aunt Iris's case."

Riley snorted but didn't let me off the hook. "You were still sure when we were eighteen. By then, we weren't really kids."

"Maybe I wasn't a kid, but I didn't know how the world works." While I'd been at Harvard, I'd learned. "I went to Harvard because I believed it was the best. But actually being there…it was so different than what I imagined. I was surrounded by people who thought the least important part of going to an elite school was what we were learning in class. What mattered to them was *who* you knew, not *what* you knew."

Of course, Riley didn't look surprised. Growing up where and how he did, he'd already learned lessons at eighteen that I had to go through seven years of Ivy League education and a couple of summers of cutthroat internships to understand.

I pushed on. "I got caught up in it. I saw the rat race as another challenge. Another thing to apply myself to excel at. And I did. I made the right friends, and they introduced me to the right people, and suddenly I had a job lined up at one of the most lucrative personal-injury firms in the country."

"Out in LA?" Riley asked.

"Yeah. LA." I blew out a breath. "The goal of a second-year law student is to have a summer position that will lead into employment after graduation. I had that, *and* I was doing well in the job. Everything was falling into place.

"Then, one weekend in the middle of the summer, the whole firm was out on a partner's yacht. Another intern looked at me with this big smile on her face and said, 'Can you believe this is going to be us in fifteen years?'" Even the memory made me shudder. "All of a sudden, it clicked for me. This wasn't just another class I was trying to ace. I was making choices that were going to shape the rest of my life."

I'd talked so much, we'd reached the point where we had to squeeze through the gates. Riley paused with his hand on the iron rungs. "What did you do then?"

"I... um, I marched up to the managing partner at the firm, made an over-the-top speech that ended with me telling him I quit, and then I realized I couldn't storm out dramatically because, you know, we were at sea. So I sat in a corner, drank the premade cocktails, and avoided eye contact until we got back to the dock."

Riley tilted his head, face solemn. "Well, you never were into boats."

I burst out laughing as Riley turned away and squeezed through the gate. I couldn't see his face, but I still knew he was smiling along with me.

I slipped through after him, more easily, because I lacked his luscious chest and ass. "Hey," I called softly, very conscious of exactly what had happened the last time we'd entered the park.

He turned, the flush in his cheeks suggesting his thoughts were traveling along similar lines.

I rocked on my heels. "I've missed this. Talking to you."

"So have I."

"And the day before yesterday, when we..." I didn't know how to put words to the experience. Anything I could have said out loud would have sounded crass instead of transcendent. I looked at him helplessly, and he saved me with a tiny smile.

"I've missed doing that with you, too."

"So have I." I swallowed. "You should have answered my calls, back then."

I saw a crease in his cheek like he was biting the inside. Then his jaw flexed, and he nodded. "I know. I was a coward."

"I was afraid, too. I stopped calling after a few weeks, and I think it was because if you'd answered and told me you didn't want to talk to me again, it would've felt more real."

He stared at me with open shock. "I was sure you'd be fine without me. Maybe even better off. I didn't believe I could really hurt you."

"Well, you could. You have," I corrected. I'd spent eight years learning what it felt like to leave things unsaid that I should have told Riley Meadows. I'd learned my lesson. "I didn't know what to do without you. I still don't."

Riley's breath hitched. "The day before yesterday, after we were together, you got weird," he said softly. "It seemed like you thought it was a mistake."

I shook my head. "I know I didn't handle it right." I glanced at him. "I was scared."

He only had to close two steps between us to have me in his arms.

It wasn't like two days ago, when all I wanted was to get naked, and we'd staggered by mostly unspoken agreement into the office. This time, I already felt naked, stripped bare in a way that left me much more vulnerable than just losing my clothes. He folded me in, and I wrapped my arms around him in turn and pressed my face into his neck. We both shuddered as though feeling the same bone-deep relief.

"I missed you too," he said into my ear, his voice and his beard somehow both soft and rough against my skin. "So much."

I held him tighter and felt his breath stutter before I forced myself not to squeeze quite so hard. "Sorry," I muttered against his neck. He grunted and hauled me closer.

"No, *I'm* sorry. You have nothing to be sorry for."

"I should have tried harder to talk to you."

He huffed. "You called a hundred times."

I laughed shakily. "A hundred and one times, actually." The phone had kept a handy little log to taunt me with.

He leaned away from me and cupped my face in his hands while my arms stayed locked tight around his waist. His thumbs were warm and rough on my cheeks, and I realized he was brushing away a few tears I hadn't even noticed I'd shed.

"I'm sorry," I said again, then rolled my eyes at myself. "I'm not really crying."

A few more tears burst loose to prove I was a fucking liar. Riley calmly brushed them away, too.

Then he kissed me.

A tiny sound escaped me, along with a couple more tears, and I lifted myself on my toes so I could press our lips together more deeply. His tongue grazed the seam of my parted lips. His hands were still gentle on my face, his fingertips making tiny strokes against my neck, and I didn't know what to do with the feeling that came along with holding one another like this.

I'd thought I couldn't fall further for Riley. I'd been wrong. I was in free fall, in all its scary euphoria, with no idea what was waiting for me when I finally landed.

Part of me was terrified at the prospect of that future pain. But pulling away now would be agony, too.

Pain now, or pain later. Maybe it was a vice, but I'd choose pain later, every time.

We weren't able to put in a full day because Gene had an appointment in town. When it was time to stop, I peeled off my gloves with a groan, finding a fresh blister on the side of my hand. While I was distracted by examining it, Riley stepped close and caught my hand in his. He inspected the blister for a second, and then brought my hand to his mouth.

I'd always thought of the concept of healing a wound with a

kiss as an innocent gesture, but there was a wicked heat in his eyes as we stared at each other over our joined hands. And then I felt the tip of his tongue on my skin, the burn of soreness turning into a blaze of more pleasant pain.

"Don't *do* that when it's time for me to go home," I complained.

He smiled almost shyly, and kissed my hand again, this time on the back, just above my knuckles, like a gentleman in an old movie.

"I wish I didn't have to go," he murmured.

But he did. So I went home.

My parents had lived in the same house since they married, a couple of years before my mom got pregnant. Back when they bought it, the house had been a mess. I'd seen the *before* photos a million times. I always sighed when they broke them out, eager to show a new acquaintance the transformation, but in reality, I found it pretty cool that in their twenties, they'd taught themselves how to lay hardwood floors, replace drywall, and swap out old corroded pipes for PVC. Now their prized Victorian was in meticulously restored condition, and at three stories with a wrap-around porch, a proud addition to the historic register.

And then I came along, and the entire third story became my territory, a warren of sloping ceilings and irregular rooms formed by the steep-pitched roof and turrets that topped the house. When I moved in at the beginning of the previous summer to study for the bar, I found everything exactly as I'd left it, including the squashy old sectional and the television in the open room at the top of the stairs. The door to the tiny widow's walk balcony was still nailed shut, the way it had been since my parents first made the upstairs my playroom. There was both comfort and claustrophobia in the familiar space.

But the memories of my childhood's ups and downs, the crappy furniture, and my younger self's ill-advised poster choices didn't stop the third floor from feeling like a sanctuary.

Without the privacy, I couldn't have stood living with my

parents as an adult. I loved them, but they'd always been overly involved in my life, and ever since I'd finished school without a job, they'd convinced themselves I was derailed and it was up to them to get me back on track.

Both of my parents' cars were parked in the driveway, which was a surprise because I'd only expected Mom to be around. But when I came inside and the house was quiet, I assumed they'd taken their bikes somewhere.

I headed upstairs, and was halfway between the second and third floor when I heard their voices and slowed, puzzled. Mom and Dad hardly ever came up here.

The door at the top of the stairs was open, and a third voice carried along with their familiar ones. I stepped onto the landing to find them talking to a tall person, who didn't look much older than eighteen, with braided pigtails, Coke-bottle glasses, and a deep, melodic voice.

My mom saw me first. Along with surprise, a hint of alarm flashed across her face before her expression settled back into a smile.

"Peter! We didn't know you'd be home so soon." She shot my dad a glance, and he grimaced, much worse at concealing his feelings than she was.

The stranger turned to me with a wide smile. "So you're Peter! I'm so happy to meet you. I've never had a roommate!"

What the fuck?

I didn't ask the question out loud, but my face must have given away my shock because my dad cleared his throat again so vehemently, he made himself cough several times.

Mom smiled brightly. "Peter, this is Chris! Chris, Peter."

I was probably supposed to offer to shake Chris's hand or something, but I only managed a dazed nod.

Smile faltering, Chris glanced at my parents. "I'm sorry if I assumed... It's just, you mentioned letting me look over the lease, so I thought..."

"It's yours if you want it, Chris," my mom rushed to say,

holding out a manila envelope. Then she looked at me with a tight smile and explained, "The north bedroom."

There were two bedrooms on the third floor. The one on the north side was technically a guest room, although most of the time my parents used it for storage. There was also a shared bathroom and the open room where we stood now, with the sectional, the television, and the pseudo-kitchen I'd cobbled together using the original wet bar and stocking the cabinets with a hot plate, mini fridge, and three sizes of electric skillet.

My little sanctuary. The only thing keeping me sane. And now I was going to have a *roommate*?

"I'll let you all get back to your day," Chris said cautiously. With any luck, our undercurrent of family drama would scare Chris off.

"I'll walk you out," said my dad, transparently jumping at the chance to get away. He often said that my mom had a pressure cooker for a temper, and that I'd inherited the pressure-cooker gene, too. He always made himself scarce when Mom and I threw down, and it was obvious that was about to happen again.

As soon as the door at the top of the staircase closed behind Chris and Dad, I put my hands on my hips and glared at my mother. "So after spending my formative years at war with the city council over zoning stuff, you're going to rent out a room?" My parents used to go on and on about how student rentals were ruining the neighborhood. When I was in junior high, they'd gotten a neighborhood group together to pressure the city council to change the regulations.

"The zoning allows it, so long as there aren't more than four adults here."

"Only because you guys didn't get your way back then!"

She pointed a finger at me, and her voice turned cold. "Don't you shout at me. You're an adult, Peter. If your father and I decide to rent out a room in our own damn house, that is not a decision you're entitled to have an opinion about."

My face got hot. "*You're* the one who suggested I move

back in!"

"Of course, honey!" She threw her hands up in exasperation. "You're our son and we love you. You're always welcome here. We're not kicking you out. It's one room!"

"How much is the rent?"

My pivot threw her off-balance. She frowned at me. "The amount we gave Chris?"

I nodded.

She gave me the number. "Utilities included. Why?"

"Because I want to pay, too." I knew I was just being stubborn, but it felt good.

She looked at me in total bewilderment, which gave me a twisted feeling of satisfaction, like kissing Riley Meadows had somehow transformed me back into an angsty teenager who was inexplicably desperate to roughen the calm seas of my parents' lives. "We're not charging you rent, honey. That's not what—"

"I'm an adult, like you said. If you're renting rooms in this house, then I should be paying the going rate."

She rolled her eyes and folded her arms. We stared at each other for a long second with narrowed eyes. She was the first to turn away.

"You're being ridiculous," she said over her shoulder as she started down the staircase.

"I'll have your money to you on the first of the month," I assured her, but she only shook her head and muttered something to herself too softly for me to hear.

When I was alone, I dropped onto the squashy sectional, wanting to scream, anything to drown out the niggling thought in the back of my head that I was acting like a spoiled brat.

The last time I'd been tempted to self-reflect, I'd been off the coast of California on that damn yacht, and I'd imploded my whole life when I gave in to the impulse of looking inward. Maybe that meant I was postponing an inevitable reckoning, but so be it.

Pain later over pain now. Every time.

12
RILEY

I counted under my breath as I walked. "One, two, three—"

"No, stop. Stop," Peter interrupted.

We were just inside the gates of the park, one of the few areas that wasn't either overgrown or dotted with the soft mounds of refilled holes from two weeks of digging and having nothing to show for it.

I was measuring off ten paces while Peter stood to one side, clipboard in hand, observing with a frown. "Why are you walking like that?"

I frowned back. "What do you mean?"

He gestured vaguely with the pen in his hand. "I mean... unnaturally. Just walk like Gene would walk."

"Gene can barely walk," I pointed out testily.

Peter winced, then nodded grudgingly. "But that's recent. When he buried the money, he was in good enough shape to haul the money out here and dig a hole in the dark. He was probably walking normally."

"If you don't think I'm 'walking normally,' maybe you should be on this side of the experiment." The experiment being: how far was ten paces, exactly? We were trying to fine-tune the order in which we searched the quadrants on Peter's map.

After almost two weeks of searching, we'd found nothing. I was beginning to worry that Grandpa had imagined the whole thing and the money wasn't in the park at all. Or if it was, we'd need more time to find it than we had left.

From what I could tell, Peter was as confident as ever, working methodically through the plan.

"You two are almost the same height, though," Peter said matter-of-factly, and I arched an eyebrow. Grandpa was several inches shorter than me even when he wasn't perpetually hunched over, and that would put him closer to Peter's height. Peter added, "And you're related."

"Related? What does that have to do with anything?"

"Family members are more likely to have a similar gait."

"You're so full of shit."

He pretended not to hear me, but his mouth quirked in a smile as he looked at his clipboard and poised his pen. "Okay. Again. But..."

"More normal. Got it." I rolled my eyes as I went back to the starting line Peter had drawn in the dirt with his shoe and began counting paces again. "One, two—"

"Okay, no. That's even worse. You look like a marionette. What are you doing with your knees?"

I squinted at him. "What is this, a fucking field sobriety test?"

He grinned at me and cocked a hip, tapping the pen against the clipboard. "I don't know. Do you want it to be?"

I breathed out an incredulous laugh, somehow both incredibly annoyed and turned on by the suggestion of role playing cop and suspect. "You gonna place me under arrest?"

His smile widened, and his eyes turned bright as he took a slow step closer. "I should. You clearly have no respect for authority." His tone was playful, but his eyes were sharp as he took another step closer.

After getting our hands on each other the first time, we hadn't been able to keep them off. Peter was serious about the schedule he'd made, and so was I, because worrying about the missing money had formed a pit in my stomach that grew every day. But we were still too ravenous for each other to resist, and we'd fallen to our knees for each other right out in the open once or twice when we couldn't slow down enough to make it to the office first.

I lifted my chin defiantly, playing along with the game. "You think *you* can teach me a lesson?"

Peter's smile turned into a smirk, and his voice was rough as he answered, "Keep giving me attitude, and you'll find out." He prodded me firmly in the sternum with the knuckles of a loose fist. "Now, I said *walk*."

I groaned. "Why is this so hot?" My body was so attuned to his that it could have been our proximity that made my heart race, or maybe it was the thrill of playing cop and suspect. I'd grown up in a neighborhood where people feared and hated cops, and my family had more than its share of run-ins with law enforcement. Funny how the thinnest of lines separated what was frightening from what was a turn-on.

His expression was positively wicked. "It is hot, isn't it?" He dragged his knuckles down my chest a few inches, then spread his palm over my left pec and my rabbiting heart. "You're not walking," he pointed out, almost whispering. He tossed the clipboard aside, and I barely heard it land somewhere away from us on the grass. "Does that mean you want a lesson instead?"

"Fuck you," I said, trying to stay in character but just sounding like what I actually was—desperately turned on in broad daylight while Peter touched me with one hand.

"Mmm…" Peter cocked his head like he was thinking it over. "Is that what you want?" His blue, blue eyes bored into mine. "To fuck me?"

Holy shit. I nodded slowly because yeah, of course I did.

He dragged his teeth over his lip, a moment's vulnerability before he put on his cocky cop mask again. "I bet you do. But I think if you don't straighten up, you're the one who's gonna get fucked. What do you think about that?"

Honestly, I'd be fine with that, too. At least in theory. I'd never been on the receiving end. I wasn't philosophically opposed, but it had never come up. Guys I'd hooked up with had always wanted to bottom, if we'd done anal at all, and I was happy to top them, so that was how it had always gone.

Peter was bi. I knew that probably didn't mean he was necessarily a top or versatile, but... odds were good, right?

I'd bottom for Peter.

I'd let him do anything he wanted to me, or do whatever he wanted me to do to him.

Happily.

"Riley," Peter said, his voice gentle. He touched my cheek with the hand that wasn't still cupped over my heart. "Hey. I was just playing around. You okay?"

I opened my eyes and blinked at his face, at the wrinkle of concern between his eyebrows. I was still holding my hands slightly away from my sides, a leftover from the little game we'd been playing. I slid them around his waist and pulled him to me.

"I'm okay. My thoughts got carried away, though." I gently rubbed my cheek against the side of his neck, so my beard rasped against his sensitive skin the way I knew he liked. "I know we were only messing around just now. But... do you want to? Fuck me?"

His breath stuttered. "Jesus. Yeah, I do." He paused. "Do you like that?"

"I don't know. I haven't ever done it."

He leaned back in my embrace so we could look at each other. "You haven't bottomed, or you haven't...?"

"I haven't bottomed," I confirmed.

He smiled ruefully. "Me neither. But I would, if that's what you wanted."

Like they had a mind of their own, my hands slid down his back so my fingertips grazed the curve of his ass. "Yeah?"

He nodded only once, but hard. "I've thought about it. I just never... I haven't been with a guy. And none of the women I was with were very interested in it."

"I used to think about doing it with you," I admitted.

Peter grinned. "Me too. Honestly, sometimes I didn't think about anything else for weeks."

"I can relate."

We both laughed, and then Peter tilted his head and said, "We never talked about it."

"It never came up."

"I was having too much fun with everything we were already doing." He pressed his face back into my shoulder.

I kissed his neck again. "Same." I'd thought we'd have plenty of time to explore all the ways we could be together. All the time in the world.

My hands had been unconsciously roaming lower, and I dared to run my palm between the pockets of his jeans; the denim was pulled snug, and my hand ran through the valley of his cleft. "I like what we're doing now, too."

Peter rolled his hips against mine. We were pressed together, hot and hard, but I didn't have any particular urge to hurry. Maybe because when Peter had shown up that morning, Grandpa was out of the house, and we'd seized the opportunity to go into my room and suck each other off on a bed for once. I could get hard for Peter five times a day at least, but the recent orgasm had taken the desperate edge off.

Still...

"Grandpa isn't coming back until this afternoon, if you want to go back to the house."

Peter laughed against my shoulder, then eased a step back, his hands lingering on my hips and mine sliding away from his body reluctantly. "You don't mean that. We have a quadrant to do today."

I sighed. He was right. It would be hard enough if the search failed. I wouldn't forgive myself if we didn't get our plan executed in time because we'd been fooling around.

"You're right," I agreed. "But after it gets dark..."

He reached down to pick up his clipboard. "Actually, I'm

supposed to go to Vino and Veritas tonight. It's board game night."

"Oh." I couldn't help feeling disappointed, which was stupid. Peter had his own life, his own friends. It would be better if I didn't forget that.

"If you wanted," Peter began, shrugging, "you could come with me. My friends can be...extra, but they're all good people. And a lot of fun."

My chest felt tight with equal parts excitement that he'd asked and dread at the prospect of being around his friends. And I remembered the wine bar now... It was similar to the restaurant where I'd worked in the city. The kind of place where if I belonged at all, it was in the back, out of sight of the customers.

I'd hesitated too long. Peter waved the clipboard at me. "Don't worry about it. You can say no. I just thought—"

"Yeah, I'll go," I said before he could take back the invitation. "It sounds fun."

His mouth hung open for a moment, like I'd surprised him as much as I'd surprised myself. "Yeah! Fun. Great. It'll be great." He looked down at the clipboard and cleared his throat. "But first, ten *normal* steps, please?"

Peter had to go home to shower and change, leaving me to do the same.

After he was gone, I realized I didn't know when Grandpa was supposed to be back. He usually didn't drive after dark, so I assumed he'd return soon, and I was pretty sure he'd say yes if I asked to borrow his truck.

Still, I got increasingly nervous as I showered and looked at my crappy selection of clothing choices. I hoped like hell Grandpa wouldn't balk at letting me take the truck because I did *not* want to be the twenty-six-year-old guy whose grandpa had to drop him off and pick him up.

I ran into the foyer as I heard the door open and close, dodging the stacks of magazines I'd sorted from the newspapers the other day, when Grandpa had given me permission to throw away one but not the other.

"Hey, Grandpa," I said, slightly out of breath.

"Something chasing you, kid?" he asked, looking bewildered, and then he smirked. "You got somebody back there in your room you don't want me to see?"

"*What?*"

"I've seen you and Pete circling each other," he said, looking proud of himself for shocking me. "Tell him to come out." He held up a greasy paper bag. "I brought fried chicken."

"Peter is *not* here."

Grandpa winked at me. "If you want to play it like that, then I'll just eat the chicken myself." He headed for the kitchen, and I noticed absently that he was getting around more easily. When I'd first arrived, I worried he'd fall without both hands free to balance himself against the furniture or one of his canes as he went. Now, he moved slowly but surely even with a bag of chicken in one hand and his hat in the other.

"I'm serious," I assured him. "He's not here. Actually, we're supposed to meet up in town. If that's okay with you? I'd need to borrow the truck."

He paused in the doorway between the entryway and the dining room. "Is this a date?"

"Grandpa," I groaned. "Can I borrow the truck? Yes or no."

He unrolled the top of the bag and reached inside for a piece of chicken. "Why are you the only one who gets to ask questions?" He took a bite of a chicken leg and looked at me expectantly.

I relented with a sigh. "*No*, it's not a date."

"Why not?"

"Because it's just not. He's hanging out with his friends and asked if I wanted to come. He was probably being polite." Peter had been surprised I'd accepted his invitation, and now I wondered if he regretted asking me.

Grandpa chewed and swallowed another bite. "Well, I hope you two are being careful. Physically *and* you know." He dropped his chicken back in the bag and tapped his temple with his forefinger. "Emotionally. You two did a number on one another back in the day." He shook his head. "You're both good boys. I hope you'll take better care of each other this time."

"We're not *together*, Grandpa," I said honestly. Sure, we were fooling around, and it was the most fun I'd had in eight years, but I was well aware that this was just another stolen season with him. When he found the right important job in the right big city, he'd be gone.

Grandpa caught me off-guard with a shrug and a, "Whatever you say." He dug in his pocket and tossed me his keys. I almost didn't catch them. "Have fun, kid. You deserve it."

Giving up on setting Grandpa straight, I just waved at him and jogged out to the truck.

I drove into town, at least once every quarter-mile talking myself out of turning around and driving straight back to Grandpa's house.

My nerves ratcheted higher and higher after I'd parked and started walking down Church Street, but my agitation vanished when I saw a familiar, tall figure at the building entrance, leaning against the brick wall. Peter's legs were crossed at the ankle, and he was effortlessly sexy in a pair of snug, navy-blue pants like the ones that had probably gotten all messed up that first day getting Lemon through the mud.

His shirt was pale blue with some kind of pattern on it. Swirls and flowers. I knew it had a name but couldn't remember what. His golden hair glowed in the reflected light of the streetlamp.

He looked up, saw me, and smiled. The last lingering bit of tension flowed out of my body. I smiled back and broke into a jog to close the last of the distance between us, but when he was within reach, I didn't know what to do.

For weeks I'd gotten my hands on him whenever possible. But that had been at Grandpa's and around the park, not out here in the real world where people could see. I stuffed my hands in my pockets so I wouldn't slip one of them around the back of his neck and kiss him.

"Hey," I said.

His smile of greeting lingered in a quirk on the left side of his mouth. "Hey. I wasn't sure you'd come."

"Really? But you asked me."

"I know." He shook his head. "Never mind. Let's go inside."

"Okay."

But instead of turning and leading the way through the doors, he hesitated, still facing me. "Look, these guys all mean well, but if they say something, or ask anything…" He lifted a hand as though to run it through his perfectly styled hair, then seemed to consciously stop himself before he could mess it up.

I could barely follow what he was saying, which was weird. Peter was good at making sense. My hands literally itched to smooth down his arms, to soothe him however they could.

"I'm not going to tell anyone that we're…um, that we've been messing around." *Messing around.* I hated the words as soon as I spoke them. From my point of view, the blowjobs and frotting and jerking each other off were the way Peter stitched his soul to mine, along with his laugh and his touches and his crazy dares, the same way he had during our summers together long ago. Nothing could be more serious.

"Right." Peter's cheeks were flushed, the high color obvious even in the shadows of the late evening. "Okay. Glad we got that settled." He flashed a smile that looked forced. "Let's go in."

13

PETER

Riley and I walked into the bookstore after my friends had already retrieved the extra tables from the storeroom and pushed them together.

We bumped into Lexy first. I'd gotten to know her through Jeremy and Aaron a few months before when I finally decided to stop being a recluse. "Hey, Peter," she said, pausing with the chair she was carrying toward the tables. Her bright-red eyebrows drew together as she registered Riley's unfamiliar presence beside me. "Who's this?"

"Riley. He's...an old friend." Glancing past her, I saw Jeremy staring our way from the other side of the tables.

"Is that him?" he mouthed. He was so completely unsubtle, he may as well have yelled across the room.

"Cool. Hi, Riley. I'm Lexy. And this is Briar," she added as Briar appeared from the wine-bar side, where he'd apparently gone to steal two chairs. "Briar, this is Riley. Peter's friend." She winked at me. "I thought we were Peter's *only* friends. But look at you, Peter. I'm impressed."

"Riley *Meadows*, right?" Briar asked, smiling politely, but also stealing tiny glances in my direction that made it obvious Aaron had told his brother, Jamie, who'd told his boyfriend, Briar, that there was something going on with Riley and me.

"That's right," Riley confirmed.

Lexy gave Briar a puzzled look, then shook her head, turning back to Riley. "We're playing the most boring game invented," she announced cheerfully, pointing to the box on the center of the table, its lid propped upright like it was another book on display at the store.

Riley squinted at the box and then shrugged. "I've never played."

"It's basically trivia," Lexy explained. "But at least the set pieces look like pie. So, what are you bringing to the table, Riley?"

"Um..."

Even standing a couple of feet away, I could sense the discomfort radiating from him. When we were kids, he'd been nervous about talking to new people, and I could see he hadn't outgrown the anxiety. I sidled closer to him and nudged him with my elbow. His head whipped in my direction, and I smiled. "She's wondering if she should try to poach you for her team."

"*Poach?*" Lexy scoffed, hoisting her chair up again and walking toward the table. "Don't suffocate your friend, Peter. He doesn't have to play with you if he doesn't want to. He has options."

"Did you hear that?" I asked Riley with a wink, grapevining a few steps beside Lexy so I could hold Riley's gaze and waggle my eyebrows. "You don't have to *play with me*."

He rolled his eyes, but the corner of his mouth that had been downturned with strain was now tugging up in a smile, so I counted that as a win.

Lexy said, "Everyone, this is Riley. Riley, this is everyone," and then pointed out all the gathered persons by name. Most of the people there were our age or younger, with the notable exception of Luke, the not-quite-silver fox dating Scott. Scott himself was an adorable human marshmallow with a surprisingly vicious competitive streak that had first come out the night we played Candyland.

In addition to Lexy, there were a few single people who'd always made me feel less like an odd-numbered wheel at board-game night, like Autumn and her older brother Bowen, a guy with an enviable ability to pull off pastels and still look masc.

"To start, pick a partner," Autumn instructed. Like Lexy, she was red-haired and freckled, but her hair was a soft, strawberry-blonde, and her freckles more vivid. Also like Lexy, when Autumn spoke, everyone listened. The group stopped talking and obediently paired off.

I smiled at Riley. "Well, what's the verdict? Will you take your chances with me?"

He huffed, which made me laugh, and then he smiled and glanced away from me, wrinkling his nose like he was trying to hang on to his composure. My heart skipped all over itself, and I wanted to touch him so badly, I had to slip my hands into my pockets just to make sure I kept them to myself.

"I'll take my chances," he said gruffly, and I got the distinct feeling he wasn't just talking about board game night, which left me reeling a little as we settled next to each other at the tables. As we sat, I nudged my calf against his, and even the slight contact instantly grounded me.

Jeremy interrupted the moment when he plopped down on my other side and rubbed his hands together. "Okay, team. What's our strategy?"

"Wait, are we a team?" I asked, baffled.

"Yeah," Lexy answered, sitting down on the other side of Riley. "We choose pairs, and then the pairs are randomly paired *again*."

Board game night's administration always seemed more complicated than necessary.

Lexy took a swig from her reusable water bottle, then fixed us with a solemn look. "We need to determine our strengths and weaknesses. Nerds have the advantage in trivia." She looked smug. "In other words, we got this." She pointed her water bottle at me. "Peter is the sports nerd." She pointed at Jeremy. "Jeremy is the pop-culture nerd. I'm the science nerd." She turned to Riley with an easy grin. "What kind of nerd are you?"

Riley pressed our legs together a little harder. "Um, I'm not really—"

They set up the game, and Lexy dived for the game pieces, looking proud of herself when she snagged the brown one. "Choosing brown is a show of strength," she explained, without actually explaining anything.

"Did I mention my friends are weird?" I asked Riley conversationally, and Jeremy laughed. I turned to him. "How's Aaron? Freaking out?" He'd been tapped to help a professor research a law review article, which was a huge fucking deal and totally deserved. Aaron had taken a few hits to his confidence while we were in school, and it felt awesome to see him get more recognition.

"Oh, that's an understatement." Jeremy grinned with a combination of affection and pride that made me reflexively smile back at him. "Fortunately for him, he has me to keep him sane with a constant barrage of cow memes. Speaking of..." He pulled out his phone, presumably to fire off another one. I shook my head, chuckling. If I'd met Jeremy separately, I didn't know if I could have pictured Aaron with him. But Aaron had been right the other night: they were alike in the ways that mattered.

"Phones down!" Autumn said harshly. "*No* phones. Obviously. It's a *trivia game*."

There were twelve of us, which made it crowded around the table and left us with three teams. When we drew our first card, I was instantly crushed by Jeremy leaning over me to read the question, but I didn't even care because it gave me an excuse to lean on Riley.

Riley, who was of course squinting at the card and rigid as a board beside me. I twisted around so I could murmur into his ear, "It's okay. We just read the question to the other team." I turned back to face the table and read the question. Then learned by glancing at the answers on the back of the card that Leonardo da Vinci had been strong enough to bend horseshoes with his bare hands.

After Autumn, Bowen, Luke, and Scott's team missed our question, Lexy and Jeremy high-fived like we'd had something to do with it.

We played for about forty-five minutes, and even though Lexy had been right that this wasn't the most exciting game we'd ever chosen, there was something about sitting next to Riley in a room full of my friends, my ankle twined around his, that made me want to stay there forever.

As our game piece and another team's became nearly full, though, the game got more heated. We landed on a square in the color we needed to win, and a thrill of excitement coursed through me. I leaned forward intently along with Jeremy as a card was drawn for us, and under the table, I gripped Riley's knee.

Our question, read in a prim voice by Autumn was, "What is the dominant grape in Chianti?"

"Wine? Are you kidding me? *Boo*," Lexy groaned. But then she looked at Jeremy and cocked her head. "You're pretty bougie. Do you know anything about wine?"

"Besides that it's tasty? Nope."

"Peter?"

"No," I said distractedly because I felt a faint tremor where my thigh and Riley's were pressed together. I couldn't tell if he was upset or... Was he trying not to laugh? Surely that couldn't be right.

"Let's break this down," Lexy muttered. "What the fuck even is a dominant grape?"

"The one with the whips and chains?" Jeremy suggested.

I snorted. Lexy rolled her eyes.

"Sixty seconds," Autumn reminded us cheerfully.

"Maybe the answer is just Chianti," Jeremy suggested. "Aren't a lot of wines named after the grape?"

Lexy frowned. "That seems like a dumb answer. Doesn't it seem dumb, Peter?"

"Well," Jeremy shot back, "it's better than not answering at all!"

"Sangiovese," Riley said. All three of us looked at him, and he cleared his throat. "The dominant grape in Chianti is Sangiovese."

"That's correct!" Autumn confirmed.

"Holy. Shit. Riley!" Lexy whisper-shouted. "You're a wine nerd!" She held up her hand, and he high-fived her.

This time it was Riley's hand that slipped over my knee, and when we looked at each other, his smile was as warm as the palm of his hand.

In the end, we were nerd enough to win, and after we'd cleaned up the bookstore, most of the group wandered over to the wine bar.

"Okay, I'm buying a round so we can toast our VIP," Jeremy declared. "Riley, dude, that was some serious wine-nerd shit. Do your parents own a vineyard or something?"

Riley caught my eye with a rueful expression, and I couldn't help a laugh at the idea of Gene running a vineyard. His chuckle was a half-second behind. Then he shook his head. "I worked in a restaurant for a long time. I realized I had a knack for figuring out wine, and after that I got kind of interested. It's no big deal."

That was a story I needed to hear more about later.

"That's awesome. So, what are you having, then? Maybe you should order for all of us." Jeremy picked up a wine list from the bar and handed it over. Riley took it with a tense smile.

I wasn't sure what to do. Snatching it out of his hand would be too obvious, so I just watched uneasily as he looked down at the page, tracing his forefinger down the rows of print. He'd described his dyslexia to me before we'd known what to call it by saying that when he tried to read words on a page, they jumped around. By the time we were teenagers, though, he could read even small print and complex sentences, given enough time. But he didn't read by choice if he could avoid it.

Jeremy slung an arm around Lexy's shoulder, and they talked about a mutual friend I didn't know, not seeming to notice anything was amiss. They probably assumed Riley was analyzing the list.

Riley's expression cleared after about fifteen seconds that seemed to tick by in slow motion, and then he looked up and said definitively, "This Pinot Noir." He pointed to a row of print on the page. "But I can only have one glass. I drove here."

"Or, alternate plan," Jeremy suggested, "you can share a bottle or two with us and then stumble home with someone. I can vouch for Lexy's excellent couch. Or I can offer the comforts of The Pink Monstrosity."

"The pink...what?"

"Jeremy lives in a giant old house that's aggressively pink," Lexy explained.

"Also," Jeremy went on innocently, "Peter's place is within walking distance. Just saying."

Riley breathed out a laugh and pushed a hand through his hair. "I'm going to the bathroom."

I wondered if I could casually pull off following him. Even if I did, what was I going to do with him in there? V and V wasn't *that* kind of place. But it had been torture sitting right next to him all night and not being able to feel him up.

"Bathroom is a good idea. Be right back." Lexy slipped out from under Jeremy's arm.

"You have some explaining to do," Jeremy said, stepping toward me with an ominous grin, but then his phone rang and he scrambled to answer, because of course it was Aaron. Jeremy forgot his need to interrogate me entirely in favor of talking to his boyfriend. When he stepped outside to escape the noisy bar, I decided I'd do the generous thing and buy the wine Riley had picked out, which, incidentally, cost more than I'd ever paid for wine. That wasn't saying much, though, because what I got came in a box.

I spared a thought for my shrinking bank account. I'd saved all the money I'd made working in LA two summers before, and it had added up. But it would spend fast once I started paying rent.

I needed a job, but that was a problem for Future Peter. Tonight, I was going to drink wine and marvel at the hidden depths of the guy I was crazy about. A wine connoisseur? He'd been holding out on me. What else didn't I know? The list was probably long. I kept thinking of him as the kid I'd known everything about, but he wasn't that person anymore.

The bartender tonight, Murph, greeted me with a bright smile. "Good evening! What can I get for you?" As always, he radiated a happy energy that would be over-the-top if it wasn't completely sincere. His smile broadened when Scott joined me at the bar. Scott and Murph were good friends.

"Go ahead," I told Scott, letting him order first. While Scott and Murph chatted, I noticed another guy sitting a few stools down from where I stood. Or, more specifically, I noticed his chestnut leather wingtips, which I would have traded a limb for.

"And for you?" Murph asked, turning back to me.

"One bottle of the Ankida Ridge Pinot Noir. Unless you'd give me a discount if I bought two?"

Murph's smile was apologetic. "Unfortunately, no discount."

Recalling that there was no way Riley would follow me home no matter how much I wanted him to—not when it would mean leaving Gene alone all night—I sighed. "Just the one, then. And four glasses, please."

Murph went to the wine rack to find the bottle.

"I thought Jeremy was buying that," Riley said, leaning against the bar beside me and nudging my foot with his.

He'd been gone about three minutes, and I still grinned, slightly giddy, at his reappearance. "Well, I wanted to."

Riley looked like he was about to respond when he saw something over my shoulder. "Hey. Chase, right?"

I turned toward the wingtips guy, who glanced up, recognition registering when he saw Riley.

"Yeah. And you're Gene Meadows's grandson."

"Riley."

I looked back and forth between them for a second, and then Riley awkwardly introduced me. I shook Chase's hand. "How do you two know each other?"

"We don't, really. We just met one time," Chase explained. "At Baylor's."

"*You* have coffee at Baylor's?" I was pretty sure the dress code at Baylor's was muck boots and overalls.

"Sure. It's a Burlington institution."

"Ken Landry is Peter's dad," Riley said.

I frowned harder at Chase. "You know my dad?"

"Sure. From the ED committee in the Chamber of Commerce." He winced. "I really shouldn't call it that. The *Economic Development* Committee. Anyway, Ken gave me Riley's name. He said the owner of Meadows Park might be interested in exploring grant opportunities."

Murph had just returned with the bottle of wine and a tray of glasses. "Meadows Park is gonna reopen? That would be amazing."

Riley and I exchanged a glance. I'd never actually heard anyone under the age of fifty acknowledge the park's existence.

Murph looked at Scott. "Your parents would flip out." He turned back to us, smiling. "Scott's parents went on a date there when they were teenagers. They have this cheesy picture of them kissing next to that building that looks like a turtle."

I chuckled.

"The greenhouse," Riley clarified absently, tilting his head toward Scott, who smiled and nodded.

"Is there really a chance it will reopen? That would be so great for the community."

"Would it?" Riley looked completely bewildered. "It's a really old-fashioned place. Not exactly Disney World."

"Some of the most successful local businesses around here are old-fashioned," Chase said with a wry smile. "There's a letterpress just down the street that's even older than your park, and it's doing booming business."

Murph nodded. "Scott was just saying earlier that he wished there were more family-friendly places to visit close to home."

Scott confirmed this with a nod and a shy smile. "Luke and I are always looking for places to take Addison." Right, because Luke had a daughter, and if I remembered correctly, he and Scott had met when Luke had hired Scott as her nanny.

I expected Riley to be eating up all the encouragement, considering that when we were teenagers he could talk nonstop about getting the park going again one day. Now there was a real possibility that Gene could fund it, with or without some kind of local investment from the Chamber. All we had to do was either find the buried money or try to get a grant.

But Riley just shrugged, clearly uncomfortable. "Well, the place has changed a lot."

"I've always wondered if my parents were making this part up," Scott said thoughtfully, "but they claimed there was a live tortoise there that weighed like a hundred pounds."

"That does sound made up," I agreed, and shot Riley a glance, grinning. But his eyes were fixed on the floor. "Um, thanks for this," I said, sliding Murph my card as I picked up the bottle and tray. "Can you run it and then hang on to it? I'll be right back."

"Sure thing," Murph said cheerfully.

I took an uncertain first step, and the glasses on the tray rattled alarmingly. Riley lifted the tray away from me and carried it instead. In his steady hands, the wineglasses didn't so much as tremble as we found a table.

We set everything down, and I looked at him cautiously as I

pulled out my chair. "Don't you think it's cool that there's support for the park reopening?"

He shrugged, taking the glasses off the tray and then setting it aside on the empty table next to ours. He picked up the wine bottle and pried off the loosened cork, then sniffed it. "Maybe that means an investor will buy it at the auction instead of somebody who wants to knock it down and build a few big houses."

I narrowed my eyes. "Nobody's buying it at auction."

He'd been running his thumb up and down the bottle label, his eyes tracking the path of his finger intently. Now he looked at me, his expression bleak. "What if we don't find the money?"

"We will."

His mouth twisted. "You don't know that for sure, Peter. It could be lost forever. And if it is, Grandpa will be totally screwed."

"But we're going to find it," I repeated.

"You don't *know* that!" he snapped.

I leaned back in my chair, baffled. "Why are you giving up already? We're only halfway through the search."

He ran a hand over his hair, his frustration evident. "This is why I didn't bring it up."

"What do you mean?"

"I knew you wouldn't think there's any way your plan could fail. That's how you've always been. You plan the thing, you do the thing. In the end, you get whatever it is you wanted. But that's not how things go for most people. It's definitely not how things go for me."

"Um, is everything okay?" Lexy asked quietly.

At some point, she and Jeremy had approached the table, and now they both stood a few feet away, looking like they deeply wished they'd stayed away a little longer.

"Fine," Riley said, and pushed his chair back. "I need to get home to Grandpa. Have an extra glass for me."

"Riley," I hissed, getting up to follow him, but he was already walking away. "I'll be right back," I said distractedly to my friends, squeezing between the edge of our table and an occupied chair before my way was more or less clear to chase after Riley.

When I came out the door, he was already a dozen yards down the sidewalk.

"Hey!" I shouted, breaking into a run to catch him and startling passersby on the Church Street pedestrian mall.

When I reached for his arm, he angled his body away from me, my hand closing on empty air as he muttered, "I shouldn't have said anything."

"I'm glad you did. I had no idea you were freaking out."

"I'm not *freaking out*," he said, his voice rising.

"I mean, I had no idea you were *worried*. Stressing about the money and your grandpa." Now that I was saying it out loud, though, of course he was.

Riley's frown twisted. "I haven't been. Or, not all the time." His shoulders slumped. "Not as much as I should be."

Much more slowly than it would've been for someone with more emotional than academic intelligence, the clues slid together in my mind. "You feel guilty because instead of worrying about Gene and the park constantly, we've been..." What were the words he'd used earlier? *Messing around.* I couldn't bring myself to repeat them, and he knew what I meant anyway.

He nodded.

"We're right on schedule with the search," I reminded him. "We won't do anything that will keep us from turning over every square foot inside that fence, if that's what we have to do."

He nodded a few more times, but he still looked pained. I wanted to reach for his hand, but I hesitated. We were in public, and aside from stolen touches under the table in V and V, I didn't think we'd ever done more than give each other friendly shoulder checks while we were off Meadows land.

My hesitation cost me my opportunity because Riley took a slow step back. "I do need to get home. But I'll see you tomorrow?"

"Yeah."

"Okay," he said, already turning away, but then he paused and glanced at me again. "Thanks for inviting me tonight. I had fun."

I snorted. "Of course you did. Show-off."

A ghost of a smile passed over his face, and then with a little wave, he walked away.

14
RILEY

I knew Grandpa was still downstairs when I got home because the TV was on, but since he often fell asleep in front of it, I tried not to make too much noise as I shed my jacket and shoes and put the truck keys in their place on the coat rack.

"Riley?" Grandpa shuffled into the foyer in his bare feet. "What are you doing back home already?"

I shrugged. "They played a trivia game. I stayed till the end."

"Hm." He looked at the closed door behind me. "Pete's not with you?"

"No," I irritably answered the rhetorical question. "It's not like he lives here."

"Hm," Grandpa repeated. "Did something happen with you two?"

"Why would you ask that?" I snapped.

He didn't even flinch. "These days, I figure Pete is about the only one who can rock your boat."

"It wasn't him." Not exactly. I *had* been a dick to him, which was mostly why I felt shitty at the moment, but the night had been grating on me from the start. I'd actually enjoyed the game. Peter's friends had initially made me nervous. They were college-educated, confident people—radiating that my-life-is-great-and-I-have-nothing-to-hide vibe that always made me feel like I stood out in the wrong way. But they turned out to be funny and had made an effort to include me, not to mention that it had been fun when that twist of fate in category selection had given me a chance to impress them with random wine knowledge.

But then the park had come up, and my gut had gotten all twisted up. And then I'd yelled at Peter.

"Why don't you tell me about it, then?" Grandpa insisted.

I glanced at him and shook my head. "It's nothing."

"Doesn't look like nothing."

I bent down to untie my boots. "Just leave it alone."

"Now you sound like your dad," Grandpa muttered.

The straining dam on my emotions that had been under pressure all night snapped before I could escape upstairs to breathe and count and get the family temper under control.

"You really want to know? I freaked out because a bunch of people wanted to talk about the park and how to fund it and reopen it, and I didn't know what to tell them. Because if you won't even talk to a bank, you're definitely not going to apply to the Chamber of whatever-it's-called about getting money from them."

Grandpa's brows had risen higher the longer I talked. "And that would be because I don't need a bank or the Chamber. I've got money of my own."

"How the hell does it matter how much money you have when we don't even know where it is?"

His jaw worked for a moment before he found his voice, and then it came out slightly hoarse. "You were the one who said you'd find it."

"I have a bad habit of telling you what you want to hear." I kicked my shoes under the bench and stalked off to my room without waiting for a reply.

"Are you hungry?" Peter asked me around noon the next day.

His voice startled me after an entire morning spent working in absolute silence. I'd been trying to think of how to explain what my problem had been the night before, and hadn't found the words yet.

"Yeah," I admitted, setting down my shovel and squinting at the sky. There was enough food in the house for us to put something together, although I needed to make a grocery run soon. But while I was trying to remember how much of the last loaf of bread was still there, Peter opened his messenger bag and held a paper sack out toward me with a crooked little smile.

"You brought lunch?" I reached slowly for the bag, oddly touched.

He shrugged as he pulled out another paper sack. "I probably should have thought of it sooner."

"You're saving us from seeing Grandpa and getting a lot of talk about the weather." I found a sandwich and an apple inside my bag, and reached for the apple first. "Grandpa swears it's going to snow." I looked up at the sky doubtfully.

"Seriously?" Peter looked at the sky, too. "I heard it was going to get cold for a few days, but I didn't hear anything about snow."

"Grandpa's obsessed with the weather channel, so he probably had the first word on it. He said just a couple of inches, though."

Peter unwrapped his sandwich. "That's not unusual around here. It's only March." He glanced to his right and smiled. "Someone heard the sound of rustling paper, I see."

Lemon was headed our way, one step at a time, his head stretched all the way out from his shell the way it got when he was really excited about something. Which was pretty much only when he thought someone might be about to feed him.

I turned the apple around in my hand, thinking of biting off a piece for him, but Peter pulled out a third paper sack and rolled down the top. It was full of strawberries.

"You're going to spoil him," I said, but I was smiling.

Peter snorted. "He's already spoiled." He stuffed his sandwich back in its bag and walked over to meet Lemon midway. Lemon's mouth gaped open, a sight that never failed to amuse me, and I chuckled as Peter popped a strawberry past his beak and Lemon chomped dramatically, swallowed, and let his mouth hang open expectantly again. Peter gave him another one, and silence fell around us again.

"I'm sorry I left like that last night."

Peter was feeling around in the bottom of the bag for one of the last strawberries. He paused and glanced up at me. "I'm sorry you didn't feel you could tell me how worried you were about the money."

I wrinkled my nose, surprised by the angle of his response. "It wasn't like that. When we're together, worry isn't what's on my mind."

Still crouched beside Lemon, Peter peered up at me, solemn. "I know the feeling. Sometimes I think I'm two different people. The person I am when I'm here with you, and the person I am everywhere else."

"Yeah," I said, an old fear springing up from the back of my mind. I'd always known Peter was testing out different sides of himself when we were kids. And I'd always known that the side I knew and loved best, the one that was *mine*, wasn't the one he would choose.

I'd been wrong about a lot of shit, but I'd been right about that. He'd become the guy who excelled at Harvard, and was only back in Vermont temporarily, as a short setback. He wasn't the guy who belonged here, with me.

One of Lemon's clawed feet landed firmly on the toe of Peter's boot, making him jump, then snort. "Impatient?" He shoved a strawberry in the tortoise's waiting mouth. "That's the last one, big guy." He rubbed a light circle on the top of Lemon's head with his fingertips and straightened back up. "If it's going to snow, we should get Lemon inside."

I sighed. "Too bad you're out of strawberries." The easiest way to get Lemon to go somewhere was to lure him with a trail of food.

"Come on. It's not far. We can carry him."

I groaned and rubbed my shoulder. Shuffling along in a crouch while carrying Lemon was going to wreak fresh havoc on my back, which was sore as hell from several days spent wielding a shovel.

"Don't be a baby," Peter said, squinting at me. But he reached out and put his hand above mine, then rubbed the spot on my shoulder I couldn't quite reach.

"Oh God, yes," I muttered, making Peter laugh. He put his free hand on my other shoulder, and I could have melted at how good the firm, gentle pressure felt.

Peter's eyes met mine. "If we don't find anything in another week, we can talk to Gene about other options. Together."

My lingering worries couldn't be undone by a reassuring touch and a few words, but because they came from Peter, it was a near thing. I felt better, and even managed a smile and a nod. "Okay."

I'd gone to refill our water bottles in the office when Peter surprised me by bursting in after me.

"It just started," he said breathlessly. "The wind came up, and I saw a few flakes. And I'm pretty sure there was some thunder, too. I'm going up the tower to see what it looks like over the trees." He headed for the spiral staircase leading to the office building's second story.

My stomach flipped over. "Hey. Wait." But he was already flying up the steps. I grimaced and followed him.

The rapid rhythm of his feet on the stairs slowed as he reached the top and saw what I hadn't wanted him to see. "Wow," he said. "Gene must have started one of his projects up here. Have you seen this?"

I continued upstairs, and found Peter wandering around the cylindrical room that had been an office back when the building was our childhood fortress. The windows were large, almost floor-to-ceiling, and though the glass was grimy and the sky was dim, it was still easier to see up here than downstairs.

Peter was inspecting a grid of studs and stubbed-in PVC on one side of the space. "I think this was going to be a bathroom. And another small space. Maybe a closet?"

"Yeah, looks like it." I walked to the window, my skin crawling with the weight of this old secret. The secret of the future I'd hoped for, and taken steps toward, oblivious that it would have been impossible at the time. But there was no point in humiliating myself by revealing it now. Out the window, the falling snow was a white blur. I rubbed clear a spot in the glass with my sleeve, and could see a thin layer of accumulation.

"We should get back to the house while we still can," I said, turning to Peter, but he waved away my concerns.

"Your Grandpa said we'd only get a couple of inches, right?"

"Yeah. At least a couple." Peter froze, and I frowned. "What?"

"Which is it? 'Only a couple,' or 'at least a couple'?"

"Is there a difference?" I asked slowly.

"In the language of old folks from Vermont? Yes. 'Only a couple of inches' means only a couple of inches. 'At least a couple' could be two feet." He came to stand next to me, leaning against the windowsill and staring intently through the little spot in the glass I'd cleaned.

"I think he said 'at least a couple,'" I admitted.

Peter glanced at me, and one corner of his mouth quirked. "Damn. But how bad can it really be?" He looked back out the window with a wrinkle between his eyebrows. "Do you think the heat still works in here?"

"I'll go check." I left him at the window, half reluctant, half eager for a little space to catch my breath.

Memories were tugging at me. Grandpa's grand invitation to go into business with him, to work together to reopen the park.

The way my heart had felt like it could burst with pride that he thought I was worthy of it. Then, swearing Frank to secrecy when I asked him for help plotting out the renovation of the tower's second story. The difficulty and excitement of keeping a secret from Peter, whom I'd always told everything.

The water heater and furnace were inside a closet downstairs. I flipped a few switches, and the burned-earth smell of dusty vents being warmed for the first time in years soon filled the air.

"Riley?" Peter called from upstairs. "I think it's working! I can feel it coming through the vent. Everything okay down there?"

"Yeah. Just a sec." I was about to close the closet door when I noticed a mound of shiny plastic a few inches from my feet.

The black trash bag was still stowed where I'd left it eight years ago. I crouched and loosened its plastic drawstrings, finding it full of musty but otherwise undisturbed blankets. I cinched it closed again and hauled the bag upstairs, where Peter was still leaning beside the window, looking at the falling snow.

"What's that?" Peter asked.

"Blankets. I thought maybe we could... um, use them." I looked around as my cheeks got hot. "The place isn't exactly furnished."

Peter smiled, looking curious, but didn't tease me. "Yeah, good idea."

I took out the blankets, and we folded them to form a large, rectangular stack on the floor.

"Let's see..." Peter said pensively, then sat down cross-legged on our pseudo-mattress. "Not bad," he declared, then patted the place beside him with a playful smile. "Come see for yourself."

Breathing out a laugh, I sank down to my knees next to him, then tested the give in the layers of material with my hand. "Not awful," I decided, then glanced up and found Peter's face inches from mine, angled to kiss me. Our eyes met. "Not awful at all," I murmured, and then he closed the space between us and kissed me, and I was effectively shut up.

Peter kissed me once, then again, advancing with each press of our lips, until I found myself leaning back on my hands and Peter straddling my hips. I grunted approvingly, grabbing his waist and rocking up against him. He put his hand on my chest and pushed until my shoulders hit the blankets.

Grinning, he stretched out on top of me and kissed me again, his body long and hard. I could feel the expansion of our chests with each breath, synchronized, and my pulse in my throbbing dick, which was tight against Peter's as he bore down and ground us together.

He braced some of his weight on his knee so he could shove his jeans down his hips. I raced to do the same, only getting my jeans halfway down my thighs before Peter had kicked his off altogether and was rocking against me again. Our bodies were hot where they were bared, and the hair between his legs and at the tops of his thighs rasped against my sensitive skin in a way that made me ache.

I slipped my hand down his back and grasped his ass cheek, my new favorite place to touch now that I'd discovered how perfectly the tight, round muscle filled my palm.

Peter grunted and stopped grinding our cocks together to push back against my hand, and with the motion, my fingertip delved into his cleft and grazed the tight ring of skin around his hole. We both gasped, but Peter didn't go still, just pushed back more insistently.

"You said you wanted to fuck me," he muttered against my temple, then gave the side of my face a messy kiss, just in front of my ear. His next words were whispered straight into my skin and set me on fire. "I'd let you. I think I'd love it."

My cock throbbed, but it was my finger that was poised at his entrance, and I couldn't keep myself from pressing firmly against that tiny, dry place where I knew he could somehow take me, hot and tight, and that it would be fantastic. He shivered, not letting me in. Because he didn't know how. Because no one had ever fucked him.

I could be his first.

It shouldn't matter that no one had been inside him. I wasn't a person who put much stock in any concept of virginity. And yet a wild animal urge overtook me at the thought that I could touch Peter where no one else had, maybe not even Peter himself. I hooked my free hand around the back of his neck and pulled him closer so I could speak in his ear.

"Let me in, baby," I pleaded. "Push against my finger. Come on." I knew from playing with myself how it worked; counterintuitive at first, and then, suddenly, it felt so right. I kissed him again and again—his earlobe, the sweat-damp skin just beneath—and pushed more insistently. My fingertip felt so sensitive, it burned, like it was my cock poised to fuck him, not my hand.

Peter exhaled a shaky breath, and I knew the moment he bore down instead of tightening up because the hot skin against my fingertip flexed and softened, and just like that, I was inside him to the first knuckle, and he was growling out something. Encouragement or protest? I wasn't sure, so I didn't move.

"Okay?" I rubbed the back of his neck. "You feel so good. So tight." I shifted my finger experimentally. I didn't want to hurt him, and I knew that lube was key to anal play, but his whole body was trembling needily against mine, and I could tell by how hard he was, nestled against me, that he was enjoying this.

"Yeah, okay," he said, his voice a harsh breath. "Good."

I kept playing with him with slow, tiny movements, until we were both leaking all over each other and slick with sweat.

"I wanna touch you," he said, and with a sudden movement, rolled our interlocked bodies so that he was on his side, tucked against me face-to-face. Then he caressed the small of my back, his eyes a blazing blue. "Can I?"

My finger was still locked in his ass, and my balls were high and tight from all the teasing. I'd never really understood the appeal of having someone in my ass, not even after finding that sensitive spot inside my body with my own hand. It hadn't felt bad, but it had been too strange for me to get off on it.

But now, with Peter shaking and sweating from me fingering

him, I couldn't think of anything I wanted more than to feel his touch inside me, too.

"Yeah, you can," I said, and Peter, with a grin so bright it almost blinded me, ran his forefinger down the seam between my ass cheeks. I was a lot hairier there than Peter, and my ass had more meat. If my hands were free, I would have spread myself for him. But he found his way without my help, pausing to lick his finger in a way I found so hot, I groaned.

Then his wet finger was circling me again, only teasing me a second or two before he pressed in.

My back arched at even that small penetration. Everything back there just felt like *more*. Bigger, harder, hotter. And Peter's hand felt like *everything* because it was Peter, our eyes were locked together while we explored each other. I knew the wonder in Peter's face was written all over mine, too. And I was twenty-six, not eighteen, but fuck, it didn't feel like it. My heart was as big as the moon and my future limitless because Peter was here, looking at me like that.

Because Peter was mine, if only for a moment.

"Fuck." My breath was ragged, my hips jerking, like my body couldn't decide what it wanted more: the friction of Peter's cock against mine or his finger in my ass. "I'm gonna... Peter, I'm gonna..."

"Me too, baby," he growled.

Our bodies jerked and shuddered together, and Peter, in the midst of it, pressed farther into me, his finger swirling like he wanted to feel every inch of me he could, the welcome invasion stretching my orgasm out past the moment of release into what felt like an acre, a mile, a whole snowy sky of sensation.

15
PETER

The snowfall had accumulated to some six inches since the previous day, enough to leave knee-high banks along the edge of the cleared sidewalk adjacent to the law office when I arrived there a few minutes after noon.

I met a couple of the associate attorneys outside the front door.

"Hey, Landry." One of the younger lawyers in the firm, Evelyn, grinned at me from beneath glossy straight bangs. She was effortlessly cool in a black dress and burgundy riding boots. When I'd first met her, I'd wondered how she could possibly have ended up working with Iris and Tom, but now I knew that her boots were vegan, faux-leather, and that she'd probably spend at least half her lunch giving pro bono legal advice to the residents at the domestic violence shelter, like she did every Wednesday.

"Hi, Evelyn. How have you been?"

She looked resentfully at the snowy street. "Ready for spring. If I see one more snowflake, I'm going to scream."

"I hate to break it to you, but I don't think any of this will be melting anytime soon." The sun was out, but the temperature was hovering well below freezing.

"I guess I'll be screaming, then. But don't worry. Only on the inside."

I laughed. "You can take the girl out of Florida, but you can't take Florida out of the girl."

"That's true." She tilted her head. "So, are we going to be colleagues, or what?"

I paused with my hand on the door handle. "I'm still figuring things out."

She sighed, then glanced at her phone. "I have somewhere to be. But you should remember there are a lot of people who would kill for an open invite to work here. Don't be an entitled asshole. Make up your mind," she said, already walking away.

I winced. Evelyn's words had definitely hit their mark.

I'd texted Aunt Iris a couple of days ago, but with Tom on his annual trip to the Galapagos, she hadn't been able to meet with me immediately.

I braced myself to run into Jeremy at the reception desk, but to my relief, his chair was empty. I wasn't ready to answer his questions. He'd been texting me persistently over the past couple of days, and in that form, I'd been able to ignore him. Face-to-face, it would be a lot harder to deflect.

I found the door to Iris's office open, and heard an unexpected, familiar voice.

"Tom?" I poked my head in.

Tom was a big, tall man with a ruddy complexion and long, gray hair. His typical ponytail swung as he spun around to face me.

"Pete!" Before I could escape, he'd swept me into a full-body hug.

"Hey, Tom." I patted his wide shoulders with a faint laugh. "I thought you were in the Galapagos." His trip usually lasted at least six weeks, and this time he hadn't been gone a month.

He pulled back from the hug but kept his hands on my shoulders. "Yes, but unfortunately, I had to cut my trip short. I have a client in crisis, so I dropped everything to come back. Part of the job." He inspected me with a solemn face. "How are you?"

I took a deep breath. When Tom and Iris asked that question, they weren't making small talk. They expected honesty and had an uncanny ability to tell when I tried to gloss over anything.

"I'm..." I trailed off with a frown. Different answers were competing in my head, each one paired with an image from the past twenty-four hours. The answer varied depending on whether the image was one with Riley or without him.

Was I fantastic, or was I lost?

Did I feel the closest to myself I had since I started college, or did I have no idea who I was, much less who I was supposed to be?

After a long beat of silence where I couldn't figure out what to say, Tom gazed at Iris with a stricken expression. I glanced over my shoulder at her and found her nodding sadly.

"I told you." She sighed. "He's still stuck."

Tom squeezed my shoulders. "Have you reconsidered carrying the crystal Iris imbued with peaceful intentions? A mind that never rests is prone to turmoil." He gave my forehead a warm kiss like I was still ten years old. "My poor, smart boy."

I gently broke away from him, shaking my head with a wry smile. "The crystals haven't come up again. But I did reconsider something else." I looked back and forth between them. "I know it isn't what you proposed, but would you be willing to hire me part-time? Temporarily." As I asked, I remembered what Evelyn had said and flinched. Was I being an entitled asshole?

Iris and Tom didn't seem to think so.

"Oh, finally!" Iris beamed.

Tom hugged me against his side with one arm, and dabbed at the tears in his eyes with the other. "Finally," he agreed.

I'd known—or been pretty sure, anyway—that they'd react this way, but a part of me was still relieved that they weren't going to immediately pressure me into more. The first time Iris had shown me the empty office and given me a wink and a nudge as she suggested it could be mine, I'd felt the same turned-upside-down sensation I'd had on that yacht off the coast of California. Panic. The urge to flee.

"You guys," I murmured, squeezing Tom back. "You heard the part about it not being permanent, right?"

They smiled mistily at each other, obviously ignoring me.

"His office is ready, isn't it, Tom?"

"Yes." His smile turned wry. "I *may* have stuck a couple of your crystals in the desk drawers, just in case."

"Darling Tom. You've always had such a shocking intuition."

"Hey," I hissed, stepping between them. "Not permanent. Part-time. And I'll work from home, or out of the conference room. No office." They didn't object, but I still prompted them for an affirmative response. "Is that okay?"

Tom kissed my head again. "Whatever you say, Pete."

After I left the law firm, I wandered around Church Street for a while. Between the snow and Gene needing to make a run to Morse's Line to restock Lemon's hay supply, Riley and I had called off our search for the day. Left alone after the unspeakable luxury of seeing Riley for so many days in a row, I barely knew what to do with myself.

I really should have worn waterproof shoes. Finally, my cold feet drove me home, where I was foiled again.

A pickup truck stacked with boxes was parked in the driveway, and I recognized the person sliding a box over the tailgate.

Chris. My new roommate.

I would have turned around and walked in the opposite direction, but... well, wet feet. I trudged up the sidewalk toward the front door instead, hoping to escape inside unnoticed.

"Oh, hey! Peter, right?"

I turned, resigned, and waved. "Hey. Can I help you with any of that?"

"Oh, no, you don't have to," Chris said, just as another person appeared around the back of the truck.

"What they mean is, of course you can help. Thank you for offering! I'm Kelly."

"Peter. Do I just...?"

"Grab a box," Kelly said with a grin, which faded when I reached for one of the larger ones. "Oh, no, let me get that. Here." He shoved a trash bag at me that felt like it held pillows, but was stuffed so full, I had to wrap both arms around it to carry it.

As we went up and down two sets of stairs for what felt like ten thousand times, I learned that Kelly was Chris's older brother, and that Chris was the only member of the family who was the college type. Kelly had gone directly from high school to working full-time at their parents' custom engine repair shop. Not that I had any idea what that meant, but from Kelly's explanation, it sounded like they mostly rebuilt old cars and machinery.

"This place is so cool," Kelly said as we dragged Chris's twin mattress upstairs. My job was basically controlling the angle from the top, while Kelly bore the mattress's weight from below.

"You wouldn't say that if you saw my parents' kitchen. They're really into Americana. You'll never see more plates with chickens on them in one place."

Kelly laughed, holding the mattress steady while I got my end through the doorway at the top of the stairs. "You really grew up here?" he asked.

"Yeah."

"Burlington is like a magic town, and this is a magic house," Kelly said, all wide-eyed sincerity. "When Chris sent me pictures from their college visit, I didn't think it could be real. Figured it was a movie set or something."

We finally got the mattress onto the level floor at the top of the stairs, and I leaned my end against the back of the couch and stopped to rest. "Where are you from?"

"New Jersey."

"I have a friend from New York, and he used to talk the way you do about Vermont."

"Yeah, I bet. It's amazing."

Hearing an edgy young guy with an undercut and a lip ring earnestly tell me how cool my hometown was felt surreal. "When I was Chris's age, all I wanted was to get out of here," I told Kelly before I could think better of it.

"Well, sure. No kid appreciates where they come from."

"I guess that's probably true," I agreed.

"Back when I graduated high school, I told myself I was only working at my dad's shop temporarily. I told anyone who would listen that it was just a pit stop."

I leaned against the mattress. "And then what happened?"

"Nothing."

I was startled into a laugh.

Kelly smiled, too. "I mean it. Nothing special happened. We just had day after usual day. After one of those, we locked up and headed to the bar down the street, where most Friday nights we had a drink with the other guys. We were walking along, talking about a job that had been a bitch to figure out but that we'd finally cracked that day, and something clicked in my head. I felt like I was where I was supposed to be, you know? I realized I was really happy." He crouched down to pick up the mattress again. "You ready to take this the rest of the way?"

I slowly hoisted my end while my thoughts turned round and round the story of Kelly's big, life-affirming revelation. *Nothing special happened. We just had day after usual day.*

I felt like I was where I was supposed to be.

"You in there, Chris?" Kelly called as we shuffled toward Chris's bedroom. "We're coming with the mattress. Hope you know where you want it."

While I was helping with the boxes, Riley had texted me a picture of Gene's truck loaded with a dozen bales of hay. I figured that given the distance to Morse's Line, they'd already be nearly back to the park. So after Kelly's truck was unloaded, I waved goodbye to them, got in my car, and drove out to the park. I was almost to the driveway when I realized I still hadn't changed my shoes.

I really hated having wet feet.

At the turn for the park entrance, I found the gate propped open. The fallen trees that had been blocking the way were gone, so I drove carefully up the pitted road, wincing every time my car nearly bottomed out, until the park came into view, along with Gene's truck, backed up to the gate. Riley was in the bed on top of the stack of hay, rolling a bale down to the tailgate. When he saw me coming, he jumped down.

"Hey," he said, smiling, in hay-dusted flannel.

I had to swallow hard before I found my voice to answer. I was never sufficiently braced for the sight of him, his beauty always catching me off-guard. "Hey. I thought I'd give you a hand. Where's Gene?"

"I left him at the truck stop to play cards. And Curtis came by with his tractor and dragged the logs off the driveway. That'll make this a lot easier."

"No kidding," I agreed, though the pile of hay was still tall, and the greenhouse would feel really far away when we were lugging bales the whole distance. I hated handling hay. It was itchy, backbreaking work, but I wasn't going to leave the whole task to Riley, so I put on my gloves and we got to it.

Between the two of us, it only took about twenty minutes to transfer the stack from the truck to the greenhouse. Riley scattered part of a bale for Lemon, who ignored him in favor of standing in front of the closed gate to his enclosure, rhythmically bumping his beak against the barrier.

"You can't go out in the snow, buddy," Riley told him.

I'd been doing some reading on Lemon's species, and I was pretty sure some of them *did* go out for short periods even in the snow, but the messages were mixed on whether that was safe. "Keeping a desert animal in Vermont is a challenge," I told Riley, and he sighed, bending over to rub Lemon's shell.

"Yeah. At least we don't still have the zebras to worry about. Or any flamingos," he added with a nod to the empty pool.

"Gene's grandparents must have been... interesting people."

"Yeah. He tells a lot of stories about them. And his mother was really into the animals, too. Grandpa's grandfather gave Lemon to her as a present when Lemon was just a little hatchling. 'No bigger than a lemon,' as the story goes."

I smiled, cocking my head at Lemon and trying to imagine him ever being so small. "I guess I should have wondered how he got the name, but I never did. Just seemed to fit, for some reason. I guess back then, the greenhouse would have been more than enough space for him."

"Actually, they used to keep him in the house," Riley said with a grin. "My great-grandpa built the greenhouse when he got too big to keep in the house. I'm not sure how long ago that was."

"It's on the map from back in the sixties. So older than that." I'd never thought about it too hard, but Lemon had to be close to a hundred years old. I was struck with surprise at the thought for a moment, but then I fidgeted, distracted by the awful feeling of wet feet.

Riley glanced at me, then down at my shoes. "You're wearing the wrong gear to be out here."

"I've been wearing the wrong gear to be out anywhere today," I agreed. "My socks are wet."

He stood up immediately. "Come on. I know you're miserable. Let's go to the house and get you dry."

I didn't know why I was surprised he remembered. It wasn't like I'd forgotten anything I'd known about him. "Yeah," I said, and cleared my throat. "Okay. That'd be good."

When we got back to the house, Riley led me upstairs. Gene's collecting hadn't infiltrated Riley's bedroom, and it still looked the way I remembered. A double bed, a checkered quilt, a row of framed prints of farm scenes by some Vermont artist I was supposed to remember the name of but couldn't.

I sat on the edge of Riley's bed to take off my shoes, and he surprised me by kneeling between my feet and helping me slip them off, then peeling off my damp socks. I wrinkled my nose and tried to pull my foot away.

He wrapped a firm, warm hand around my chilled toes and looked up at me. "Let me."

I bit my lip and slowly relaxed my leg. His thumb traced the arch of my foot, making me shiver, and then he slowly massaged heat back into my skin before rolling a chunky wool sock over my foot. I hadn't even realized he'd had it in his hand.

My other foot got the same treatment, and this time I relaxed and let myself enjoy it, leaning back on my hands. Riley cuffed my jeans so the wet fabric was out of his way, and then rubbed my foot with both hands this time while I stared at his bent head and wondered if he was real, or if I'd hit my head or been in an accident two weeks before, and all the days since were a fever dream.

He put on the second sock, rubbed my calves, and smiled at me. "Better?"

"Yeah." I pushed his hair out of his eyes. "Perfect."

RILEY

"Three more days of below-freezing temperatures? Are you kidding me?"

Peter sounded pissed, but it was hard not to smile at him when he was sprawled on Grandpa's old couch with his feet in my lap, wearing my socks and grousing at the weather channel.

"You're reminding me a lot of Gene Meadows right now."

Peter blinked at me and tossed the remote onto the coffee table, which I'd uncluttered two days ago. I was inordinately proud to see that the beveled glass top and worn wooden shelf had remained tidy since.

"That is the opposite of the effect I want to have on you," Peter murmured with a playful smile, wriggling his socked feet against my thigh.

I rolled my eyes, and the smile I'd been trying to restrain broke loose when Peter laughed. But he sobered quickly.

"This puts us way off schedule."

I squeezed his ankle, frowning. "But we have those three contingency days."

"Yeah, but we'll be using them all up at once. And it's going to be muddy as hell after the snow melts, which will slow us down even more." He hooked his arm over the back of the couch and drummed his fingers against the cracked vinyl upholstery. "What would your grandpa say about bringing in some people to help us look?"

I raised an eyebrow at him. "Is that a serious question?"

He sighed, throwing his head back. I held on to his ankles a little harder. Even though the topic made my blood run cold—running out of time to look for the money before Grandpa's property, and whatever was buried on it, got sold off to the highest bidder—the sight of Peter's throat, stretched out like he was baring it to me, heated me right back up.

"I can't believe I'm saying this," Peter said after a second, his voice almost a whisper, and I understood the urge. Grandpa wasn't home, but talking about him made me feel like the house might tell on us later. "If we think there's a real risk of time running out, then maybe we need to talk to Gene's social worker."

"Dolores?" Well, now I wasn't thinking about Peter's neck anymore. "About what?"

Peter pushed himself up into a sitting position, his heels digging briefly into my thighs, and then he reached out and rested his hands on my wrists where they were crossed over his feet. "About intervening. Maybe Gene isn't in a position to make his own decisions about what's best for him."

I snatched my hands out from under his. "What the fuck? Like, have him committed?"

"No! This isn't the 1950s." Peter pulled his feet out of my lap, and I stood up. "But he could lose everything. And if someone else is given decision-making authority…"

"No," I said, crossing my arms. "I'm not doing that. I *won't*."

"Would you listen? He wouldn't be *committed*. If a judge appointed you as his guardian—"

"No!" I bellowed. "Listen to yourself. What the fuck, Peter?"

Peter's eyes narrowed, and he got off the couch. "It was just an idea."

"I would never do that to Grandpa." My voice was perfectly flat.

"Fine." He swallowed, looking away. "I was just trying to help."

My anger faded as fast as it had flared. "I know that. I'm sorry for snapping at you. But trying to take away Grandpa's freedom… I couldn't do that. Not ever. Okay?"

"Okay." He still wasn't looking at me.

I took a slow step toward him. "Hey. I'm sorry."

Finally he glanced at me, his mouth a tight line, his eyes cautious.

I felt like shit for making him look at me like that. "Fuck. I'm *really* sorry. I know you only want what's best for him."

"Yeah." Peter sighed shakily and stepped toward me, and relief struck me like a punch. I put my arms around him and pulled him in, and his breath gusted as he hugged me back. "And not just him. I want what's best for you, too."

"I know," I murmured as he leaned back, and then he slipped his hands behind my neck and tugged me lower to kiss me. "Lie back down," I told him.

He nodded, and with a quick, wicked smile, tackled me to the couch.

"What the—" I began, but my own laughter interrupted me as I found myself lying on my back on the couch, Peter straddling me, his hands buried in my hair.

"When did you cut this?" Peter asked.

"About three months after the last time I saw you. Do you hate it?" He'd always had a thing for my hair.

"No. I love it. I would never have thought that, if you'd asked me before. But it's sexy as fuck." He dropped another kiss on the side of my mouth, then nipped my lower lip. "When I saw you the other day in the doorway, I thought I was having an out-of-body experience."

My chest got tight at the thought that he'd been lightning-struck in that moment the way I had been. "Yeah?"

"Fuck yeah. I thought about you so much over the years."

"Me too. But you're even hotter than I thought you'd be."

Peter chuckled huskily. "Half the time people still think I'm in high school."

"You don't look like a kid to me." I slid my hand under his shirt, and he shivered, his smile fading as he lowered his lips toward mine again.

The sound of the door being thrown open made us both freeze.

"Grandpa," I hissed, horrified, and my body gave an involuntary lurch under Peter's just as he was starting to roll off me, which resulted in him getting thrown onto the floor and crashing into the coffee table.

I struggled up on my elbows to find Grandpa already in the doorway.

"I see I'm interrupting." He had one hand braced on the frame and the other on his hip, a smirk on his face. "You okay, there, Pete?"

From the floor, Peter called weakly, "Hi, Gene. I'm fine."

With a shake of his head, Grandpa headed for the kitchen, laughing the entire way.

I rolled onto my side. Peter had sprawled on his back with his arm thrown over his eyes.

"Shit. Are you okay?" I bit my lip to keep myself from laughing, but Peter must have heard the threat of it in my voice because he uncovered his face and glared at me.

"You think this is funny?" he demanded seriously, but I saw the corner of his mouth trying to curl upward.

A snort escaped me when Peter rolled onto his knees in a swift movement and caged me in with his arms, then bent over me, staring me in the eye, the smirk he hadn't been able to hold back making him look a little devilish.

"I can't believe Gene cock-blocked us," he muttered, and I groaned, wrapping an arm around his shoulders.

"Don't use the words *Gene* and *cock* in the same sentence. God."

He snickered, which made me laugh, and then we broke apart

again when a kitchen cupboard door banged pointedly from the other side of the house.

"Maybe we could go to your place," I said, then instantly regretted it. If Peter wanted me at his house, he'd invite me himself. He hesitated, and I sat up, shaking my head. "Never mind."

He grimaced. "It's just that I have a *roommate* now."

"You do? Like, in *your* room?" This was the first I'd heard of it.

"No. Just on the third floor. There's another bedroom up there, remember?"

I nodded slowly, even though I didn't remember the layout of Peter's house all that well. I'd only been there a few times, and my general impression was that the house felt like a palace, and Peter's room like a prince's tower.

"Well, Mom and Dad decided to rent it out. My room too, I assume, but then I came back and threw a wrench in their plans. They didn't even bother to tell me until Chris was already about to move in." He rolled his eyes. "Can you believe it?"

I wasn't sure what to say, and while I was hesitating, Peter narrowed his eyes. "What?"

I shook my head. "I don't know."

"Yes you do. Say it."

I swung both legs onto the floor so I was sitting upright, the back of my neck prickling with awareness that I was stepping onto thin ice. "I don't *know*," I insisted, and then kept talking, like an idiot. "But that room was empty, wasn't it?"

He looked confused. "It had a bunch of Mom's stuff in it from when she was going to put a home gym in the basement but decided to keep her membership downtown instead."

I frowned, impatient. He knew what I meant. "No one was using it, though."

Peter shrugged.

"And you're just *assuming* they were also going to rent out your room. But all you know for sure is that they were getting a tenant for the room with the old workout shit in it."

"That's not the point. The point is that the third floor was *mine*, always. And now I'm sharing it with a nineteen-year-old stranger. And of course they were going to rent mine out, too. Why wouldn't they? So I told my mom I'd start paying rent." He'd been sitting on the floor, but now pushed himself restlessly to his feet. "Apparently that's what my childhood home is now. A boarding house."

I couldn't help a short, incredulous laugh.

Peter crossed his arms. "Now what?"

I didn't even hesitate this time, too annoyed to think twice about how he'd take my words. "It's their house. You're not a kid anymore."

"I know that," he snapped. "I'm just there temporarily. It didn't make sense to sign a lease when I... When I first got back." His eyes skated away from mine, and I had the feeling there was something beneath the surface, right there on the edge of the topic we were discussing. He snorted. "After that whole battle they organized between the neighborhood and the city council, now *they're* renting rooms?"

"Well, maybe they need the rent. Or maybe they realized that a whole floor of the house was gathering dust with you gone." Honestly, imagining two people living by themselves in that giant house felt wrong.

"The house is paid for!"

"So? Maybe they want to go on vacation or buy a boat or something." My frustration welled, and even though I was trying to rein myself in—*thin ice, thin ice*, I kept repeating in the back of my head—I couldn't stop there. "Is it so terrible if they want to do something for themselves? They've always done everything for you."

"What?" His expression turned from irritated to confused. Of course it did. He had no idea how lucky he was.

"Not just them." I stood up from the couch. "You have so many people who are crazy about you. You always did. Your aunt and Tom, your parents, Frank. Even my grandpa."

Peter looked completely bewildered. "And you think I don't care about them, too?"

"I don't think that."

"Then what *do* you think?"

That wasn't what I meant. Not exactly. And without stopping to consider what a bad idea it was or choose my words a little more carefully, I said, "I think you take them for granted."

"Everything okay in here, boys?" Grandpa asked from the doorway between the foyer and the living room, where Peter and I were now having our standoff.

Peter's eyes had been locked on mine, but now he jerked his gaze away, and dread began to unroll in my head like a dropping curtain. "We're fine," he said tersely.

"Hey," I choked out. "I'm sorry. I shouldn't have—"

Peter interrupted me with a shake of his head, then strode out of the room. I reached out to grab his arm and stop him, but it was like my movements were a second delayed, and my fingertips only grazed the empty space where he'd stood.

I unstuck my feet and followed him into the foyer, brushing past Grandpa. "Peter, I didn't mean—"

"Yeah, you did," he said shortly, shoving his arms into his coat sleeves. "It's fine. I'll call you later." He stepped into his wet shoes, not bothering to tie them, and then was out the door.

I started to follow without bothering with a coat and shoes myself, but Grandpa stepped in front of the door and raised a hand to stop me.

"Just let him cool off, kid."

I shook my head. "I don't—"

"He said he'd call you," Grandpa insisted firmly. "Both of you could use a little time to think about what to say when he does. Let's go have a sit and watch some bull riding. I'll help you straighten out the difference between a blooper and a blowup."

17
PETER

The next day I showed up at the usual time, just after nine in the morning, and we trekked out to the park.

I was waiting for Riley to speak, but at the same time, I recognized that if I wanted to wait for Riley to break a silence, I might be waiting all day.

I was used to fighting with Riley back when we were kids. Especially those first few summers, but really, in all the time I'd known him, Riley and I had often clashed. And not the playful bickering of most kids, but rather full-blown shouting matches that left us both hoarse.

Riley spoke ominously of the "Meadows temper," and my dad said I'd inherited my mom's. So maybe Riley and I had a greater-than-normal tendency to argue. But back then, we always made up before the end of the day.

Last night, we'd gone our separate ways before the fight was over.

While I was still trying to decide if I was ready to make amends or if I'd rather stay stubborn a while longer, Riley blew out a breath and extended an olive branch first. "I shouldn't have said that yesterday, about you being ungrateful."

Not exactly an apology, but his tone was contrite. I nodded. "You weren't wrong."

"Yes, I was. I'm glad you have people to take care of you. I'm glad you've never known what it's like to *not* have them."

My hackles went back up. "You do realize I lived by myself for seven years, right?" Well, I'd had roommates, but that wasn't the point. I shook myself out of the urge to get defensive. "Sorry. I don't know why I'm being such an asshole about this." Probably for the same reason I was a jerk to my parents about Chris, but I was still cautious about looking too closely into that blind spot in my self-awareness. I was worried I wouldn't know what to do with what I found.

"People *should* take their parents for granted, at least a little," Riley said. "Parents should be there for their kids, no matter what. And if they do that, the kids are probably not going to fully realize how special that support is." He started to slip through the gate, then pulled back with a grimace. "Fuck this." He shed his backpack, unzipped the center pocket, and pulled out a can of WD-40.

I really, really wanted to make a joke about lubing his hinges, but instead I just hovered close while he climbed a few feet up the gate so he could reach high enough to apply the oil.

While I squinted up at him—at his focused frown, the careless strength in his body as he suspended most of his weight from the one hand gripping the uppermost bar on the gate—I registered the subtext of Riley's remarks on taking family for granted.

He'd said kids should be able to take their parents for granted because parents should support their kids absolutely, leaving the kid to never know how good they had it. The only reason Riley could put that into words, and the reason he'd especially resented my lack of awareness, was that Riley hadn't had parents like mine.

Meddlesome, often tedious, detail-oriented parents who probably would have happily spent all their free time lobbying for funding for preservation of historic resources, but had instead double-checked my homework, driven me to debate tournaments, surprised me with trips to the city and professional football games—a sport my father didn't even know the rules of.

Parents who sacrificed a lot for me over the years, and were still making sacrifices.

Riley dropped back down to the ground and gave the gate an experimental jerk. The hinges still squealed, but the gate swung open, and he nodded at his handiwork. Then he glanced at me, turning uncertain again.

"I can understand where you were coming from," I admitted.

"Good. As soon as I said it, I couldn't believe that's what came out of my mouth. I think I was just keyed up from what you said about Grandpa."

And now I was bristling all over again. I wasn't sorry for what I'd said about forcing the issue with Gene. Maybe I hadn't approached it the right way, but I still thought it was the right thing to do. He'd said he understood I only wanted what was best for Gene. Had he not meant it?

I walked through the now-open gate. "We'd better get to work. We don't have any more time to lose."

Riley hesitated, and I thought he might say something. But he didn't, and we got to work.

The mud made the digging both easier and harder. The ground was soft and yielding, but also slippery and treacherous. I was staggering for balance with every shovelful until I figured out how to adjust my stance to compensate for the weight without falling on my ass.

After digging so many holes with no luck, maybe a part of me had decided we were never going to find anything. My mind had disengaged, and my body was going through the motions of working the grid inside the quadrant with no expectation that the shovel would turn up anything but sand.

Whatever the reason, when the shovel first struck something solid with a distinct metallic *ping*, I had to stare into the hole blankly for three or four seconds before the excitement sparked in my chest.

"Riley," I called, banging the tip of my shovel against the spot, my heart hammering at the unmistakable sound of metal-on-metal, proving it hadn't just been my imagination the first time. "Hey!" I shouted, dropping to my knees at the edge of the hole and reaching inside with my gloved hands. "I think I found something!"

The hole had been about a foot deep, and the mud wanted to ooze back over what I'd uncovered, but by the time Riley dropped to his knees beside me, I had cleared away enough of it that my eyes could confirm what the shovel had already tipped me off to: a metal box was embedded in the ground, somewhere in the vicinity of ten paces due south of the bumper cars.

"Holy shit," Riley breathed. And then, between the two of us, we were digging like a couple of animals, mud flying and my knees slipping beneath me, until we managed to move enough sediment out of the way that we could pry the box free.

It was smaller than I'd expected. The perpetual twelve-year-old in the back of my head must've been imagining a treasure chest like something out of a movie, while the reality turned out to be something roughly the size of a carry-on. It had loops in its closures for locks, but nothing there to stop us from flipping the clasps and raising the lid, right there in the mud.

Riley apparently came to the same conclusion because he threw aside his gloves and poised his hands over the two clasps. Then he stilled and turned his head my way.

I gave him a single nod of encouragement, and he took a deep breath, flipped the latches, and pushed back the lid.

Among the jumble of contents, I saw a dog-eared magazine, stacks of boxes of shotgun shells, and two glass jars with rolls of cash inside.

Beside me, Riley was so still, it was almost like he'd stopped breathing. And then he grabbed one of the jars, untwisted the lid, and spilled the cash into his hands. He thumbed through the bills, presumably counting them. They weren't the crisp hundreds of a cashed lottery payout. They were tens and twenties rumpled from a long time in circulation. They might have been in one of Gene's jars since before either of us were born.

He dropped the jar and the cash back into the case. The glass thudded against the stiff cardboard of one of the boxes of ammunition.

"Riley, are you—"

"I just need a minute."

I sat back on my heels, wanting to give him time. My stomach was tying itself in knots at the implications of what we'd found. Was this what Gene remembered burying five years ago, or had it been longer than that? Maybe he'd buried a lot of cases in the park over the years.

I looked at the random contents of this time capsule and doubted Gene's memory and his rationality more than ever.

Riley had to be thinking along the same lines, but the tension between us from last night had intensified tenfold. I didn't know if an offer of comfort would be welcome, so I just stayed there beside him while he took his time, staring at the contents like he would discover there what we'd been searching for, if only he looked long and hard enough.

Then he snapped the lid closed and fastened the closures in jerky movements, kicking mud onto me as he got up and grabbed the case's handle in one motion.

I tried to follow him as he stalked toward the gate, but one of my feet had fallen asleep while I knelt in the mud, and I staggered after the first step, wincing.

Riley didn't break stride. "This is steel," he said. "Grandpa said he put the lottery money in an aluminum case."

I finally caught up to him. "At least we know there really is money buried out here, *and* we know we can find it."

"There was only four hundred and five dollars in that jar."

"Sounds like enough for another truckload of hay."

Riley spun toward me. "Why are you acting like everything is okay?"

Surprised by his vehemence, and still emotionally raw from yesterday, I winced at his abrupt tone and the cold look on his face.

"You don't mean it, anyway." He turned and started walking again. "You *don't* think everything is okay. You think I should have Grandpa put away. And I bet you think this"—he lifted the case demonstratively and gave it a little shake, the jars inside clanking—"proves you're right."

"I never said he should be put away! I just said what you already know but don't want to admit. That maybe he needs more help than he's getting."

"If that's true, then I'll help him. But *not* by taking the park from him. There's no way that doing that is the right thing for Grandpa."

Frustration bubbled up in me, making me speak even when I knew I shouldn't. "So the right thing is what? Him being homeless? The park getting dozed? And if the park's gone, what about—"

Riley's eyes caught mine, his look suddenly turning sharp. "What about what?"

I swallowed. He knew how I would have finished that sentence if I had enough courage. I could tell by his expression. *What about us?*

But I didn't have that much courage, so I searched for an out. "What about Lemon?" I managed. "What about *you*?" I added when he'd practically rolled his eyes at my first false clarification, and I didn't blame him.

"I'll make sure Lemon's safe. Maybe some tortoise sanctuary in Arizona, or any place there's some kind of desert. He'd probably be better off."

Just like that, I went from feeling hurt by Riley's cold detachment to pissed off. "That's what you'd like to think."

"Come again?"

"You want to think that Lemon doesn't need you. That Gene doesn't need you. If nobody needs you, then you don't have to feel bad when you don't stick around. Well, guess what? People need you! And when you leave them hanging, they can get hurt." I assumed it was pretty obvious I wasn't talking about Lemon anymore, or even Gene. "You know what? Never mind." I still had my shovel in my hand. I turned back toward the hole we'd just wrenched the case from. "I have a quadrant to finish."

"You're home early," Mom said when I came through the kitchen door to shed my snow boots and coat.

She was in front of the stove, and the whole room smelled like bacon and grilled onions. Her expression was guarded. Ever since our argument and my declaration about paying rent, we'd been avoiding each other.

"Are you making corn chowder?" I asked hopefully, peering into the grill pan at the diced bacon and onion.

"Maybe. It was your dad's idea. He thinks we should talk. And I knew that if I wanted to talk to you, I'd have to corner you first."

"So the soup is the bait in your trap," I surmised with a quick smile.

She smiled faintly back, set down her wooden spoon, and turned to lean against the counter, facing me. "Honey, I say this as someone who knows very well where you inherited most of your vices from: there are ways to resolve things that don't involve picking a fight."

Ouch. I opened my mouth to argue, realized how ironic that would be, and closed it again.

"*However*, your dad and I should have said something earlier about our plans for the third floor. It was wrong of me to imply that this house doesn't belong to all three of us. We're family, and any home of Dad's and mine is always going to be a home of yours, too."

I struggled with gratitude, as well as frustration at myself for being completely unsurprised by what she said. "I shouldn't feel entitled to that, though," I muttered.

"Yes, you should," she interrupted firmly. "Maybe there aren't many things you're entitled to, but the love and support of your parents is on that list. So, that's *my* apology." She looked at me expectantly.

"I'm sorry, too. I acted like a child."

"Well, we all have growing up to do. It's a lifelong process. I promise you, we were talking about renting out the upstairs last summer, before you decided to move home." She grimaced. "What you said, about our big fight with the city council over the zoning? Believe me, I recognized the hypocrisy, and so did plenty of the people your dad sees at the Historical Society, once we advertised the room for rent."

Another wave of shame washed over me. I wasn't surprised to hear that either. While we'd argued, I'd instinctively struck where I knew it would hurt her. "Mom…" I began, but she interrupted me with a shake of her head.

"It is what it is. But after I retired last year, the taxes alone on this house, you would *not* believe—"

"Mom, stop." My lingering anger had been a thin veneer over the guilt and shame of acting like a spoiled brat. Facing it hurt. I swallowed hard. "You don't have to make excuses to me, okay? It's your house. And I don't need the whole place to stay like it was when I lived here for it to feel like home. It'll always be home, like you said, not because of an empty room on the third floor for me to crash in, but because you and Dad are here."

The tension in her expression broke, and her voice was small. "Oh, honey."

I pulled her into a hug. We were the same height, and along with the pressure-cooker temper, I'd inherited her build, which was to say, we were both scrawny people, all elbows and knees.

Hugging her always gave me the feeling of hugging myself, and it was nice.

Having a roommate wasn't fun, but my moving back in was always meant to be temporary. And that hadn't changed.

Neither had my total lack of an idea for where I'd go next. But that was a problem for Future Peter.

She pulled back, studying me. "Is there anything else on your mind? You look tense, sweetie."

There was definitely something else on my mind. But my mother was the last person I was going to mention Riley Meadows to. My dad had always liked Riley, but Mom…

"Nope, I'm all good." I smiled and did my best to look relaxed, an act I'd gotten pretty good at when I was schmoozing Harvard alums on my law school breaks. It didn't seem to totally fool her —a little wrinkle stayed fixed between her eyebrows.

"If you say so." She squeezed my arm. "While you're here, maybe you could make yourself useful and strip those corn cobs over by the sink?"

RILEY

When I came downstairs and saw that Grandpa was stuffing empty cereal boxes into a trash bag, I was confused for a second. He'd grown more willing to let *me* throw stuff away, but he still rarely tossed anything himself. Then I remembered it was Friday, and two weeks since Dolores's last visit.

"The social worker comes today," I murmured, reaching for my phone to text Peter and let him know we couldn't work today. "I forgot."

"Whether we're ready or not," Grandpa mumbled, giving the bag a few hard shakes so the boxes would settle enough for him to stuff a few more inside.

"Here, let me help you with that." I crushed down the contents with the palm of my hand, and then he held the bag open while I placed cereal boxes inside, determined to seize the opportunity to clear another three feet of counter space.

"She'll be here any minute," he said when we were done and I was cinching the bag closed and tying it off. He ran a nervous hand over his hair, which I could tell he'd combed. "How do I look? Like someone who ought to be locked up?"

I might have laughed at his attempt at a joke if my argument with Peter wasn't still ringing in my ears. "You look fine."

He tugged on his clean but rumpled flannel shirt. "Just five minutes ago, I realized I hadn't done up these buttons right."

"She told us last time that all she expected was progress." We both heard the car outside, and Grandpa swallowed hard. "It's going to be fine," I assured him, and went to the door to let Dolores in.

As usual, Dolores wore comfortable, practical clothing, and had her slightly messy hair in a clip. She smiled at the sight of me. "I was hoping he hadn't run you off," she said cheerfully as she came in, taking in the foyer with a quick glance.

An hour later, Grandpa apparently passed muster despite putting up a degree of resistance to even the simplest questions Dolores asked him—on principle, I was sure. She'd also checked each room and praised us for the cleanup progress.

When we got back to the foyer, where our slow tour-slash-interview had started, she looked down at the spiral notebook she'd been using for notes. "One last thing, and I'll get out of your hair. How is the household budgeting going? Have the two of you figured out a way to manage the expenses of the property?"

I stared at her, searching for some sign that her neutral expression was a mask. Did she know about the foreclosure?

"We're still working on that," Grandpa said after a long moment. "We'll have it tied up any day now."

"Okay. So long as you're working on it," Dolores said, refocusing on her notebook.

She probably knew about the foreclosure already, but if she didn't, she'd find out sooner or later, and it would be better if she heard it from us. So I sidled up to Grandpa and elbowed him.

"What?" he muttered.

"Tell her," I mouthed.

"What's that?" Dolores asked. "Something I should know, Gene?"

"Nothing important," he said dismissively. "Just a little past-due tax bill I overlooked. We'll get it taken care of."

"I'm glad to hear you two have become such a great team."

She turned her smile in my direction. "Riley, why don't you walk me to my car?"

Dolores didn't seem like the kind of person who needed to be escorted anywhere, so I followed her outside dubiously, where, instead of going to her car, she rerouted and sat down in a rocking chair on the porch instead.

"Anything *you* want to say to me, honey?"

I sat beside her. "Nope."

"Okay, then. Will you at least tell me how you're doing? You, not Gene. Helping him is a big job."

"I'm fine," I said immediately. She arched an eyebrow, and I felt compelled to elaborate. "You're right. It's not easy. Especially because people wouldn't tell me exactly why he needs help, so I had to figure it out myself."

"By people, I assume you mean me?" I shrugged, and she nodded. "I do what I can not to take away the dignity of the people I work with. And that includes letting them tell the people in their lives what they should know."

"I know you wanted Grandpa to tell me himself." She'd said as much that day in the car. "Well, he's never told me shit." I flinched a little at the curse word, but before I could apologize, she laughed.

"Of course he did, honey. Maybe not with words. But he showed you. He decided to show you when he chose *you* to call up to come stay with him. When he invited you to stay."

Her words sank in, making something I'd totally missed about the past weeks suddenly obvious. As grouchy and difficult as he'd been, Grandpa *had* let me see his vulnerability. I hadn't realized how hard that must have been for him. I'd been the only person from the family he'd wanted to come to Burlington to sign him out of the hospital, in part because I'd been the only person he trusted to see what he was going through.

Dolores must have seen understanding dawning on my face because she made a soft noise and reached over to squeeze my shoulder.

"What do you do when..." I began, then had to stop and swallow and start over to keep my voice steady. "What do you do when the people you're helping won't listen? What do you do when you want them to have their dignity, but they won't make the choice that will keep them safe?"

She hesitated. "Does this have to do with Gene's money?"

I tensed. "You know about that?"

"I don't have any details. Gene likes to bite my head off every time I bring it up. But I know he won the lotto, and I know that now he's about to lose this place. There's about a thousand ways for me to fill in those blanks, but I don't like to waste my time guessing."

"There are ways to stop the foreclosure without the lottery money," I said carefully. "I talked to Peter—I mean, I talked to a lawyer about it. Grandpa could probably get a bank loan against his property. But he won't even try."

"A bank might want to know how he'd make payments on a loan like that, when he doesn't have any sources of income right now," Dolores reminded me gently.

"Well, there's some chance of getting the park fixed up. Maybe restart the rides. At least a couple of them. There's a guy in the Chamber of Commerce and another in the Historical Society I talked to a little. And I could pay some rent."

She smiled. "It seems you've given this a lot of thought."

"I want to help."

"I know you do. Gene made the right choice when he called you. You're a good grandson, Riley."

I looked away. "Not really," I said tightly. "He needed somebody the past few years, and I'd fucked off." I didn't have the energy to regret swearing in this moment. I needed all I had to keep my shit together. I felt like one of the rain barrels tied to Grandpa's gutters when they got full, except instead of water, emotions were about to spill out.

"You grew up, honey. That's not the same thing." Dolores

stood up and rubbed the small of her back. "I have another appointment. But I'm going to call you soon, okay?"

I looked up at her, but the kindness in her face was too much. I looked down again, blinking. "Okay."

"And real quick, I'll tell you a secret. It's something I learned after a lot of time working with people who are going through a hard time and don't want to hear what I've got to say. If there's something that somebody needs to know, you just tell them. Plain and simple. Early on, I used to write it all down. Practice it in the rearview mirror of my car before going in to say it to their face. You tell them once, and then again, and again. Your only responsibility is to keep telling them. It's their choice whether to listen." I felt the brief, warm weight of her hand on the top of my head, then heard her feet on the porch steps as she walked to her car.

I didn't practice in the mirror. I practiced with a captive audience.

"The thing is..." I said, crouched on the greenhouse floor while Lemon watched me, chomping on his dinner. A piece of green lettuce hung out of the side of his mouth. "You're going to lose the park if Peter and I don't find the money in time. Wouldn't it be better to make sure that can't happen?"

Lemon's eyes focused on me from either side of his wide, pebbly snout. It was easy to imagine the smart-ass remark Grandpa would make when I said something along these lines. And he'd probably do it with the same unimpressed look on his face that Lemon wore right now.

"Yeah, I know I said I'd find the money. But we both know there's no guarantee I can do that, especially not in time to avoid the foreclosure."

Fuck, this wasn't even the real thing, and my voice was already getting higher, my heart beating faster.

Groaning, I put my head in my hands. "I don't know if I can do this," I muttered. I pressed the heels of my hands into my closed eyes until I saw red, like the pressure could hold in my frustration. My fear. What the hell was I going to do if the park was really gone? I imagined moving Grandpa out of his house and into one of the little apartments in Dolores's brochures about subsidized housing. And even one of those tiny places had a portion of rent to be paid by the tenant. I would help with that, do what I had to, which probably meant going back to the city and begging for my old job back.

No more Vermont. No more Burlington. No more park. No more Lemon. No more days spent digging holes with Peter. No more days spent with Peter at all.

When we were kids, the summers had been magic. But I'd thought they were the kind of magic I could make last once I turned eighteen. Later I'd realized that had been wishful thinking all along.

Even when Peter and I went out that first day a few weeks ago, armed with shovels, I'd thought in the back of my mind that this was just one last, stolen visit to our old fairy tale. I'd known I wouldn't get to stay long. And while the end wasn't coming as a surprise, facing it still hurt.

I felt a solid pressure on the toe of my boot, and when I lifted my head, startled, I found Lemon in front of me, watching me steadily.

"I'm not Peter," I reminded him. "I don't have any strawberries for you." But he didn't seem to be begging for food. His mouth was closed. I stroked the top of his head very gently with three fingers. Sometimes he ducked away from a touch anywhere but on his shell. Today, though, he hiked his head a little higher against the pressure of my fingers, and I chuckled and petted him again.

I imagined wheeling Lemon on his chariot out of the park, instead of into it. Loading him into the truck of some reptile sanctuary and watching him be driven away. Maybe it would be to Arizona or somewhere that tortoises supposedly belonged better than in Vermont. But it still felt deeply wrong.

Studying him in this moment, he wasn't just a beloved pet. I understood in a new way why Grandpa called Lemon his little dinosaur. I looked into the face of the last eighty years when I looked at Lemon. I'd never really thought about that before.

Lemon was just a tortoise. I knew I was projecting a lot of shit onto him. But somehow, picturing the park without Lemon was the hardest thing I'd imagined so far. Harder than imagining the auction or even the shadow of the fucking wrecking ball. My hand started to tremble where I petted him, so I spread my palm over his carapace instead and leaned toward him just a little.

He kept his foot firmly on mine while I knelt there, until the trembling stopped and a new resolve took its place.

Peter wanted me to force Grandpa to do what was best. I couldn't do that. But I *could* do what Dolores had said. I could keep telling Grandpa what I needed him to hear. Even if I couldn't make him listen to what I said.

After it got dark and the night's televised bull riding event switched to a commercial, I rubbed my knees where I sat on the couch and looked over to Grandpa's chair. "Hey. I need to talk to you about the park."

Of course, he got tense in an instant. "What?" He looked torn between frustration and confusion. "What now?"

"I want you to let me take you to the bank and ask for a loan to pay the taxes."

"Are you seriously going to bring this up again? Something wrong with your ears? I've said again and again—"

"I know what you've said. But you've never let me finish. Could you just listen before you talk? Please? That's all I'm asking. For you to listen."

He looked at me with his mouth in a hard line, a disturbing impression of Lemon that made me want to laugh hysterically, except my stomach had tied itself in knots and I couldn't so much as chuckle.

Finally, he nodded shortly and muted the TV.

I leaned on my knees and took a deep breath. "Thank you. If you were to apply for a bank loan, you'd have plenty of equity in the property." I was using Peter's words, and they felt strange in my mouth. "But the bank would want to know how you'd pay them back. And I know you're not dealing in parts anymore." Grandpa *couldn't* spend all day prying apart junker cars the way he'd spent most of his life earning a living, but I didn't need to phrase it like that, so I didn't. "That leaves the park."

He sat up a little straighter, and his eyes narrowed further, like he couldn't help the outburst. "I'm not selling—!"

"Hey. You said you'd listen," I interrupted quickly. He clamped his jaw shut, and it shifted like he was grinding his teeth, but he let me go on. "I don't mean selling the park. I mean earning money from it as an attraction. Maybe not like the old days, at least at first. But I talked to this guy, Chase, who's with the Chamber, and he told me what the requirements are."

I went over what Chase had outlined for me. Grandpa wasn't looking at me anymore, but he wasn't interrupting me either, which gave me an inkling of hope.

"And," I dared go on, "someone mentioned the park the other night, when I was out with Peter. These people were my age, and they were excited about the idea of the park reopening. I used to think about it too. And so did you. I remember the time you got that popcorn machine fixed up. And when you ordered all the fun-house mirrors." In hindsight, these were random, irrational efforts, starting with one small detail that only made sense at the end of the long road of fixing up the park, not at the beginning. But I could also see now why he'd always lost momentum quickly as he realized the fruitlessness of those efforts. He hadn't known how to begin. Taking on the whole park must have felt insurmountable to him.

It felt that way to me. Almost. But I could see how it could be accomplished through something like Peter's treasure hunt. A map. A plan. No matter how massive the task, anything could be broken down into steps.

The more I spoke without Grandpa jumping in, the more encouraged I became, my own thoughts exciting me. "You and I agreed to work on the park together starting at the end of that last summer. I know you must remember that."

His eyes flashed to mine, then away again, and I faltered at what I'd glimpsed in his face. Not a relaxing of his guard. Not the familiar exasperation. Something else. Something that struck me in the breastbone like a bullet.

"You've always wanted to reopen," I insisted. "I know it. Why else did we drive to Michigan for those fun-house mirrors? Why are there *two* restored antique popcorn machines in the garage?"

"That's what you remember," he said gruffly. "You remember the fun-house mirrors and popcorn machines. You know what I remember? *I* remember selling off the carousel horses the last time I was too broke to pay my taxes. I remember turning off the gas in the house so that I could heat the greenhouse for Lemon two winters ago." He looked around with a bleak expression. "Watching this house fill up with stuff. Feeling like the door handle wouldn't turn when I knew it wasn't locked, trapping me inside—" His voice broke off.

I didn't know what to say. I stared at him in horror. I hadn't really thought about everything from Grandpa's perspective this way. How lonely the years must have been, how hard. Exactly what might have driven him to burying the lottery winnings in the middle of the night. What it meant that he barely remembered any of it.

His voice was almost a whisper. "I've believed in this park since I was a boy, just like you. But believing in something is like opening a wound, and the disappointment afterward, a scar. You believe enough times, and suffer enough disappointments, that scar builds into something tough. Something you have to saw through. Opening it again that can kill you." His voice had gone flat and level. He reached for the remote and switched the sound back on, and the *clang* of metal as a chute opened, then the grunts of the bull on the screen and the clamor of the crowd, filled the ringing silence he'd summoned with his last words.

Maybe Dolores would have thought I should keep talking, but at least for tonight, I was at a loss for words. I said nothing while cowboys were slung off bulls, and nothing when Grandpa turned off the TV twenty minutes later and went to his bedroom.

I sat in the darkness for a while, and then I went outside into the night, bundling myself in my warmest jacket.

Back in New York, I'd walked all the time, routinely trekking greater distances than the couple of miles from Grandpa's house into Burlington. Sometimes I walked aimlessly, just to get out of the apartment I shared with two roommates who were basically strangers.

I wasn't aimless tonight, though. I wanted to talk to Peter, and not on the phone. Words had never come easily to me when I couldn't see the other person's face.

It wasn't until I was outside his house, its windows shining with warm light like something out of a picture book, that I realized I should've at least checked to see if he was home.

Hey, I texted, *can you talk?*

Typing and sending texts was a little easier for me than reading the responses, but not by much, so I was standing on the sidewalk with my eyes glued to my phone when Ken called to me from the porch.

"Riley? Is that you?"

PETER

I was in the conference room at the firm, reading over the closing paragraph of the document on my laptop screen. I smiled with satisfaction. If the judge ruled against Tom, I'd be shocked.

"I've heard stories about lawyers like you," Tom said from the doorway.

I looked up and rubbed my eyes. "Huh?"

"The ones who actually enjoy research." He winked and sat down in the chair next to mine.

I laughed, stretching my arms above my head and wincing when my back twinged. "For the first three hours, maybe."

"But not the last three?"

Six hours? That couldn't be right. I squinted at the clock in the corner of the screen and groaned. Eleven p.m. I'd arrived at five that afternoon to print off a letter I'd written to Marion's neighbor —the case-that-wasn't-a-case refused to completely go away. Apparently the Flemish Giants had just had a litter, and now the disgruntled neighbor had gotten himself worked up again.

Once that was done, I meant to slip out unnoticed, but then I'd seen that Tom was still in his office, and found him elbow-deep in research for a half-written emergency motion. Together we'd managed to create a pretty outstanding argument in the accompanying brief, if I did say so myself.

The work had also been *fun*. I was reminded why I'd enjoyed law school so much at the start. The whole curriculum was made up of a series of puzzles to solve and challenges to hurdle. Working with Tom had felt like that. Except here, my efforts benefited a real client in the community I grew up in, not just myself, which made finding the solution ten times more satisfying.

"Pete?"

"Huh?" I blinked at Tom.

"I said you'd better get home. I just saw I have a couple of missed calls from your folks. Have they been trying to reach you?"

"Oh, dang it," I murmured, looking around the conference room in vain for any trace of my phone. "I don't know where I left my phone."

"Over by the printer, I believe," Tom said kindly. "Thanks for your help, Pete."

"Sure. It was fun." I grinned at him, tired but still giddy.

He looked like he was about to say more but held back.

I picked up my computer and went to the copy room, where sure enough, I found my phone next to the printer, right beside the envelope for Marion's neighbor, which I'd sealed before getting distracted by Tom's case. I slid the envelope into the outgoing mailbox while I scrolled through my phone.

Two missed calls from Dad. One text from Mom that made my eyes widen.

Mom: *Will you be home soon? Riley's here.*

And then a text from Riley himself, time-stamped at eight p.m., forty-five minutes earlier than my mom's.

Riley: *Hey, can you talk?*

I called Riley with the car's hands-free speaker on my way home, but he didn't answer. A few minutes later, I was running up the steps to the back door. The kitchen was empty, but before I could head upstairs, Mom stuck her head in from the entrance to the dining room.

"Peter. He's upstairs."

My dad appeared behind her and put his hand on her shoulder. "He looked worn out, so we sent him up there to wait for you."

"Is he okay?"

"He just wanted to see you, I think," my dad said.

I bit my lip, hesitating against the urge to run upstairs and see Riley. I had to let it sink in that Riley had been sitting down with my parents. Weird.

"I got caught up helping Tom at the firm," I said. "I didn't have my phone."

"It was nice to have the chance to visit with him a little," Mom said. "Your dad made grilled ham and cheese sandwiches."

I had no idea what to say for a moment. I settled for, "Thanks for making him welcome."

"Of course," Dad said. "We know he's important to you."

My mom nodded. "Yes, we do."

With *that* surreal statement chasing me, I surrendered to the urge to flee upstairs.

The third story was dark. Chris's door was closed, but I knew they'd gone home for the weekend. My door was ajar, casting a bar of light on the carpet outside.

"Riley?" I called softly, pushing the door open. Then I paused because he was curled on his side in my bed, sound asleep.

Had I ever seen him sleeping? I didn't think so. I'd have remembered. I walked slowly up to the side of the bed, studying him. His beard needed a trim. Or maybe it didn't. Without the sharp edges, it looked more like something a Vermonter would wear than a New Yorker. His face was relaxed in sleep, too. His lips parted. He looked young, vulnerable.

I perched on the edge of the mattress and ran my hand up his blanket-covered thigh. "Riley?"

I felt the moment when he woke up. His leg tensed under my hand, and then he relaxed again as he blinked at me in the dim light.

"Peter."

Slowly, giving him every chance to pull away, I stretched out beside him, my hand settling on his hip. "I got caught up helping Tom at the office, but I would have come home earlier if I'd known you were here."

"It's fine. I should have called before I walked over."

"You *walked*?"

He grunted, looking down a moment, inhaling like he was summoning his strength along with his breath. "I'm sorry for what I said about you and your parents."

I breathed out a chuckle. "Don't be. You were right about that. I apologized to my mom last night, actually." I raked my teeth over my lower lip. "I'm the one who's sorry. I shouldn't have pushed you about Gene. You know him better than I do, and I have to respect—what?"

He was shaking his head against my pillow with a tiny smile. "Don't apologize. *You* were right about *that*. Grandpa needs my help. And that means pushing him on certain things." His hand emerged from under the blanket, and he put his palm against the side of my head, cupped over my ear, and threaded his fingers into my hair. "I tried to explain it to him again, but he wouldn't listen." His thumb brushed my cheek, and then he pulled away, the blanket falling into his lap as he sat up.

I pushed myself up, too. "That doesn't sound fun," I said quietly. If he'd been arguing with Gene, no wonder he looked so exhausted. They were both stubborn, to their credit *and* detriment.

"No," he agreed, rubbing the back of his neck. "What were you and Tom working on?"

"I can't really say much," I reminded him, and he nodded. "But it was for a motion he has to file first thing on Monday. I think it'll be granted. We wrote a really good argument." Even giving the barest details, a little excitement returned to me, and Riley smiled slightly like he could hear it in my voice. "So, I hear you ate sandwiches with my parents."

His smile widened for a moment, wry. "Yeah. It was nice."

I laughed softly. "I hope my mom didn't... I don't know. Interrogate you." She had always made Riley uncomfortable. I'd never told him she had reservations about our friendship, but he seemed to sense it anyway.

"She didn't. We talked about their stuff, mostly. The board they're on. Your dad's job. And I didn't realize your mom was a librarian now?" She was an archivist, technically, and had been for three years, but I just nodded. "You don't talk about your parents very much. You never did."

"Neither do you."

"But that's different."

"Is it?"

Riley searched my face for a moment. "You and I both said we were sorry. So why do I feel like we're still in the middle of a fight?"

"Because," I began, the truth coming to me as I said it aloud, "we *are* in the middle of a fight. Not the one that started two days ago. The one that started eight years ago."

I saw the flicker of hurt in his expression, and I instantly wanted to swallow what I was about to say and soothe him instead. But I couldn't. I'd been holding in all these feelings for too long, and the thought of keeping them in for another second made me sick.

"That day," I went on, the words coming in a rush through my rough throat, "I'd just gotten called off the Harvard waitlist. I was so excited to tell you. On some level, I had to have known you wouldn't be happy about it. You always acted weird when I talked about college."

I looked away from Riley's very still face, my eyes tracing a path over the curve of his shoulder, letting myself remember him as a boy, with patchy scruff on his cheeks and his hair in a messy bun, the grin on his face as he'd bounded down the driveway when I'd pulled up in my crappy old Camry.

I hadn't revisited the memory of that day in this level of detail. And now that I was doing it, I frowned as I recalled something else, a detail that had been lost in the blur of anger and pain that had come later that day.

"Right when I got there, you said you had something to tell me. What was it?"

"It's not important."

I wasn't going to let him off the hook that easily, but I could circle back to the question. I pushed ahead. "We went up to the park. It felt like if I was going to tell you something important, it should happen there." But looking back, studying the memory more closely than I'd ever dared, I realized Riley had suggested we run up to the park before I had a chance.

What had he wanted to tell me?

I slipped back into the memory. "You wanted to go up to the basket in the Ferris wheel, where we first kissed." I smiled faintly. We'd never worked up the nerve to climb any higher than that basket—number eleven, perpetually wedged at two o'clock, if you looked at the ride from the park gates and imagined it as a clock face.

We'd climbed there a dozen times, but we'd still been left breathless from the strain on our bodies and the exhilaration of doing something silly and dangerous.

"Once we got there, I turned to you, grinning so hard my cheeks hurt, and blurted, '*I got into Harvard!*' And you were..." I stopped myself, still unsure how to describe the look of utter pain on Riley's face back then.

"Shocked," he said quietly.

I nodded. That was one word for it. "You asked if I was really going to go."

"And you laughed."

I winced. I'd been incredulous at the question, but of course my reaction had been all wrong. "I knew I'd messed up."

We looked at each other in the half-light of my bedroom, our words from eight years ago ringing between us.

Riley had said, *"So that's it, then? What about us? What about the park?"*

And I'd answered, in a voice full of condescension, *"You don't seriously think you and I could fix this place up? And even if we could, there's a reason it closed in the first place."*

I rubbed a hand over my face. "I shouldn't have said what I did."

"I shouldn't have said what I did, either."

Our eyes snagged again. I'd never forgotten his words, and I repeated them now, my voice a little hoarse. "You told me, 'You want to go? Fine! Go to your fancy fucking school. Enjoy your fancy fucking life! I don't need you either.'"

We'd both been on our feet at that point, and when I'd staggered back from Riley's words like they were a slap, the basket had rocked violently.

"And the next thing I knew, I was falling."

I wasn't sure how I'd wound up with my foot on the edge of the basket, or why my hand had slipped. The loss of balance had felt like it happened in an instant, time slowing when I'd realized the inevitability of the fall.

"You were right, though," Riley said, a muscle jumping in his cheek as he looked away. "It was one thing for me to throw away a few years trying to do something impossible with the park. What did I have to lose? But you... your future was worth more than that. It would have been a waste."

"That's not true. *Riley*. It's *not*," I insisted when he shook his head. I cupped his face in my hands until his eyes met mine again. "Don't you know how amazing you are? I wish you could see yourself the way I see you."

A small sound escaped him as he searched my face, and then he let out a long breath and brushed his knuckles against my cheek. "Sometimes I think I do see myself that way. Just for a second."

"Good." I smiled lopsidedly, exhausted by the revelations of the past seconds. A part of me just wanted to push Riley flat on the bed and tuck myself next to him and sleep for a year. But I still had a nagging thought that wouldn't quite let go. "What were you going to tell me that day?"

He dropped his chin to his chest so fast, I almost missed the way he winced. "Nothing."

"Bullshit. Tell me."

"It wasn't just what I wanted to tell you." He cleared his throat. "I had this whole ridiculous *thing* planned. I was going to… I was going to tell you I loved you." He pushed back his hair, sheltering his face from view, while my heart caught fire in my chest. "And then I was going to show you something. You know —a grand gesture."

Show me what? I wanted to know, but I couldn't get past the first part. "You were going to say you loved me?"

He sighed and lifted his head. His eyes were dark and intense. "Peter. You know I've always loved you."

The lump in my throat was too big to swallow. He was right. I did know.

"Always," he repeated simply.

Always. The same way I had always loved him.

I had known, but hearing him say the words was different than simply knowing the truth underlying them. Those words in Riley's deep, rough voice were the cool rain on the flames of my wrecked heart. Blinking, I reached for him, my vision narrow and dark, and he caught my hand, linked our fingers, then slipped his other hand around my waist, pulling me close.

I tilted my head, and as our chests pressed together, so did our lips. The kiss was long and sweet. I felt the tip of his tongue on my lower lip and grazed mine against it. I framed his face with my hands and breathed against him. I wanted to kiss him forever.

I wanted to say with that kiss what he'd said with words. *I've always loved you.*

But he deserved more than that. He deserved everything. Including the words, which were so wonderful to hear and so frightening to say. He'd given them to me, a gift, and I wanted to reciprocate.

I opened my eyes and found his watching me. I stared into them. "I love you too, Riley. Always."

He pulled me toward him as he fell back against the bed, and I caught myself on my hand, then lowered myself so he'd feel my weight against his chest, moving to straddle his thighs without breaking our kiss.

Then he tugged at the hem of my shirt, and we broke apart, panting and frantic, to strip in a tangle of arms, legs, and fabric, until I could stretch out over him again, both of us now gloriously naked.

We hadn't been together quite like this in the park. The musty office and the open outdoors in Vermont spring didn't lend themselves to being fully nude *and* horizontal. I wanted to see him, but I couldn't stop kissing him long enough for a good look. He grasped my ass so our hips pressed together more tightly, and I rocked into the pressure of his cock against mine, the roughness of his body hair on my sensitive skin almost painful, had I not been so desperate for the heat of him, the friction.

"I love you so much," he murmured between the kisses he was laying along my jaw. I put a hand between us so I could grip his shaft, and felt the gust of his breath on my neck as he exhaled in surprise, then moaned.

"Me too," I said hoarsely. "Wanna show you how much." I managed to escape the firm hold of his arms so I could kiss his sternum, then the soft skin below his navel, as I sprawled between his spread legs, continuing to stroke his cock with my hand and putting my tongue to work on his balls.

"Oh fuck," he breathed, gripping my hair. I sucked one of his testicles into my mouth and gently tugged, and his cock jerked in the slack grip of my hand. I tightened my fist around him and stroked again in the same rhythm I sucked on the hot, round mouthful I'd taken, before letting him go with a wet *pop* and pressing my face lower, where his hair was thick and fine between his ass cheeks.

"Peter," he gasped, sensing my objective. "Are you…?"

I answered his question by spreading his cheeks with my thumb and forefinger and running the tip of my tongue tentatively over his rim.

I wasn't sure what I would feel, doing this, only that I wanted to make Riley feel better than he ever had before. His body trembled and his voice turned to a whine, so I had a feeling I was on the right track. But I quickly realized this wasn't going to be a service I performed just for Riley's pleasure. I was startled by how hungry I was for my own sake. After the first cautious pass, my tongue grew bold, and I worked him with my mouth until my chin was wet, until his crease was dripping with my saliva and his rim was soft and yielding to the tip of my tongue.

At some point, Riley had grabbed his knees to hold himself open for me. I realized this as I resurfaced from the daze of having my tongue all over him. I'd been holding him hard by the back of his thighs, and I could see the shapes of my fingers imprinted red on his skin. They'd likely bruise.

"Peter, God," he moaned. "Are you gonna… *fuck!*" He interrupted his own question with a wail as I pushed my forefinger inside him where my tongue had just been. "Not your fingers," he said tightly. "I want your cock inside me."

I stared at his reddened hole with longing. "Don't you want to…?"

"I want you to fuck me," he insisted. "Please, Peter."

Maybe I needed to be asked twice, but not three times. I massaged him gently with the finger that was in his ass. "I've got lube and condoms." I hesitated. "I haven't been with anybody since the last time I was tested."

"Me neither."

The idea of not just being inside him, but taking him bare, made me see stars for a second. And then I launched myself off the bed to fumble in the nightstand for what I needed. Riley was still laughing at me when I resettled on the bed, kneeling between his legs and rubbing my thumb around in the pool of lube in my palm to warm it.

"You think this is funny?" I murmured, unable to even pretend to be anything but deliriously happy, a silly grin making my cheeks ache. I needed to kiss the smile he was flashing in return, so I leaned forward to take his mouth while I gently massaged the lube just inside his rim, then stroked the excess onto my cock, which was so hard, I shuddered at my own touch.

"I'm sorry. This is supposed to be serious, isn't it?" Riley asked when we broke our kiss.

"Damn straight." I grinned, glancing down and biting my lip as I lined myself up. I wrapped my dry hand around his hip, pushing a little to adjust the angle. "Do you want a pillow under you?" I asked tightly as the crown of my dick nudged him. If he asked me to do anything but get inside him, I might die. But I wanted him to be comfortable.

He shook his head, smile gone, lips parted. "No. Put it in."

I pushed against him, my heart jumping into my throat at the sensation of breaching the tight ring of his outer muscle and feeling the silky sheath of his body beyond.

"Fuck," he keened, his head falling back. I stopped, even though all I wanted in the world was to thrust. "Keep going," he said through gritted teeth. "Put it in."

I pushed forward slowly, then paused again when he protested. Little by little, I found my way in, until I was fully seated.

"You feel amazing." I eased forward, pressing his legs toward his chest. His face was red, his hair dark and shiny with sweat, and little breaths puffed past his parted lips. "Are you okay?" I murmured, pushing his hair off his temple and kissing his cheek. "Does it feel...?"

"Just...don't move for a second. Let me..." His body shifted beneath mine, and the tiny movements were amplified a thousandfold where I was buried inside him.

"God," I groaned.

"Just... I... oh fuck," Riley said as he got me where he wanted me. "There. Right there. But—slow."

I obediently rocked against him as slowly as I could manage. We were both sweat-slick, our hearts pounding in sync. As I moved, Riley made more and more feverish noises, and I knew I was rubbing against his prostate with every deep, short stroke as my hips found a rhythm.

"Okay," he said, and I felt the brush of his calves against my ass as he crossed his ankles behind my back, pinning us together. "Okay."

I stared into his face. "Now?"

He gave a tiny nod, his eyes dark and fathomless as the night, and I knew what he was telling me, just as he knew what I was asking, without words.

I rose on my knees, pulled back, then drove back into him in a long, hard thrust that made him cry out.

"Yeah, baby. Like that. Just like that," he pleaded, and I gave him two more thrusts, pushing myself dangerously close to the edge.

"It feels too good," I said, pulling back and burying myself again. "I'm gonna come."

He grasped his cock and stroked it, eyes locked on mine. "Do it. Make us both come."

God, he was the hottest thing I'd ever seen, and that *voice*, rougher and lower than ever and saying *these things*... I lost control of myself altogether, fucked into him over and over, so lost to the urge to leave a mark on him that I missed the moment when my orgasm crested and felt the climax as one huge, slow wave instead of a single burst.

As it washed over me, Riley's hand kept flying, and then his body seized my cock hard and he came too, just like he'd promised.

Later, tangled up together and with no intention of moving either until morning or until my body rallied and I could try to make him come again, I dared to ask my burning question. "How was it?"

"Bottoming?" He sounded amused.

"Yeah." I was lying on my side, stroking his stomach while he ran his knuckles up and down my back. I tensed for a second when his hand swept from the small of my back to my ass, then relaxed with a breath of laughter as he brushed against my hole with his fingertip.

"You could say it exceeded my expectations."

I couldn't help feeling smug.

"I guess you must be curious, too," he said, his probing finger continuing to stroke up and down, brushing my rim over and over. "You'll find out for yourself soon enough."

"Is that so?"

He pressed more deliberately against me, and I bit my lip against the faint burn as his fingertip slipped inside. "Mm," he murmured. "Yeah."

A combination of nerves and excitement took me over. "Anytime soon? Should I mark my calendar?"

He closed his eyes as a slow smile eased across his face, and slowly pulled his finger out. His hand returned to its place, splayed against my back, as he yawned. "TBD."

20
RILEY

"Ready, kid?" Grandpa called from downstairs. "Don't want to be late!"

I came down to join him in the foyer as he shrugged into his coat.

"Board games don't start for another forty-five minutes. I'm not going to be late." Grandpa had offered to drop me off a block from Vino and Veritas on his way to his own outing.

"I don't care when board games start. Bingo cards are getting passed out at seven sharp."

I chuckled as we went out to the truck. Things were back to normal with me and Grandpa after our clash of tempers a week and a half ago, but my unease still simmered under the surface of every conversation we had.

I was frustrated with myself for being too cowardly to follow Dolores's advice and keep trying to get Grandpa to face hard truths. Instead, I'd just been trying to get along with him.

But I was about to pick another fight, as soon as I mustered the nerve.

"Damn mud," Grandpa muttered when the truck's wheels spun at one of the spots on the driveway where the gravel was most thin. It had rained for two days straight this week, putting Peter and me even further behind our schedule for searching the park.

When we got to the blacktop and Grandpa accelerated, the tires flung mud that peppered the pavement with a sound like distant machine-gun fire.

Peter had clearly been afraid to broach the topic of the schedule with me, but he'd done it anyway the night before. I'd agreed with the suggestion and promised to bring it up with Grandpa.

Now, I couldn't find the words. But I had to hurry up because we were already halfway through our short drive to town.

"The rain has set me and Peter back on the search. I don't know if the two of us can finish it in time."

"Oh?" He frowned. "Tomorrow I'll come up there with you."

"That would be good," I said slowly, even though the idea of having him work with us made my head ache. I would be so busy trying to keep him from hurting himself, I wouldn't get any work done myself. "Also, a few of Peter's friends offered." At his sharp look, I quickly explained, "They don't know what we're looking for. Just that we've got a plan to dig up the whole park."

Grandpa shocked me by not immediately saying no. But at the stop before turning onto the street that led into town, he twisted around in his seat to look at me. "These friends of Peter's—what kind of friends are they?"

"Good ones. Aaron went to Harvard with Peter, and he's going to work for Iris and Tom at the law firm. And his boyfriend is really great, too."

A car pulled up to the stop behind us, its headlights glaring through the rear windshield.

"You know them? Or are they just Peter's friends?"

"They're my friends, too," I said, and was surprised to find I meant it. I hadn't had to spend much time with the group to feel like one of them.

The car behind us honked, and Grandpa grumbled and faced forward again to turn onto the road. "If you need some help and these are people you can trust, then *I* trust *you* to be smart."

I was so startled, I couldn't think of anything to say until he'd pulled into the public parking lot adjacent to Church Street to drop me off.

It had meant a lot to me when he'd trusted me to find the money. But it meant even more that he trusted me to include people he didn't know. I knew how much he had to hate the idea of so many strangers on his property, even when they *weren't* combing it for a lost fortune.

"Thanks, Grandpa." There was more I wanted to say, but I didn't know how, and anyway, I didn't think Grandpa needed to hear it.

"You bet, kid. Now get out of the damn truck. I told you I'm gonna be late."

Laughing, I obeyed, shutting the door a split second before Grandpa drove off. Then I walked through the alley between two buildings, and spotted Peter waiting for me like he had the last two board-game nights, leaning against the wall next to the entrance, smiling at the sight of me.

"Hey," he said, taking a few steps so we met in the middle of the sidewalk.

"Hey." I started to bend my head down to kiss him, then hesitated. I'd never kissed him in public before.

He smiled and reached for my hand but didn't take it, just grazed his fingertips against mine. "How did it go with Gene? Did you talk to him?"

"I did, and it went shockingly well. He said we can have help."

Peter's eyes widened. "Wait, *really*?" He grinned and reached for me again, this time squeezing my forearm hard for a second before letting go. "That's amazing. Wow, what a relief. We can talk to Aaron and Jeremy tonight. And I was thinking, I'm sure a bunch of the others would help, too. I mean, if you think it would be okay with Gene."

"We shouldn't push Grandpa too far. But a handful of people we know well, yeah, that would be good. The problem will be trying to explain what we're doing without telling them exactly why."

"I think that part will be okay. It's a treasure hunt. They'll just be excited. And then by the time they realize that a treasure hunt is actually backbreaking labor, we'll have guilt and pizza to make them stick around."

"Hey, Peter! Hi, Riley!" Lexy was coming in, arm-in-arm with another woman who I didn't recognize, but who also waved at Peter like she knew him, smiling curiously at me as they passed by.

"We should go in, too," Peter said, taking a step sideways to get out of the way of another cluster of pedestrian traffic. Then he hesitated. "I know the first time we came, I introduced you as a friend. But *certain people* may have made some assumptions anyway."

I chuckled. "Your ankle was molesting mine most of the night. I'm not surprised someone noticed."

"I think your ankle was the instigator," Peter said in a serious, low tone. "So… it's okay with you? If they know?"

I nodded. "Is it okay with you?"

A relieved smile broke over his face. "Yes." He reached for me again, and this time, threaded our fingers together.

I glanced around us instinctively, but the passersby who were paying any attention at all did so with absent smiles. I was from one of the largest and most progressive cities in the world, but I still hadn't ever expected to be comfortable with public displays of affection. But then, it had never seemed relevant. The only person I wanted to hold hands and walk down the street with had been Peter, and I'd assumed I missed my chance.

"Just to be clear," I wondered, "what exactly are we okay with them knowing?"

Peter grinned and squeezed my hand with his right as he hooked his left forefinger through one of my belt loops and tugged gently. "That we're..." He trailed off.

"That's where I got hung up, too."

We loved each other. We both said it every day. We wore ourselves out every day looking for Grandpa's money, and still managed to stay up for hours in my room or Peter's, exploring each other. I still intended to top Peter one of these days, but not until I got over the joy of having him fuck me instead. And at this rate, it might be awhile.

Were we boyfriends? I couldn't decide if I loved the word or if it seemed too small for our relationship.

"I guess our label is *to be determined*," Peter said. "Like so many things between us," he added meaningfully.

I laughed and tugged on his hand. "Come on. All the good seats are going to be taken."

He let me lead him toward the door, frowning curiously. "What exactly constitutes 'good' and 'bad' seats for board games?"

The day after the next, I was in Lemon's greenhouse, shoveling out his enclosure while I waited for Peter to arrive, when I heard voices outside. Neither of them were Peter's.

It was Grandpa, looking a little flushed and unsteady but smiling, and with him was a middle-aged man in a sharp navy suit, paired incongruously with a pair of Grandpa's mud boots, apparently on loan.

Grandpa was gesturing proudly to Lemon, who was a few feet away and seemed interested in having a closer look at his guest. Said guest was nervously walking backward to keep his distance.

"Oh, there he is," Grandpa said cheerfully at the sight of me. "Riley, this is Nelson Bantham, from the bank. If they're handing out money, I may as well take it," he added grimly. "And if it means they have eyes and ears in this park, well, I've got nothing to hide."

I wondered if he was deliberately alluding to what he *had* hidden in the park, but I was too surprised by his one-eighty on the matter of borrowing money to pay the tax bill to analyze it.

"Hello, Mr. Meadows," Nelson said distractedly, continuing to walk backward as Lemon, clearly locked onto his target, advanced. "Mr. Meadows, I am compelled to clarify that I would not describe the loan and mortgage process as 'handing out money.' Also, does the turtle bite?"

"Young man, Lemon is a sulcata tortoise, not a turtle. As for the biting, certainly he *can* bite, but I don't think it's likely he will, so long as you keep your hands to yourself." Nelson blinked at Grandpa, looking not at all reassured, as Grandpa began shuffling toward the office. "You said you wanted to see the structures? Well, aside from the rides, we have this tower here, built in 1921 for the ticket office and concessions."

I didn't dare interrupt them, but I followed at a safe distance, listening nervously to their conversation and expecting the whole thing to blow up before they parted ways.

Miraculously, it didn't.

Grandpa and I walked Nelson back to his SUV, parked outside the gates and with only a light coating of mud on its tires.

"The property needs a lot of work to be operational," Nelson was saying matter-of-factly, "but the acreage itself has considerable intrinsic value. I can extend this loan to you, Mr. Meadows, but you need to think about how you're going to make the annual payment. I understand you're not willing to sell your land voluntarily, but that means you're going to have to figure out another way to pay annual taxes going forward." He paused, looked back over his shoulder and up at the Ferris wheel. "I rode that when I was five years old."

After hearing nothing but business from Nelson for twenty minutes straight, I was surprised by the personal insight.

Grandpa looked where Nelson was looking. "I'd give just about anything to see that wheel turn again."

"I… would appreciate seeing that, too," Nelson agreed after a moment's pause.

When Nelson had gotten in his car and drove away, I rounded on Grandpa. "What was that?"

"What?" he asked irritably. "I was taking your advice. And now you're going to grouse at me about it?" He shook his head. "Damned if I do, damned if I don't."

"That's not what I—I'm *glad* you took my advice. But you could have *told* me you were going to take it." When I said the words aloud, they sounded nonsensical, but they made perfect sense to me. I'd spent however much time panicking about the park's ticking clock while Grandpa had already decided to talk to the bank. It was time wasted.

"I see," Grandpa said, nodding solemnly. "I need to make sure and report my thoughts and actions to you immediately. Maybe we should check in before every meal. We can keep a chart."

I sighed. He was deeply aggravating, but I was too swept up in euphoric relief to care. "Thank you, Grandpa. I think you're doing the smart thing."

"Better safe than sorry. But we won't need his money anyway. You're going to find ours."

"Well…"

"You have that search party coming to help, don't you?"

I snorted at the phrase *search party*, but nodded. "Yes. On Saturday." It was still muddy, but if we waited any longer for it to dry out, we risked getting even more rain or snow. "But there's no guarantee we'll find it."

"You will," Grandpa said comfortably, then frowned. "How do you feel about walking back to the house and bringing the truck around for me? These days, that walk through the woods is an accident waiting to happen for me."

That image felt like it described Grandpa's whole life. A house of cards, and the keystone was being slowly pulled loose. I just hoped that before it fell apart, we'd have finished building another, sturdier house, and he wouldn't be left hanging out in the cold.

21

PETER

Somehow, in the four days since Gene had agreed to the plan and we'd talked to Aaron and Jeremy, our four-person party of treasure hunters had grown exponentially.

Jeremy had pointed out that Jamie and Briar would want to help. And with that suggestion, Riley and I realized that most of our crowd from Vino and Veritas met the criteria for joining in: we trusted them implicitly, and they were likely to be motivated by the wacky idea of a treasure hunt with pizza as their only reward.

We'd chosen Saturday for the search so that the students among them wouldn't have to worry about missing class. And now the group that had gathered in a loose circle inside the park gates to receive their instructions included the entirety of the board game night crew and a few other familiar faces from the Vino and Veritas staff, too.

Riley nodded to me, his appointed search coordinator, and I cleared my throat. "Thanks for coming, everybody. If you look at your maps, you can see there's a grid over the map of the park. Certain points are marked on the ground with flags for reference. The sections you'll dig are color-coded. Go down at least three feet in your designated areas, then fill in behind you. Any questions?"

Lexy raised her hand. "I was promised a giant tortoise."

Riley smiled and nodded toward the greenhouse. "I guess we can start in fifteen minutes, if you want to go see him first."

They all did, of course, and as the whole group headed for the greenhouse, I stepped up beside Riley and touched his hand. "You okay?" He looked as nervous as he'd been during our first game night, even though he already knew everyone. So I assumed his anxiety had to do with something else.

"Yeah. Just…" He pulled off his right glove and dragged his hand over his face. "This is it, you know? If we finish digging up the place today and don't find anything…"

"Then we go over it again and dig six feet instead of three."

He snorted, but his eyes were soft. "Oh, is that the plan?"

"Yeah. We can get those sexy headlamps and work from dawn till dusk, if that's what it takes." I looked at him, uncertain. "But if your grandpa gets the loan…"

His eyes widened. "Oh shit. I forgot to tell you. He did."

"What?" I exclaimed. I punched him in the arm, and he winced and clenched his bicep. "When?"

"They called late yesterday. Sorry, I—oh." I'd interrupted him by flinging my arms around him.

"Shit, that's a relief."

Riley disentangled himself so he could meet my eyes and glare at me, half-serious. "You said it was a sure thing!"

I laughed. "I was pretty sure." Conceptually, I'd known the loan wouldn't be a problem, but my understanding of mortgages was one-hundred-percent abstract, and knowing it had actually happened flooded me with relief.

The loan didn't solve every problem, but it solved the most pressing one.

There were voices from the greenhouse, and I glanced over to find our friends coming back, chattering as usual. Lexy caught my eye, formed a heart with her hands, and mouthed, *"So cute."*

For a half-second I thought she was talking about me and

Riley, standing there within kissing distance, but then I realized she meant Lemon.

Riley squeezed my waist and let me go. "I guess it's time."

I caught his hand. "Hey. We're going to find it. But even if we don't find it *today*, everything will be fine. Gene can pay his taxes. The park isn't going anywhere."

He smiled, and his thumb stroked the side of mine. "Yeah. Okay. You're right."

"You two coming, or were you planning to have a strictly supervisory role?" Jeremy asked, picking up his shovel and leaning it against his shoulder. "That would be unacceptable. I'll unionize this crew and come for you in court."

"Okay, okay." I laughed, reluctantly letting go of Riley's hand. I reached for my shovel and took a deep breath, swallowing all the uncertainty I hadn't wanted Riley to see. "Let's do this."

At noon, we were ahead of schedule, but our workers were getting restless. Luckily, my dad showed up right on time with a stack of pizza boxes.

"You kids have been busy. Wow." He looked around, laughing, as twenty-somethings stepped out of shallow holes throughout the park, drawn to the pizza boxes like moths to a flame.

I took off my gloves and took a few boxes off the top of the stack. "Thanks for bringing these out here."

"No problem. Where do you want 'em?"

"In the office."

"Sure thing." He started for the office tower, and I fell into step behind him.

I'd preemptively cleaned the ticket counter for this very purpose, and Riley had positioned a shop light so the space was well lit.

"Thanks again, Dad."

"You bet," Dad said with a warm smile. "Well, I'll get out of your hair. I'd offer to dig, but I wouldn't be able to move tomorrow."

I walked back outside with him and toward his car. His gaze swept over the park, and his smile turned wistful. "The place sure has changed."

"Has it?" I knew Dad had spent time at the park, but it wasn't something we talked about. "Uncle Frank brought you here back when everything was still running, didn't he?"

Dad chuckled. "Not everything." His expression turned sober as he nodded toward the bumper cars and the empty carousel shelter. "I was the last kid to take a spin on the carousel before it was taken apart and sold."

"Wow. I didn't know that."

Dad nodded. "That was a hard day for Gene. Frank didn't bring me out here again after that. Plus, I was getting older. I wanted to be with my friends, not adult family members. But some of my best memories as a kid are from this place."

I stared at him, wondering how we hadn't had this conversation before. "You never told me that either."

He shot me a wry smile. "No? Well. You had enough to say about the park for both of us when you were a kid. I didn't think you'd want to be bored by your old man's nostalgia."

To my embarrassment, I knew he was probably right. "I'm sorry. I was kind of an asshole back then."

Dad laughed and gave me a quizzical look. "Buddy, you were a kid. A kid who worked hard and made his parents very proud. Did I sometimes wish we were closer? Sure. But mostly, I was impressed by how independent you were. How sure of yourself."

I wrinkled my nose. "I haven't felt very sure of myself lately."

Dad put his hands in his pockets and fixed me with a serious look. "Is there something you want to talk about, honey?"

Today wasn't supposed to be about me. Today was about Riley and the park. But my dad was searching my face like he really wanted to know the answer to his question. I swallowed.

"I'm not that independent. I'm not that sure of myself." My

voice faltered, and Dad made a little noise of concern, but didn't interrupt. After a second, I went on. "I know I *should* be those things. I know that the only person I should rely on, or, like, condition my happiness on, is myself. But I..." I wrapped my arms around myself. "I've never been really happy since I left home. I don't think I *can* be happy without...without Riley."

Dad smiled faintly. "Spoken like a man in love."

I hadn't had to tell my parents that Riley and I were...whatever we were. Together. We'd made no secret of spending almost every night together for the past couple of weeks. And honestly, they'd probably known before that, too. I had a feeling I wasn't as good at playing it cool with them as I'd always thought.

"Loving somebody is like anything else that's really worthwhile," Dad went on quietly. "Scary as hell. And a little bit easier the longer you do it."

By the time the sun was setting, Riley and I were alone, sitting in the bottom basket of the Ferris wheel, where one of us could trip and fall without breaking a bone, and watching the gold-and-crimson-soaked sky over the trees.

I didn't know what to say to him.

I hadn't known what to say as the day wore on and we crossed more and more squares off the grid without finding anything except the occasional strange artifact of the park's past, like a rusty pair of antique binoculars and a few pieces of twisted metal from a damaged ride.

I hadn't known what to say when our friends had driven off with apologies that we hadn't found what we were looking for.

I hadn't known what to say when Riley climbed into the Ferris wheel basket, so I'd just climbed in after him and sat at his side.

Riley was the one to break the silence. "I want to show you something," he said, and hopped off the ride.

I followed him, running to catch up. He led me into the office, where the unexpected brightness of the shop light made me blink. Then he jogged straight up the stairs to the second story, with me right behind him.

At the top of the stairs, he turned to face me like he was waiting for a reaction.

I looked around but didn't know what I was supposed to see. It looked just like it had when we'd lain up here during that heavy snowfall a couple of weeks before. The memory made my heart speed up, but I still felt like I was missing something.

"That last day here, eight years ago..." Riley hesitated. "Remember how I said I'd planned a whole grand gesture?"

There wasn't much light, but I could still see him clearly. His eyes were fixed on mine, steady, but there was tension and uncertainty in them, too. "Yeah. You never said what it was."

"I know. I didn't think it mattered anymore, but..." He took a deep breath. "Back then, Grandpa wanted me to move to Vermont. I was done with school. There was nothing keeping me in the city anymore."

"I never really got it," I admitted. "Why you went back to the city. Even after what happened with us... I don't understand why you stayed away. The park was everything to you."

He broke eye contact for a moment while he seemed to compose himself. "I'll get to that. But first, the grand gesture." He smiled wryly. "I was going to ask you to live here. In the tower. With me." He motioned around us. "Frank and I had barely gotten started, but we had a plan to revamp the place into an actual apartment. It would have been really nice."

I blinked, looking around again with fresh eyes. And I swore I could suddenly see it, the little home Riley had pictured making for us. And I could imagine his excitement and nervousness at telling me about it. At inviting me to share in it. His burst of frustrated anger when I'd told him about Harvard made more sense now.

I was trying to come up with words when he started speaking again. "You said the park was everything to me. I know you always thought that. But it wasn't the park. It was you. It was always you. Being here without you... I couldn't have stood it."

My eyes felt hot with sudden tears. I knew what I wanted to say, but fear was like a knife, digging into my side, whispering that I shouldn't dare. I thought of what my dad had said just a few hours ago, though, and made myself be brave.

"I know. It's the same for me. I spent all the years at Harvard pretending I wasn't homesick. And then when I came back to Burlington, I didn't feel any better. Not until you were here, too. Because I can't *have* a home without you." I sucked in a deep breath. "*You're* my home. You know?"

"Yeah." He strode over to me and put his arms around me. I clung to him. "I know. God, I know."

I needed to be kissing him. I grabbed the back of his neck, rose on my toes, and angled my mouth against his. He immediately gripped my ass, pulling our bodies tighter together.

By unspoken agreement, we began stripping each other's clothes, kissing the whole time, and when I finally got him naked and stepped back so I could see him, the light had shifted in the window and he was awash in the violet hue of early night instead of the warm glow of sunset.

"You're *gorgeous*," I whispered roughly, skating the back of my hand across his chest so he shivered. His nipples were taut, and so were the muscles of his abdomen. He cupped his hardness and squeezed. I wrapped my fingers around his, and together we gave his cock a few slow pulls.

"I want this," I told him, meeting his eyes boldly. "I want you to top me."

His hand stilled as he groaned, like my words had a deeper effect than my touch. He wet his lips, and his eyes seemed to glow. He gave me a gentle, gentle kiss on the corner of my mouth and murmured, "Get on your hands and knees."

I dropped to my knees so fast, a bolt of pain shot up my thighs despite the cushion of our bed of folded blankets, but it didn't faze me. Riley sucked in a breath from behind me, out of sight.

The room felt too cool, raising gooseflesh all down my back. I felt a moment's uncertainty as my own vulnerability struck me, but then Riley knelt behind me and rested his chest on my back, his warm body covering me, and he stroked my chest and rubbed his face against my hair.

His hand wandered from my chest to my cock and stroked me until I was fully hard, while he kissed the back of my neck and pressed his own swelling dick against my ass.

"Do we have what we need?" I breathed, the logistics of the situation striking me suddenly. As blindly eager as I was for him, I was pretty sure that if I tried this for the first time without lube, I'd regret it. I didn't want to regret anything about giving myself to Riley like this for the first time.

He kissed my shoulder and lifted himself from my back, holding my hips, his thighs pressed to the backs of mine, and rolled his hips against me. The tease.

"I do, actually," he said. "I wanted to be prepared. Even though I was imagining me as the one on his knees."

The thought made me moan. As happy—and nervous—as I was to be in the position I was in, thinking about being inside Riley was never not going to go straight to my dick.

"Next time. But right now…" My voice was a little high and breathless.

He ran a hand up my back. "I know, baby. I've got you." His hand ran back down my spine, and then his fingertips traveled farther down, into the crease of my ass. I was shaking with anticipation even as the pad of one of his fingers touched my hole, the way he'd touched me so many times over the past weeks, but now, with the imminent promise of even more than his fingers, my heart felt like it might break out of my chest.

"Come on." I lowered myself onto my elbows and rocked back toward him. "Don't tease me."

22

RILEY

"Fuck," I breathed, "you're so hot like this." By some miracle, my discarded jeans were within reach, so I grabbed them and dug into the hip pocket for the lube packet I'd stowed there. I'd been keeping one handy out of optimistic preparedness, but it was only one, so I squeezed some of the contents onto my fingertips with care, then applied the lubricant to Peter, rubbing his hole with a slippery forefinger until he arched his back and pushed without me talking him through it. Smiling, I bent and kissed his bowed back while I stirred my finger inside him, coating the tight ring of his inner muscles.

"Good job, baby," I said approvingly. Peter was silent, but he whimpered and rocked toward my touch, which I interpreted as him being overwhelmed, but in a good way. I worked a second finger into him alongside the first, which made him groan, but in moments he'd relaxed again. "Fuck, Peter," I said roughly. "You're doing so good."

"I want you," he said breathlessly. "Come on."

I knew he didn't mean that he wanted a third finger, but I hesitated. I had to make this good for him. And not just because I wanted to make him feel as good as he made me feel when our positions were reversed. My sense of responsibility ran deeper than that. Giving Peter anything less than the best of me felt like sacrilege. The pressure of the moment left me frozen for a second.

"Riley, goddamn it," he growled, breaking my reverie, as he glared at me over his shoulder, a debauched angel with tousled golden hair and stormy blue eyes. "Fuck me right now, or I'm going to hold you down and do it myself."

"Is that supposed to be a threat?" The idea of him pinning my arms over my head and riding me for his own pleasure was probably the hottest thing I'd ever imagined. But that was not what we were doing right now. *I* was taking care of him.

I pushed my fingers deeper inside him, making him bite his lip, but the fierce glint in his eyes didn't falter.

"Okay, okay," I said, breathing out a laugh, my hand shaking as I withdrew it and worked the residual lube onto my hot, sensitive skin. "I've got you," I promised, and lined myself up.

I'd fucked guys. In some ways, fucking Peter was nothing like fucking anyone else, but the basic mechanics were the same. I knew what to do and was pretty sure I could make him like it. So I just breached him and froze, rubbing his back while he adjusted to the stretch.

"Oh, fuck." He leaned his head down on his forearms, which repositioned us so that I could stroke into him more easily.

"You feel fucking amazing. Just hang with me. I'm about to make you feel so good."

I reached around to stroke him. He was harder than I'd expected him to be, and within a few strokes, I felt him leak against my palm.

"You like this?" I asked, giving the tiniest thrust. "You like the stretch?" That part wasn't my favorite. I toughed it out for what came later, but I knew it was different for everybody.

"I like feeling you." He grunted. "I want to see you. Can we... I want to be on my back."

"Yeah, whatever you want." I slipped out of him, and he immediately twisted to lie on his back. As beautiful as he'd been on his hands and knees, I loved seeing him like this even more, and the sight of his face made me need to kiss him.

I lowered myself over him, bracing my weight on my hands, and he looped his long legs around me and pulled me to him, making me laugh against his mouth.

"Come on," he whined. "Don't make me wait."

I reared back so I could fit us back together. This time, he didn't make any noise, but his mouth fell open as I sheathed myself slowly inside him, his legs dragging me forward when I might have paused if it'd been up to me.

However, it was pretty obvious who was running the show. Peter didn't stop pulling me to him until I was all the way in, and then he only took one shaky breath and met my eyes in silent command.

Slowly, I withdrew and thrust again, staying deep, reveling in how it felt to have my hips flush to his body, to feel the clutching heat of him, the strain of his strong body. "Amazing," I murmured, turning my head and kissing his splayed knees. "You're amazing."

Peter canted his hips in a tiny rocking motion, the most he could move when I was pinning him to the floor, filling him. "More," he demanded. His hands roamed down my back, then clutched my ass, pulling me, spurring me into a steady rhythm.

I had a feeling he didn't know exactly what he was asking for, but my self-control was seriously slipping. I wanted to come undone and fuck him senseless. Inexorably, I sped up, and our bodies met with a firm slap that made Peter cry out.

"Are you okay?" I panted.

"Keep going. Just like that."

This time, I didn't doubt my orders, just surrendered to them, pounding into him. It felt amazing, a frenzy, but I still needed—

"Oh fuck," I hissed when Peter's hand, a bruising grasp on my ass, shifted an inch so his fingertips could press against my hole. For a second I thought it was an accident, but then I saw his grin. The fading sunlight turned his body to silver and shadow, and in monochrome, his eyes were mercury. I buried myself all the way inside him and stilled, letting him drive his finger inside me. I was dry, and tight from the strain of thrusting, but as he stroked inside, I gasped at the combined sensations of being inside him while he was inside me, even just with a finger.

"I want to fuck you while I can still feel you inside me," he whispered.

I blinked, my thoughts foggy from the blissful exertion of pounding into him, but my heart started beating faster like my body understood his intent a second before my thoughts caught up.

His finger still inside me, Peter said. "Give me the lube."

Somehow, the supplies had ended up within arm's reach, so I obediently passed him what he needed while our bodies stayed joined. My dick throbbed and my thighs shook at the sensation of being buried inside him without giving over to the insistent urge to thrust.

He made a bit of a mess, but managed, one-handed, to slick his fingers with lube before pushing them back into me.

My hips rocked helplessly, and I gasped, not sure what I wanted more—to thrust into his ass or back against his hand. I couldn't believe I'd ever had a single reservation about having him inside me. Now, it sometimes felt like all I thought about. But being inside him was amazing, too.

I pushed my face into his neck and exhaled shakily. "You're going to make me come."

"No," he said, even as his fingers worked me, wicked and dexterous and *merciless*. "Not yet."

When I couldn't stand it anymore, I pushed myself back up onto my knees. His hand fell away, freeing me to pull out of him in a single, slow motion. Then he grasped my waist and urged me to lay down facing him. I hooked my elbow under my knee, lifting it.

"Jesus Christ, Riley," he panted, then cut himself off to kiss me hard on the mouth. His hand skated up my thigh and between my cheeks, rubbing me between my hole and my balls, then fondling my shaft. "I love you." He transferred the residual lube from his hand and my cock to his own. It wasn't much, but I didn't care. "I love you," he repeated, his eyes boring into me along with his cock as he pushed against me.

I grunted at the friction, but I was so caught up in the wild ride of our fucking that the spark of pain in my body didn't slow me down. I pulled my knee closer to my chest, Peter straddling my other leg as his long, lean body shuddered with each slow thrust.

He leaned over me, and I pushed myself up to meet his kiss.

"I feel you," he said when we broke apart, rolling his sweaty temple against mine. "I feel you everywhere."

Funny, I thought, as he picked up speed and came with my name on his lips. I felt Peter everywhere, too, all the time, and not just when we had sex. All the time. Everywhere, anywhere. He was a part of me I couldn't live without.

We lay tangled in the dark, on musty blankets that offered little protection from the hard floor, but the moon was shining on us through the windows of the tower in our park, and somehow I'd never been more comfortable.

"I'm going to work for Iris and Tom," Peter said into the quiet. "Just so you know. I'm not planning on going anywhere."

I couldn't see his face. His head was resting on my chest, his ear just over my heart, and I wondered if it was deafening him as it started to pound. I smoothed his tousled hair. "Are you sure?"

Peter breathed out a chuckle that tickled my skin. "Are *you* staying?"

I swallowed. "Yes."

"Then I'm sure."

23

PETER

For the first time since we'd finished our search of the park almost two weeks before, I showed up at Gene's house wearing old clothes and a pair of gloves. The week before, Gene's social worker had said she'd close his case if the house got completely cleaned up, and after a few days of grumbling about it, he'd finally decided to let Riley and me take care of his stuff.

He was on the porch when I arrived. "Hey, Uncle Gene."

"Morning, Pete." He gave me a tense smile. "How's the office lifestyle treating you?"

I hadn't technically revised my status with the firm from part-time to full-time, but I was there more than forty hours per week anyway. Not too much more, though, because Iris and Tom took work-life balance just as seriously as chakras. "Oh, it's not too bad."

"Riley's inside," Gene said, gesturing to the door. "I think I'll just sit out here for a bit."

I nodded, trying to keep my tone level because I knew he wouldn't like hearing me feel sorry for him. "Okay. We'll see you in a bit."

Riley was in the foyer, already putting stacks of magazines into a plastic bag. He turned as I came through the door. "Hey."

He dropped the bag to squeeze my arms and kiss me hello. "I can't believe you showed up. You should have pretended to have something come up at work and saved yourself. I would have understood."

"That's not how this works," I reminded him, but I couldn't conceal my trepidation as I looked past the foyer into the living room, then in the other direction, toward the dining room. Towers of stuff piled on the table almost reached the light fixture overhead.

"We'd better get started," I murmured, "before he changes his mind."

I could see from the expression on Riley's face that the enormity of the task was overwhelming him. I put my hand on his arm. "Hey. We just need to take this slowly and systematically. One room at a time."

Riley smiled at me. "Should I imagine each room has four quadrants?"

I snorted but didn't laugh. "Because that plan worked out so well in the park," I muttered.

Riley sighed. "You've got to stop obsessing."

"I'm not *obsessing*," I protested, taking the empty trash bag he handed me. But I was. Just a little. I couldn't accept that we'd carried out the entire search and had almost nothing to show for it.

Where was the money?

Under a hidden trapdoor in the funhouse, or maybe in its walls? In the hollow branch of one of the old trees that stood sentry on the west side of the park? Had someone sneaked in and taken it, like Gene had originally suspected, a theory I'd thought paranoid?

We might never know. I recognized that, but I didn't know if I would ever come to terms with the mystery.

I knelt on the living-room floor next to Riley, helping him shovel the aluminum cans piled in a corner into one of the plastic bags.

"Your grandpa drinks too much caffeine," I muttered when we'd filled one bag and started in on another.

Gradually, we revealed a few framed pictures on the floor, leaned up against and facing the wall.

"What are...?" Riley began, trailing off when he tipped the first frame back and saw what it was.

"The maps," I finished for him, reaching for another one.

The one in my hands was the one I remembered best. It was drawn with a 1950s aesthetic, designed to fold in half like a program. On the front side was a drawing of a string of people lined up to enter the gates of the park, which were thrown wide open in welcome.

"I don't remember this," Riley murmured.

I looked over his shoulder. "I think I do. But it didn't look as interesting as the other ones when we were younger." I swiped some dust off the glass with my wrist. The map was much more detailed than the one in my lap, almost like an aerial view on a modern-day digital map, except in colored pencil. Sunlight and time had faded patches of the colors and lines almost to nothing.

"It's older than the other one. It shows the walking trail." Riley traced a finger in a twisting loop around the outside of the main park fence.

"Wasn't it put in so that your great-great-great-great-grandmother could show off her pet bear?"

Riley chuckled. "He wasn't a pet. But yeah. He had a cage that must have been...here." He put his thumb beside a dark icon that, if I squinted, I could have said resembled a bear. "And the zebras," he added, tapping another spot along the trail that definitely showed a cluster of horse shapes with stripes.

"Do you remember the summer when Gene had those guys come out with the bush hogs and mow the trail?"

Gene's parents had been the ones to give up maintenance of the trail to focus on the park. Gene had fought the overgrowth the summer we were eleven, clearing trees, but the sawed-off trunks and mowed brush had regrown almost as dense as before.

"Maybe we could still find the pond," Riley said, catching my eye with a half-smile.

I felt heat creep into my cheeks, which was ridiculous, because we'd just been kids. The original trail had edged past a shallow pond, where an old iron support for a swing set and a tilting merry-go-round still stood. That was the spot where I'd boldly taken Riley's hand and asked him to be best friends. Later, he'd broken out in a nasty poison-ivy rash I seemed to be immune to, and we never went along the walking trail again. "You remember that?"

Riley squeezed my knee. "I remember all of it."

We smiled at each other. His hand inched higher on my leg, and I leaned toward him, suddenly itching to be kissed.

"Taking a break already?" Gene said from behind us, sounding disapproving. "I suppose at this rate, we might be done by Easter. What's that?" He ambled over, obviously unconcerned about whatever he'd interrupted. "Oh," he said, his voice lowering at the sight of the maps. "There they are. I'd been wondering." He reached out his hand, and Riley passed him the older map.

"We didn't remember there was a map with the walking trail. I bet Peter's dad would be interested in a copy."

"The original Meadows Park," Gene said quietly, studying the map with a slight squint and a smile. "You know, if it were up to me, I might have kept it like that. Gotten a few more animals. Kept the rides nice and simple."

I felt Riley tense, and looked at him, puzzled, as he quickly got to his feet. "Rides?" he asked sharply. "Along the trail?"

"Just the simple ones, like I said. You know, the cabin, the jungle gym. When I was a child, the merry-go-round was the only ride we really needed."

"That and a bear on display," I said, amused, but still distracted by the strange look on Riley's face. "Are you feeling okay?" I asked him, getting to my feet. "Do you need a break, or…?"

"He called the merry-go-round a ride, Peter," Riley said

tersely, his eyes latching on to mine with an intensity that took me aback.

And then my surprise subsided just enough for understanding to register. "Oh shit."

"Grandpa." Riley took the framed map out of Gene's hands and gave his shoulder a shake to get his full attention. "When you said you buried the money ten paces from one of the rides in the park, we thought you meant *inside* the park."

Gene nodded slowly. "I did. That's what I meant." Then he pressed his lips together, and his eyes narrowed. "But I told you, it was late, and I... It was like a dream."

"Is it possible you didn't go up to the main park?" Riley insisted. "Did you go somewhere along the old path instead?"

"I don't know," Gene said slowly. "It's possible."

I stared at the map, my mind racing. "You said the merry-go-round was your favorite." The zebras had watered at the shallow pond for decades, helpfully treading on the young forest growth. That made the shores of the pond one of the only places along the old walking path that Gene could have driven up to on the ATV that night.

I met Riley's wide eyes with my own dismayed stare.

Was it possible...?

I could read what was on Riley's mind in his expression. He was a second away from racing out the door and up to the pond. "We really need to clean up the house," I said half-heartedly. "And it's going to storm any minute." Also, we didn't know for sure if the safe was buried south of the merry-go-round, but we did know the social worker was coming the next day.

Riley looked at me plaintively. "We have to look."

I couldn't really argue. I nodded, and relief broke in Riley's face. By unspoken agreement, we rushed to pull on our rubber boots.

"You think it's still out there?" Gene asked, his voice fragile but with a note of hope that squeezed at my heart.

"Maybe. Only one way to find out."

Outside, Riley started the ATV, which turned over on the first try for once. I threw the shovels in the back, and had barely sat down before Riley took off. I worried we were only setting ourselves up for another painful disappointment.

The clouds rolled overhead, burgeoning with the promised rain, as the ATV bumped over the rough terrain on the far side of the creek. It was a jerkier ride than usual, Riley's foot heavy on the gas pedal and straining the creaky old engine, which protested with a sustained, high whine. I held the grab bar and focused on staying in the middle of my seat, while around us, the sky began to turn noticeably darker with each moment and a cool wind broke, pushing my hair into my eyes.

The merry-go-round was anchored in a slab of concrete, but it had been placed at an unwise proximity to the wet bed of the pond, and at some point before I was born, the earth had shifted underneath the foundation, tipping the ride onto its side like a fallen flying saucer. Needless to say, it had never been able to turn in my lifetime, and as a result, had never interested us when we were kids.

Riley pulled the ATV straight up to the north side of the merry-go-round and put it in park. When he killed the engine, the silence felt sudden and left a ringing in my ears.

Our haste from a moment ago seemed to abate for an instant as we each drew breath. Without turning to me, Riley reached for my hand and tangled our fingers together.

"If it's not here, then it may as well be nowhere," he said.

I didn't have a response. He was probably right.

In the distance, thunder cracked, and the reminder of the threatening storm pushed us out of our seats and had us reaching for the shovels in the back, which somehow hadn't gotten thrown out by Riley's wild driving.

Riley counted off the paces, and the moment felt so solemn, it didn't even occur to me to tease him for the stiff, awkward strides he took. He dug his toe in at the ten-paces mark, and then we began digging.

Even though it had been two weeks since we'd stopped digging, my body was still accustomed to the rhythm of the work. I felt a pleasant strain in my shoulders, and my thoughts fell quiet. Underlying the familiar movements, though, was the knowledge that one way or another, our search was about to be over for good. I hadn't had that sensation at the end of our day searching inside the gates with our friends. But the same mystic energy that had made this place feel like a guardian, a playmate, and a friend since the day I'd first come here as a child seemed to be speaking to me now, telling me this was it. An ending. A beginning.

The thunder rolled, and Riley and I dug.

When I was knee-deep, my next shovelful of dirt went wider than I expected, the ground offering markedly less resistance to the tip of my shovel than it had in the movement immediately before.

My heart sped up at the possibility of what encountering less packed earth could mean, but my arms were already repositioning the shovel, just as Riley did the same. The tip of his shovel landed so near mine, they grazed with a clash of sound like crossing swords.

We looked up at each other, startled, our shovels resting together in the ground, just as fat raindrops began to fall.

Smiling and shaking our heads, we pulled our shovels back again in unison, and the next moment, we both saw a scrap of metal beneath the soil where our shovels had just been.

Our eyes locked again. My heart pounded, and Riley's chest heaved, too.

"Could be just another box of random junk," Riley said, but he was already sinking to his knees. I stepped back, tossed aside my shovel, and knelt across from him. It felt just like that day in the park when we'd found the steel case and thought the hunt was over—the soaring hope before the gutting disappointment.

We scooped with our hands as fast as we could. The rain fell heavier, sluicing down the collar of my shirt, plastering my hair to my head. Falling with tiny little *pings* on the aluminum lid of the case we finally unearthed enough for Riley to undo the latches.

Then he hesitated, his eyes finding mine. His face was blurred by rain, but I understood what he wanted without him having to speak. The result of nine summers together. Nine summers, and one wet, confusing spring. I slid my hands alongside his so that we could lift the lid together.

Riley looked down at the case as the lid rose. I kept looking at Riley.

His wide eyes turned wider still. His parted lips pressed together, and he swallowed. And then he let the lid fall closed again, planted his hands on top of it, leaned forward, and kissed me.

I'd never believed in the park's magic more than in that moment, a magic of shared secrets. The gift of the solution to the Meadows's problems in the wet earth between us, and in the way the wash of rain cooled my skin, flushed from Riley's kiss.

And Riley's kiss itself. His touch. The park's original gift—him and me.

RILEY

One week later

"We'd better hurry up," Grandpa said gruffly, checking his watch. "I don't want to be late."

"Don't worry, Grandpa," I assured him as I got out of the driver's seat and Peter slid across the bench seat to get out behind me. "We'll make sure you aren't late to Bingo."

"I still don't know why you couldn't drop me off first and run this errand yourself," Grandpa went on, slowly making his way around the back of the truck. He was steady on his feet, but moved slowly and cautiously these days. According to his doctor, he was doing better. He'd had a few unexplained cardiac events, one of which had necessitated the hospital stay I'd signed him out of a little over two months before. But the doctor said he was drastically improved, which made Grandpa believe the problems had been stress-induced.

He'd finally invited me along to a doctor's appointment and given his doctor permission to answer my questions about Grandpa's recent health issues. After weeks of bugging him for information, it turned out that what I needed to do to get him to trust me was ask if he'd let me stay and work on the park with him, just like we'd talked about eight years ago.

"Gene," Peter said, his expression dismayed, "this isn't just an *errand*."

"I don't know what the point of having a business partner is if you still have to go to all the appointments," Grandpa went on, like he hadn't heard Peter.

Peter caught my eye with a disbelieving look. I fought a smile. What did he expect? Grandpa was who he was.

I lowered the tailgate and reached for the canvas suitcase we'd strapped into the bed of the pickup.

"Careful," Peter murmured as I slid the suitcase off the edge of the tailgate and onto the ground.

I raised an eyebrow at him. "What? It's not like it's fragile."

He rolled his eyes and closed the tailgate, then shoved his hands in his pockets. "I can't believe we just drove it over here." Peter held open the door for me. "We should have let them bring the armored car."

Grandpa gave Peter a severe look. "I don't know why they plaster their business all over those vehicles. Like they're begging to be robbed."

Peter, in turn, gave *me* a look that invited me to share in his apparent thought that Grandpa was being eccentric.

But I just shrugged. "It *is* pretty ridiculous if you think about it."

"Yeah," Peter hissed, "it's much less ridiculous to transport cash in the *back of a pickup truck*." He shook his head at us reprovingly. "You are two of a kind. I swear."

"You love us," I said, grinning at him.

"Well, yeah. But I must have questionable judgment."

We walked into the lobby, and one of the tellers smiled politely at us, sparing only a brief, curious glance at the suitcase. "Can I help you?"

I nudged Grandpa forward firmly. He glared at me, then cleared his throat. "Yes, ma'am. We're here to make a deposit."

EPILOGUE: PETER

Two months later

I was still getting used to the new wooden sign at the turn into the park and the fresh asphalt my tires glided over smoothly as I drove up. The gates stood fully open on repaired hinges, and they shined silver in the setting sun.

Riley and Gene and a small army of people of various trades had begun transforming the park about two months before, and every time I noted one of the small changes that marked the revival of the park to its former glory, it left a bittersweet taste in my mouth.

But I had zero mixed feelings over the sight of Riley waiting for me under the archway, a bottle of wine under his arm and the stems of two glasses threaded through his fingers.

Soon, I'd be coming home to Riley at the park every night. The apartment in the office tower was almost done, but for now, we were still splitting nights between Gene's and my parents'.

I parked and walked up to him, unable to help my smile. "What's going on here? Are we celebrating something?"

Riley's warm hand cupped the back of my head as he bent to

kiss me. "Well," he said as he pulled away, "kind of. It's the first day of summer."

The summer. Our season.

"Oh," I murmured. Every time Riley was sweet to me, my heart did a somersault. It had been doing those somersaults for over a decade, and I knew it wouldn't stop for many decades to come. He took my hand, and we walked through the gates.

All traces of the excavations were gone. A crushed stone path led from one ride to the next, bordered by patches of fresh sod. Lemon's outdoor time had been strictly relegated to the land *outside* the gates, where Riley had used landscaping timbers to form a short fence around an acre or two of tortoise-friendly terrain.

"They got the carousel horses installed today." Riley poured wine into my glass, then his. "Come see."

As though driven by the same mystic force I credited with us finding the money that had expedited the work on the park, other aspects of the park's restoration had fallen into place, too. Chris's family's small-engine repair shop knew how to work on the rare, antique engine that powered the Octopus. Lexy had created an Instagram profile for Lemon that had gone viral, resulting in a slew of unsolicited donations for the construction project to link the greenhouse to his outdoor habitat.

And when Gene had sold off the carousel horses years ago, breaking his own heart in the process, the buyer had been Mr. Davis, a local man who had only bought them because he had memories of summer afternoons at the park as a child, and he couldn't bear to see them auctioned off to the far corners of the country. When he'd found out about the park's reopening plan, thanks to the PR campaign Chase's firm had spearheaded for us, he'd offered to donate them back.

"Wow," I said as we rounded the bumper-car pen and the carousel came fully into view. "It's spectacular. Wait…" I turned to Riley, grinning. "Are those tortoises?" The pair of beatific, smiling tortoises were sculpted in the same style as the classic horses and had the same gold-embellished saddles.

"Yeah," he said, laughing. "Of course."

He recounted Mr. Davis's stories about the park, and how he'd brought a picture of himself riding the carousel at about eight years old. My dad would add it to the growing digital collection of memories that was displayed on the park's new website.

When it was too dark to see the carousel well anymore, and with a little alcohol in my system, I stopped paying attention to the words coming out of Riley's mouth and focused on his mouth, period.

He must have noticed the intent in my expression because he laughed and walked backward a step. "Don't distract me. I've got a surprise for you."

"This wasn't the surprise?" I asked, nodding at the carousel, but I couldn't resist a little mystery. I followed him toward the center of the park.

"Nope," Riley said. "That would be right over here. Just stand there. Yeah, right there. Now give me a sec." He jogged toward the Ferris wheel and hopped up onto the loading platform, then pulled a lever on the control box.

A few at a time, the lights on the Ferris wheel flickered and came on, until it was a blazing ring of lights, stark against the muted charcoal of the early evening sky.

I stared. The wineglass almost slipped from my hand, but I rescued it at the last instant, the liquid sloshing dangerously.

"Isn't it great?" Riley was beaming, glowing inside and out, the multicolored lights of the wheel shining on his face.

I nodded, unsure what to say. I agreed. Of course I did. If anything, *great* was an understatement. But something was stifling my excitement, and I knew what it was.

"Baby," Riley murmured, taking my glass and setting it beside his on the ground. He squeezed my shoulder. "What's the matter?"

"I don't know," I said with a brittle laugh. "I'm excited about the park reopening. I really am. But...it's like we're inviting the whole world into a place I've always thought of as just for us."

Riley held me against him and rubbed my back. I put my cheek on his shoulder.

"I don't know why *I'm* freaking out about this," I muttered. "You and Gene are the ones who greet strangers in the driveway with a shotgun."

I felt the rumble of Riley's laugh vibrate in his chest, but when he pulled back to look me in the eye, he was solemn. "I'll make you a deal. During operating hours, it'll be everybody's wonderland. But when the gates close, it'll just be ours."

That was a deal I was happy to make.

Our lips were a half-inch apart when a distinctive voice interrupted us. "You slippery little—oh, don't mind me, boys. I think Marion's neighbor might have been right about these little beasts. I know I closed the door behind me when I went in to feed them..."

Smiling at Riley's sigh of irritation, I slipped out of his arms and turned to find Gene in a half-crouch, one white rabbit under his right arm, and reaching slowly for a second.

"Grandpa, you shouldn't be—" Riley began to protest, but I squeezed his arm and glanced at him significantly, and he fell quiet. Gene was doing better all the time, and he looked steady on his feet despite the fact that the adolescent Flemish Giant he was holding already weighed several pounds.

"Easy there, little fella," Gene murmured, but as his fingertips brushed the snowy fur on the rabbit's back, she bounded out of reach. "For the love of..." He straightened up and scowled at me. "This is all your doing, Pete."

Riley folded his arms and fixed me with his own version of the Meadows scowl. "You should have insisted that lady pay her bill in cash," he agreed, walking over to stand next to Gene and tickling the captured rabbit behind the ears. The touch made her sneeze, and they both laughed. Gene cuddled her under his chin.

"Yeah, you both look really broken up about it," I muttered to myself, fighting a smile. "And for your information, I didn't send Marion a bill at all." She'd volunteered the payment—and the payment method. Her rabbits' most recent six-kit litter. They were all females, and they were all white, so how to name them was a challenge we hadn't quite tackled yet.

"They're going to be a hit when we have the open house next weekend." We'd planned to invite guests to ride the carousel, tour the park, and learn about the planned restoration in return for a free-will donation. "Lemon might even be upstaged."

Gene and Riley made noises like I'd blasphemed, but I ignored them. I was busy plotting a few strategic steps to intercept the bunny, and then I managed to grab her. She struggled for a half-second, then relaxed in my hold, tipping her head back to sniff me, her whiskers tickling my neck.

"Give her here," Gene said, reaching for the second rabbit. I helped him tuck her under his arm. "I'll get these little renegades back to bed," Gene said. "You kids get back to your...wine." With a parting eyebrow waggle, he headed for the far side of the funhouse, where the rabbits' hutch stood.

Shaking our heads and laughing softly, Riley and I turned back to face the Ferris wheel, which was still ablaze with light. He put his arm around me and tugged me against his side. I slid my arm around his waist and leaned my head against his shoulder.

Maybe it was Gene's interruption. Maybe it was thinking about the open house, and imagining people lifting their grandchildren onto the carousel horses that had been their favorites when they were kids.

The magic that filled the park wasn't imagined, wasn't make-believe, no matter what I'd told myself for years, and neither was the way Riley and I had loved each other. I'd been so, so wrong.

The park, and Riley and me...the magic had always been real.

And if Riley and the park had taught me anything, it was that magic was always better when shared.

Milton Keynes UK
Ingram Content Group UK Ltd.
UKHW040754030324
438788UK00004B/194